Supernova 1 *SF Introduction*

Supernova 1

SF Introduction

FABER AND FABER
3 Queen Square, London

First published in 1976
by Faber and Faber Limited
3 Queen Square London WC1
Printed in Great Britain by
The Bowering Press Ltd
All rights reserved

ISBN 0 571 10984 5

PZ
1
.S957

Acknowledgements

The publishers would like to express enormous gratitude to Philip Pollock for his devotion to this project, and to convey their appreciation not only of his undoubted ability as a reader but also of his unfailing sense of fun which made the selecting of these stories so enjoyable.

Contents

Biographical Notes   *page* xi

Robert Holdstock
THE TIME BEYOND AGE   3
THE GRAVEYARD CROSS   29

Robin Douglas
AGAPÉ   49
NIGHT OUT   66
THE TUNKUN   75

Martin Ricketts
A MATTER OF LIFE AND DEATH   97
LIMBO GIRL ON THE FLAT SHE
    WALKED   110

Michael Stall
GAMING   123

Edward Allen
CRATER   163
LITTLE BIG MAN   171
THE TREE   178

Cliff Lawther
SPIDER BELT   185

Biographical Notes

Robert Holdstock

Born 1948 on Romney Marsh. Turned on to SF in 1957 by simultaneous exposure to Dan Dare and the Quatermass TV series. Swiftly discovered H. G. Wells, Olaf Stapleton and Angus MacVicar. Wrote first novel in 1959. Unpublished. Read Applied Zoology at Bangor University, then Medical Zoology in London. Ph.D giving trouble. Once worked on a banana boat, and on another occasion for the Welsh underground. Recently turned to writing full time. Passions include ancient British history, very heavy rock music, spaghetti westerns, parasitology, Ireland, Asterix and science fiction. Married with one cat and lives in Hertford. Faber and Faber have published his first novel, *Eye Among the Blind*, and are publishing his second, *Earthwind*, in 1977.

Robin Douglas

Born 1949 in the Isle of Man, third daughter in a medical family. She was educated in Wales, and at St. Anne's College, Oxford, where she first became interested in SF. Since graduating in 1970, she has worked among other things as a teacher, a library assistant and a bookseller.

Martin Ricketts

Born in Bristol in 1946. An undistinguished grammar school education was followed by an equally undistinguished apprenticeship in the aircraft industry which left him with no illusions about his engineering talent. Took up a musical career in 1968 when he joined a band of musicians calling themselves "Johnny Carr and the Cadillacs". After several metamorphoses this became "MacArthur Park" which made several appearances on radio and TV and released three records; all three sank without trace. Returned to respectable employment in 1972 as a credit controller. Now lives in Bristol with his wife Maureen whom he married in 1972.

Michael Stall

He is in his early thirties; a Yorkshireman; and currently in marketing administration. Among his interests he lists the desultory study of exotic languages; SF; and above all, writing.

Edward Allen

Edward Allen is aged 40 and married. He is a member of the Institute of Patentees & Inventors, British Mensa and was a founder member of the World Future Society in the U.K. He is particularly concerned with the long-term effect of science and technology on natural systems, and is currently engaged in writing two books on this topic.

Cliff Lawther

Born Berlin, 1948, and immediately airlifted out when they realized their mistake. Early life spent in the coalfields of the North-East. Following acceptance at Southampton University, went on to do joint honours in judo and electronics. Hitchhikes everywhere, and enjoys playing folk guitar in between times. Married, with one son aged 5, and another of indeterminate sex on the way. At present, searching for the fabled flat screen television to finish his Ph.D at Kent University.

Robert Holdstock

The Time Beyond Age:
A Journey

The day before the experiment was scheduled to commence, Martin and Yvonne, our two M.A.A. grown subjects, were allowed into the observation laboratory for the last time.

As usual they caused chaos, thundering around the small room, arms flying, bodies taking unexpected turns until every technician in the place was clinging to his or her equipment for dear life. As Martin, a small figure clad all in white, raced past me I made a grab for him and sat him firmly upon the desk by my typewriter. Yvonne squealed (brake-like) and stopped behind me before deciding which way she would jump onto my lap. She chose to arrive from the left; I had been expecting her from the right and her arrival was painful!

Through her visor she watched me typing. Martin, sitting remarkably still, studied the posters and pictures all around the walls, twisting his protective helmet so that he could see further to each side. I told him not to do that, since the seal would loosen if the helmet were twisted through more than one hundred and eighty degrees.

I was typing a pre-experimental report for *Nature*, and was trying to get a decent title. Yvonne watched my fingers at work, every so often adding a letter of her own. Thus I typed:

NEWZ STU DTITES ON THE ACECELERAT⅓ION
OFXLIFE BY CHEMBIC AL MEANS%

"What does that say?" she asked, pointing to the line.

"A little more than I intended," I replied. *Chembical* I quite liked. I read the proper title to her and Martin launched himself from the bench, made a motor-cycle like noise, with appropriate hand gestures, and accelerated around the laboratory again. He was stopped by a middle-aged nurse (whose eyes popped open with hilarious effect when the human motor cycle collided with her) who picked him up and carried him, complaining, into the small decontamination cubicle. Coming outside she waited for the air inside to sterilize then snapped instructions to him to disrobe. He complained again, but stripped off his protective suit and the nurse placed her arms into the arm-gloves that reached into the chamber and reduced Martin to hysterics as she tried to administer the various prophylactics with which our two subjects were pumped every day.

The following morning the experiment began.

The first stages, of course, were the familiarization procedures, and our two subjects were introduced to the closed environment that was to be their home for the rest of their natural and unnatural lives. There was something almost depressing in watching the children, conceived, grown and matured to the age of six in a Morris Artificial Amnion, now facing an incarceration in a second womb, this time for good.

The environment itself was an enclosed area nearly a quarter of a mile wide and exactly a quarter of a mile deep. In the middle, directly outside our laboratory, was a park ground, equipped with trees, benches and bushes. This was the environmental focus and the area within which Martin and Yvonne would be conditioned to spend most of their time. Outside the park was a mock city, houses and offices, detailed on the exterior but empty within. Only ten buildings were complete—the parental homes of our two subjects, their subsequent married homes (two, one far larger than the other) and the offices where they would work during their lives.

Into this environment they were led and left alone, under a light hypnosis necessary to guard their awarenesses from the falsity of the city.

Martin, to our surprise, reacted against the environment in a difficult and worrying way. He lost his sense of security in the open space of the park—it didn't frighten him, but it made him unhappy and this was something we had not expected to happen.

I watched him carefully during this acquaintance phase. At first he walked among the trees very slowly, seeming very dubious

that anything so irregular could be at all efficient. His examination of the town was almost perfunctory, an acknowledgement
of its existence. He returned to the park and I watched him chip
bark from the bigger of the two oaks we had grown in the environment. He spent a long time scrutinizing the carefully selec-
ted microfauna that seethed beneath the fragment. He had no
conception, of course, of the essential artificiality of the ecology,
although it was plain to him—and we did not hide the fact, save
as regarded the town itself—that the environment was contrived.
The extent of our contrivance it was not necessary for him to
know for the familiarization to have its effect.

Yvonne, by contrast with her chosen mate, warmed immediately to the environment and it was all we could do to get her to
return to the laboratory. It became a game—three or four sterile-
suited technicians chasing one giggling sterile-suited girl in and
out of the shells that comprised the town. In conversation with
her later in the evening, as I implanted one more of the inter-
minable number of monitoring devices she would carry to her
death, she told me how wonderfully free she had felt sitting on
actual grass, picking flowers that were actually growing. It was
an unpleasant thought to me that the young girl, knowing only
sterility and starkness of the complex prior to this time, was now
finding in an equivalent piece of unreality all the reality she
would ever need. She had yearned to see the outside world,
longed for nature and pined, perhaps, for the instinctively
realized sensation of wind and rain on her face. Now she was
content with a park that encapsulated all her dreams. And she
sat in the middle of a construct, half knowing the fact, but finding it completely adequate.

Yvonne was a very chubby child, round faced and pretty. She
had dark brown eyes and she chose to wear her hair in an elab-
orate display of curls, but had been complaining, as she matured
these last months, that her hair was getting greasy. By the time
we closed her off in the artificial world beyond our laboratory,
she had begun to wear her hair straight, in a style that didn't
suit her. She was growing quite fat, nothing that wouldn't soon
vanish as she grew to adulthood, and it didn't seem to bother her,

whereas Martin was naturally, and almost pathologically, ashamed of his protruding ribs.

It was May of '94, a feverish summer forcing itself upon us. The environment looked inviting and in the final weeks when children and technical staff both were in frantic final preparation for Closing Off Day, it was regarded as almost criminal that the cool parklands should be a prohibited area. After all, the disease-free status of the ecology was secured every day, now that Martin and Yvonne were spending time inside without their protective suiting.

In time, towards August, the atmosphere in the laboratory became almost unbearable as our two subjects underwent full acclimatization. We watched as they played and explored their new territory, Martin gradually coming to terms with the area, but obviously still unhappy; and as we watched we sweltered and wondered who the true masters of the situation might have been.

It was at this time that the last member of our team joined us. She was a young woman, Josephine Greystone, only two years out of her basic training, and she brought to the laboratory not only reasonable looks, but a great enthusiasm for biology in general, and it was she who precipitated what were to become almost routine late-night sessions evaluating the utility of biological research as a whole.

She soon became very interested in Raymond McCreedy, a man in his mid thirties, unmarried, unforthcoming about himself, a scientist totally involved with his work, to the great benefit of the scientific community, but to the detriment of any personal relationships between the members of the various teams. McCreedy was the head of our team, and had supplied the initial impetus for this particular experiment; it was also his own applied pressure that had secured the necessary funding from the Rockefeller Foundation.

Josephine worked hard trying to draw the man out of his test-tube shell, and indeed, before the full programme had begun, he was amenable enough to conversational foreplay; but any emotional involvement was destined to be just a dream on

Josephine's part. The full programme began and McCreedy's interests became centrally directed upon the two human subjects behind the observation wall.

In September the programme of deep hypnosis began: hours and hours of factual adjustment and psychological disguise. Martin's prevailing disquiet with the environment was buried very deeply. In tests in the next few days there were signs that he would accept the environment long enough for it to become so familiar to him that he would be able to control the insecurity as it crept back to his awareness.

Three weeks before the first of the rapid growth treatments was administered, the two subjects received their Life-Education. The Life Plan team, led by Doctor Martin Rich, had spent six months devising and recording nearly four hundred years of everyday experiences. A complete catalogue of friends, ac-quaintances and enemies, of events and non-events, of tragedy and success. One for Martin and one for Yvonne, the two systems knitting together gradually as they grew together themselves according to blueprint. The events they would live through were implanted first, followed by the complex series of visual and sonic codes with which the Life Operator in charge could direct events beyond the wall.

Finally, the enormous bank of experiences that they would never actually participate in—the twenty-nine days that would pass as they slept each night, giving them the illusion of a full and active life.

On the first day of November there was a promise of snow, but the skies, overcast and depressing, vanished into night without releasing their burden in any form. This was the day the full programme began.

I was lucky to draw my Christmas leave over the Christmas period itself. I returned to the Institute on the 27th December to find Josephine, two nurses and two of the technicians in attend-ance. The Life Plan team had left an autoprogramme in operation for seven days, and McCreedy himself had succumbed to the need for rest and was spending time in London.

"You could have taken your leave with McCreedy," I remarked to Josephine, tactless as ever. "Any of the technicians who were here over Christmas would have been glad to swop."

"Why should I have wanted to swop?" she asked as we prepared for the day's observation.

"To be with McCreedy?" Oh hell, I thought. I've put a foot in somewhere.

Her look at me was pure contempt. "Why should I have wanted to be with Doctor McCreedy?"

I had received all the warning signals, but momentum carried me to desperate conclusion. "I'm sorry, I just thought. . . ."

"I very much doubt, Doctor Lipman," she said stonily, "if you thought anything at all. What you laughably call thinking rarely transcends a naïve and superficial curiosity."

"Look, I'm sorry, let's drop the subject, shall we?"

Her look changed from contempt to distress. "Yes, why not. Let's drop the subject of McCreedy, let's forget him for three days and have ourselves a real ball. For your information, and to ensure that you don't open your mouth again, Doctor Lipman, I have nothing going with McCreedy, and have no desire to try and change that state of affairs."

I couldn't think of any suitably cutting remark with which to extricate myself from my wretched corner, so I fell silent and monitored the two subjects, aware that Josephine was sitting staring at nothing in particular.

In the five months of Yvonne's life that I had missed—by taking a five-day break—she had altered remarkably. Her hair was very short, now, cut in the style of her currently favourite singer, and she was beginning to discover the versatility of cosmetics. She was still living in a separate building from Martin, ostensibly with her parents, but, as dictated by the programme within her, she was finding Martin's pre-adolescent form an attraction. He, according to script, was not too keen on his playmate. She was still plump, but the lipid-metabolism figures were indicating that soon this would fall away.

She was approaching adolescence at the late age of fifteen.

Although it is difficult to admit to such predictable behaviour, it was about now that I realized that my affection for the increasingly beautiful girl went far beyond fatherly emotion. On that first night back from my break I followed Josephine and the nurse into the environment and approached the sleeping form of Yvonne with a strange sensation of anticipation. The nurse seemed oblivious of my feelings and in the matter-of-fact mannerism of a woman who regards the human body as an organism to be stripped, scrubbed, powdered, plugged and buried, she exposed the maturing body of the girl and proceeded to inoculate the ageing-chemical known familiarly as *Chronon*. The hiss of the parcutaneous inoculation snapped me from my lingering contemplation of Yvonne and I performed the ritual of recording with an almost blank mind: I took whole body temperature scan, a tiny skin biopsy that would not be noticed the following day; I took smears and scrapes, tested reflexes and conductivity, obtained a ten-second recording of the girl's heart (probably the most vital organ she possessed, and the part of her body likely to give us the most trouble in later years), and finally stood back, flushed, shaking, aroused.

Perhaps the nurse was not as insensitive as I had thought, for she was suddenly very quiet, watching me curiously. My embarrassment became acute and I glanced at Josephine who was standing silently beside me, looking at Yvonne. Quickly I said, "I can't decide if she's losing weight or not...."

The nurse nodded slowly, then covered Yvonne's body, blowing the sound signal to bring her back into normal sleep.

As we walked to Martin's "house" I considered my feelings. I was not really surprised that now, December of '94, I should be feeling love for a young woman, since my marriage, never a satisfactory affair from the beginning, was now awaiting legal dissolution and had been doing so for six months. What perturbed me was that I should have responded to the experimental subject and not to one of the technicians or nurses, or even Josephine.

Josephine. Had she noticed my momentary lapse of self-discipline? As we examined Martin so I studied the girl and I decided that she was too preoccupied with her own troubles to have read anything into my actions.

She suddenly said, softly, perhaps afraid of rousing Martin although she knew that he was in deep sleep: "What do you make of people who are so one tracked they can't think of anything but work?"

"McCreedy?"

She looked at me. She seemed sad, and after a moment, "He's an example, yes."

"Annoying," I said. "Pointless."

"You don't believe in dedication?"

I concluded the examination and we walked from the environment, sealed it and sterilized it again.

"I don't believe in isolation," I said. "And McCreedy is becoming isolated because of what you mistakenly label as dedication. His reactions, his behaviour, his approach to all of us working for him is becoming unreal. He begins to think we're machines, and should never turn off."

Josephine said nothing. After a moment I asked, "How do you see him?"

"With increasing difficulty," she said after a while. "It's something I can't explain."

Perhaps these days, or if you prefer, these months, were the worst. By the end of February '95 Yvonne was a fully grown woman of twenty, and Martin, though the same age, was an immediately post-adolescent young man, still self-conscious, still unsure of himself, still given to the sort of tantrum directed at the ghosts who surrounded him, that one expects in a normal male in his late teens.

The two months of my subjective time had done nothing to drown my desire for Yvonne, but more worrying to me, as a supposedly impartial observer, was the feeling of resentment I began to nurture, resentment directed at the young man I now watched and monitored as he devised some scheme to avoid parental retribution for his being out so late.

Josephine watched over my shoulder as Martin walked across the environment, oblivious of his watchers, concerned only with the non-existent forms awaiting him in his house. Yvonne, whom he had just left, was already in bed and—as our monitors showed us—peacefully asleep, about to age a month in the passing of her dreaming hours.

Tonight they had approached each other as adults, that much was apparent. I had watched them kiss in the shelter of the first oak that Martin had ever interested himself in, fourteen of his years ago. He had held her and explored her, and I could feel what he was feeling as his fingers had invaded her body.

Josephine turned away and sat staring into space. I was glad because my face was burning and I could feel my hands shaking as I directed the remote sensors to record all heartbeat and temperature changes, and instruct me if there was anything abnormal in their physical and physiological response to love-play. There was no satisfaction in the green panel that flashed 'normal' in a repetitive insult to my stricken ego.

That night, as the nurse and I monitored and examined each of them, it was with Martin that I lingered, noting his emerging masculinity and the involuntary ejaculation that occurred as my fingers brushed him during perfunctory examination. I hated his youth, and I hated his good looks; I hated his smugness as he lay in sleep, I hated the fact that he was fully entitled to everything that was Yvonne. I hated his dreams. What he dreamed I shall never know for certain, but in my uncertainty lies an impression that choked me at the time. And I hated him for that too.

Three days of my night shift passed in the Institute, and I received promising news from my lawyer—that the separation would be made legal within days—and received a substantial cut-back of my monthly stipend which would make even my bachelor life very difficult. Josephine had finished her spell on nights and it was the intense and disinterested McCreedy who sat with me at the beginning of March. I wondered if he knew of Josephine's feelings, I wondered if he had detected her waning enthusiasm. . . . Almost certainly he had. Perhaps he had even told her of it. He was becoming more abstract with every passing day.

Since there was nothing to talk about with the intense young man who gave the orders, I watched Yvonne with greater concentration than was usual or than I would have liked.

Now she was long-haired and slim, her breasts small and perfect and seeming fuller behind the attractive blouses she wore.
She worked in an imaginary office and took every opportunity
to meet Martin in the park, and on the third night of March,
my last day on nights. . . .

I shall record it for the sake of completeness.

In each other's arms beneath that tree they passed a few
minutes, petting and kissing, then undressed and he made love
to her, and the recording instruments said, heart beat 137/minute,
deep body temperature 0·5 degrees high, slight blood loss, loss of
lachrymal fluid. . . .

And so on, and so forth, as Yvonne cried and a significant
moment in the life plan was reached and passed.

The loss of her virginity was five years in Yvonne's past before the pain of that incident faded from me. It was the beginning
of May, and the first really hot day of the year. Long-range
weather predictions were for a summer as hot and stifling as '94,
and the thought of it was not welcomed by the staff of the
Institute.

I looked at Yvonne, and at Martin, and saw mature people,
Yvonne a full and lovely woman, delighting in life and love, almost passionately hungry for her husband. Martin was a strong,
lean man, full bearded and fierce-tempered. It was hard to remember that just a year ago they had been infants.

The years between twenty-five and thirty passed normally and
uneventfully, and our first report, on the 5th August, was sum-
marized by the words: "In all aspects of their lives the two subjects are normal thirty-year-olds. The effect of the chemical
Chronon is seen only in the acceleration of their developmental
rates, and the false experience implants seem fully capable of
compensating for their accelerated lives. There is no evidence at
all that mentally the subjects are anything but reasonably secure,
reasonably stable thirty-year-olds. There is no evidence that either
subject suspects their true situation. The experiment is continuing."

It was heartening news to our sponsors, and a mood of exhilaration enveloped our laboratory. We began to feel that we had a breakthrough in our grasp.

A breakthrough into what was difficult to say. The kudos for the original discovery of *Chronon* was not ours. The chemical of age, the simple protein that accumulates in body cells at a steady rate and dictates the phenomenon of ageing, was the discovery of a Swedish biochemist seven years before. The acceleration of development, and of ageing, under the influence of artificially high concentrations of synthetic *Chronon* was the contribution of a Scottish behaviourist at the University of Edinburgh, four years later.

The fact that synthetic *Chronon* worked as well on human beings as on rats would make a name for us, but hardly a reputation.

McCreedy was well aware of this, and we had both been aware of this when we had met nearly two years before to discuss the phenomenon of ageing, and the newly discovered facts about its chemical dependence.

With old age, McCreedy had said, comes a lowering of resistance not just to disease but to the environment and to life itself. We think of age as a barrier that none of us will pass. But is it? If we remove those agents of death that find they can operate better as a person gets older, will age *itself* be a barrier? Might not something, some form, some existence that we are unaware of lie beyond our four score and ten?

In rats there was nothing. They lived twice as long as normal and became twice as old. But rats were without souls, McCreedy had declared, and we should not be disheartened.

This was the first time that McCreedy had referred to a metaphysical concept, and it rather surprised me. He made no great play of his religious beliefs, and directed his actions towards no religious dogma. I came to believe that he equated self-awareness with the concept of *soul*, and that he extended his favour towards the metaphysical only to the unscientific degree of regarding self-awareness as having an effect upon the physical form. He believed in mind over matter! But detailed consideration of such things was beyond his scope. At the time this narrowness did not seem significant to me, and it was not until well after the experiment had begun that I remembered his words, and his idle reflections.

Not until late November did any serious psychological stress symptoms begin to develop in the subjects. They were now into their thirty-eighth year and the monitoring consoles were still reporting their physical and physiological condition as completely normal. Certainly there was a slight increase in the incidence of embryonic cell formation, but—with our help—they were maintaining completely adequate control of their body systems. Martin was an enviable sight, advancing into middle age with muscles that were as firm and hard as a twenty-five-year-old's. And Yvonne, whilst showing signs of age in the lines that were tracing themselves around her eyes and on her legs, was still a beautiful woman. But now I felt only sadness when I looked at her, for more and more I was remembering her childhood, her innocence and her fixed gaze from which it was almost impossible to escape.

There was no trace of that innocence now, and the beautiful eyes were narrower and more canny. When she made love to Martin she was physically demanding but seemed no longer to need the concomitant affection.

Martin, whilst undoubtedly in love with his wife, was tending more and more towards solitariness, and in this I saw a reflection of his first acquaintance with the enormous environment. He was unhappy with his situation, seemed restless and morose, and returned again and again to the realistic-looking oak tree that he had first scrutinized so long, by his terms, in the past.

Here he sat for hours, during the day and often into the night, brooding, staring, perhaps trying to identify some feature, some element of his Universe that would give him a clue as to why he felt so wrong.

Perhaps—again—such speculation by those of us who monitored and watched was just a sublimation on our parts of the fact that the experiment, stuck as it was in the "normal" years, had become unbearably boring. We were looking for trouble, or so it seemed to some of us.

With the inevitable slackening of attention, I found ample

opportunity to modify the Life Plan of the ageing Yvonne. It was an impulsive move, but had, as an idea, been in my mind for a long time. The team was small—three biologists and three technicians working in shifts, two nurses and the four members of the Life Plan team. It was inevitable that we should all learn to cope with the other aspects of the experiment, and I had become relatively adept at the surgically precise process of removing or implanting information/ideas/events into the two subjects.

I implanted my own character, my own physical description, as one of the ghost lovers that Yvonne was taking. There was something akin to the erotic when I thought, thereafter, of what she was seeing and doing, but after a few days the futility of the action came home to me.

Nevertheless, she retained me as a lover and I never found the opportunity to remove that programme. When I heard her murmuring my name, voicing the words of her ascending passion as she went through the movements of intercourse, I felt my face burn, and my imagination stretch to its limits.

When she was with someone else I became depressed and touchy. No one in the laboratory ever found out what I had done, but they might well have gathered the truth if they had bothered to listen to the tapes of what was said in the darkness of her bedroom.

Time passed and a depression settled upon the laboratory. Perhaps the movement of Martin and Yvonne into their middle years, and into a quieter phase of their lives, reflected itself in our subdued interaction and the almost lethargic approach that we began to show towards the experiment as a whole. McCreedy, I hasten to point out, in no way suffered depression, and the technicians were, I suppose, too distant from the possibility of kudos to have any great enthusiasm at any stage of the project. But the nurses and the Life Planners, myself and Josephine all became very broody.

Josephine in particular was labouring under a black cloud. Her relationship with McCreedy was abysmal. Everything he said she disagreed with behind his back. She took her only pleasure in putting him down, contributed nothing to any discussion at which he was present, but depended on me to relay her ideas to him.

In the rapid ageing of the two subjects she saw an inevitability that frightened her.

"That's us in so very few years," she said as she stared at the two subjects during one of their persistent rows. "And there's nothing any of us can do about it. It's a stab at our human pride —there are some things that àre inevitable, that man cannot control, and his decreptitude is one of them. And what do we do? We accept it! We are *Eos* watching the ageing of *Tithonus* and afraid to ask the great ZEUS to add youth to immortality. *Afraid,* I said—and that's what I meant, but even so, man is ageing like each of us individually and his racial fear stops him asking for an injection of youth. It's so horribly . . . predictable! I want to live with youth and youth's dreams. . . . I'm rambling aren't I?"

I see what she meant, now, as I complete this chronicle. In the satisfaction of completion of the project there would come a rationality that I had lost during those years. At the time I didn't understand her at all.

I became infatuated with the watching of Yvonne, staring at her for endless hours, trying to find some trace of the eleven-year-old . . . but all her youth and beauty were now imprisoned behind a wall of years. With each day, with each inoculation of *Chronon,* she aged before my eyes, now whiter, now more wrinkled, now a little more stooped.

She and Martin fought persistently. There was not a day passed without them shouting and swearing at each other, and ending the tussle with a cold and slippery silence, that only mellowed towards evening.

Martin spent a great deal of time alone, and the monitor reported that he indulged less and less in conversation with the ghosts around him. He retired from his work, and from his social life, whilst Yvonne remained socially active and very hostile towards her husband.

She flirted with numerous ghosts, most of them the ageing lovers she had taken during earlier years. Now, instead of the imaginary copulation that she performed before our eyes, she seemed to indulge in painfully unconcluded flirtation. When I watched her one evening, and heard her mention my name and knew what she was thinking, instead of the thrill I had felt when first I had entered her pseudo-awareness, I now felt only disgust and dismay, and I became deeply embarrassed at what I had done, but still no opportunity to remove my existence presented itself and there was nothing I could do to eliminate these scenes from my memory.

The time came when all sexual, and much social, contact ceased, and she sat and remembered, staring out from her body at the invisible monitors that brought her heartache to us as we watched from the laboratory outside the environment.

Martin, now, was alone, spending his time staring directly at the edge of the environment as if he was aware that he could not move beyond that barrier. Within his head, recorded triggers were depressing his interest in wandering beyond the confines, but it seemed to the more analytical among us that he had come to realize that there was nowhere to go anyway.

It was December of '96, and they were old people, seventy years into their lives, as healthy and sturdy as when they had been born, but old, none the less. For me, when on my shift, there was just discomfiture in administering examination to the thin, craggy torso of the girl I had once watched grow with the beating of my heart. In sleep she stirred, talked, cried. The monitors said all was well, but it was hard not to believe that she had lived too much too fast, and that all the empty days in her past were calling for fulfilment, and the brief and unsatisfactory time she had actually spent with Martin was calling for completion.

Now, however, a new sense of excitement crept into the laboratory. I felt it myself. For the subjects were at the beginning of the age barrier, and with every day took a step nearer to the figure of one hundred years, our first goal, and the age which, when reached, would be accompanied by our first report to the scientific community at large. And yet, a sort of natural caution prevailed. Within our hearts, as those weeks passed, we all began to imagine what, if anything, lay beyond the barrier of age; but within the microcosm that was our scientific community we never discussed our private fears and hopes. McCreedy talked loosely about possible regenerative processes, and we all talked among ourselves about the rationale behind thinking that age itself did not necessarily mean death. But of what was to come, there were just the imaginings and the anticipations of our scientific hearts. And, an acknowledgment to mythology, above McCreedy's desk an enormous picture of a cicada, watching us with an expression verging on amusement.

On the day that they were both ninety-nine years and eleven months old, McCreedy prepared his press statement while the rest of us accumulated the massive files of data and decided on an allotment for processing. The following day, 5th March '98, that momentous event occurred . . . the centenary of two human beings, and there was a feeling of great relief within the whole Institute, and for the first time ever we drank openly in our laboratory, and it was not just coffee, surreptitiously sipped with back to the health-hazard notice, but vintage champagne, eight bottles of the stuff !

I drank with restraint since it was to be my night shift, but somehow we all felt, now, that the years of narrow-minded application had been worthwhile, that there would be an end-product; even Josephine seemed brighter, more cheerful.

I watched McCreedy's press conference on a small portable TV while I waited for the frail figures in the environment to sink, again, into deep slumber. There was an atmosphere of great excitement in the vast hall from which the programme was coming, and I could see McCreedy, evening-suited and proud, seated between medical experts and two politicians, confronted by a vast array of microphones, and waiting for the hubbub of human movement and whisper to die away.

The Institute itself seemed to vibrate in sympathy with that meeting of the world, away to the south, in London.

Yvonne sat for a long while that night, at the edge of the park, listening to the ghosts in her head, and staring through eyes that were as big and innocent as they had been ninety or so years back. The camera lingered on her and I returned her gaze through the monitor and I seemed to hear her laughter and her crying, and her passion, but all so far in the past, now, so long ago.

Martin was by himself beneath the oak, turning a piece of bark over and over, examining the artificial life which crawled beneath. The "moonlight" was intense and highlighted his rigid expression, the bony crags of his face, the deepset lie of his eyes. What thoughts, I wondered, did he think at his great age? He was not senile, and Yvonne was certainly not senile, and yet there was a calmness, an abstractedness about them, that suggested mindlessness.

Did they themselves feel something significant? Were they experiencing a quieter excitement within themselves, a personal triumph? They believed themselves ordinary people, and as ordinary people they were a hundred years old. The flesh would not fall away to reveal firm skin and agile muscles and time would not fall away to reveal them in their youth and beauty, but in the mind is a store of ages and perhaps, on this night of nights, a barrier within their consciousnesses had dissolved for a few hours and they were living, ghostlike, as they had lived in reality, for the last seventy years.

On the television screen McCreedy's angular features were emphasized by the arc lights above him as he calmly informed the conference of the progress we had made and were continuing to make. He talked about the impossibility of the experiment using ordinary human lifespans—an experiment lasting two hundred years (assuming it was successful) could be run by a computer, but not by mortal scientists. He stressed that the only purpose of the experiment at this time was to evaluate whether or not we were correct in thinking that death in old age was nonetheless a disease-caused process, taking disease to mean—at the least—the gradual failure of vital body cells due to the accumulation of the toxic by-products of mild infection throughout the life of the individual. At one hundred years of age, he said, our two subjects, reared from artificial wombs, screened from all disease or body malfunction, showed all the elastic changes of age, were to all intents and purposes very old people, and yet their cellular complement was as vigorous and efficient as it had been when they had been teenagers. All the symptoms of age were built into the genetic message, he explained when prompted further, and all that had been eliminated were the non-genetically coded acquisitions of disease by-products.

The all-important questions: how long did McCreedy expect the experiment to continue for? And what did he expect to find out as the decades progressed? And was he morally justified in using human beings for experimentation outside the understanding of normal human life?

The experiment, said McCreedy, would continue for as long as circumstances permitted. He *expected* to find nothing—no scientist ever did. He hoped he would find whatever was to be found; a scientist's nightmare was to fail to observe the facts of significance in an experiment.

I could have put it better myself, but the statement was met with a respectful silence.

As to the moral question, he had a licence permitting him to work with artificially grown human beings, and he had not yet abused that privilege. Since the effective natural lifespan of the two human subjects was now ended, in a sense they were living on borrowed time, time borrowed from McCreedy himself, and they had no future, really, but to remain as a part of the experiment.

This was in March of '98, and it precipitated a phase of observation overshadowed by our burning enthusiasm. We were eager to discover what lay beyond the normal years of life, and there can be no doubt that privately we all had the wildest of visions.

Truth to tell, mine were perhaps the wildest of all. I sketched possible metamorphoses, imagined arriving at the Institute and facing the subjects walking through walls, of transporting themselves instantly into the future to observe the progress of our study. I was, I confess, convinced that the apparent decay of body and—to a certain extent—mind, was a transient phenomenon, and that greater power lay at some indeterminate time in the future of our subjects.

Confiding my belief to McCreedy, I was received with hostility.

He condemned me for my lack of discipline. Expect nothing, he said, because if you fervently expect anything at all, then you will tend to see what you want to see.

And then he told me of *his* secret imaginings and they so closely paralleled my own that we talked seriously, thereafter, of the possibility of such a state of existence following naturally upon a span of five or six score disease-free years.

Man had never had a chance to exploit his genetic freedom completely. He was killed, trampled, diseased so early in life that the protective mechanisms that might have come into operation to protect the body cells from poisoning just never came into play. What we see is man with a lifespan dictated by the length of time his body can survive an increasingly hostile microclimate. But what was his original potential? What great beings have our neotenous forms never been able to reach?

A man of religious inclination, McCreedy could not conceal from my scrutiny the fact that he believed some manifestation of Godhead lay as the ultimate destiny of our two subjects.

They grew older. By day and by night they aged weeks, and the flesh sagged, their movements slowed, and the compilations of data mounted in volume, but amounted to nothing. The incidence of disease tried to rise within them, but all was monitored and prevented and they reached the middle of their second century free from infection, from tumour or other bodily breakdown.

It is impossible to chronicle those passing months and years in detail—little happened either to the subjects or to us. We talked and read, participated in any number of short-term projects, wrote papers and took long vacations, all expenses paid. Sanity was—miraculously, I sometimes think—preserved.

In retrospect I can see how, within our scientific microcosm, we became individually insulated, erected barriers behind which we guarded our memories and preserved our philosophy. Thus, I learned nothing of my companions, and—at the time—found no interest in so studying them.

At the age of one hundred and fifty-five Martin's skin seemed to regain its firmness, the loose folds tightening, and he became

B

skeletal, gaunt. Yvonne, by contrast, sagged more, the flesh lying around her neck in three great folds, her legs becoming wrinkled and bowed.

Nothing magical or unexpected happened, however. They just became older, frailer, quieter.

The excitement of year one hundred passed into *our* distant past, and over the course of weeks, then months, the enormous ages reached by the subjects failed to arouse even the slightest whimper of joy. We worked virtually full-time countering the efforts of each of their bodies to spring into a disease condition, but all the time our eyes were watching the loose, trembling folds of skin on Yvonne and the drawn, scaling flesh of her husband. They passed towards their second century with virtually no change, virtually no movement. They were static hulks, house-bound where they slept most of the time, ate slowly through tiny mouths that hardly seemed to open for the pre-masticated food they consumed.

Yvonne watched the monitor all the time, and when she was at her most alert, her eyes were huge, deep and penetrating, and there was a terrible sadness in them.

They passed their second century and the atmosphere in the research centre became appalling.

What was the point of it now? demanded Josephine. Why continue when all we were doing was prolonging the agony of gross body decay? There were no great secrets to be discovered. Stop the experiment. Admit defeat!

McCreedy, not surprisingly, refused. His face, these days, was showing signs of great mental strain. He was white, heavily sagging under the eyes, and he seemed . . . old. He dressed in disorder, and had stopped giving press interviews. The Ministry officials who bombarded us every month were given cursory briefings and hustled away, and letters demanding that we show some results for the financial support to be proven worth while were answered abruptly and stingingly, and somehow—don't ask me how—those who put money into us continued to do so.

At about this time Josephine left the group. She said good-bye to me, but there was a distance between us that made our smiles and handshakes just meaningless gestures. She never glanced at McCreedy, and McCreedy paid no attention to her.

"It's all so pointless," she said, reiterating what she had said so many times before. "Man's destiny was always to grow old and die, and what we're demonstrating here is that no matter how he comes to terms with the forces that oppress him, man's destiny will never be anything but a slow decay. What we see in a pair of individuals reflects our whole race. We have to live with our dreams, not our realities."

She left and for a while I felt moody and listless. McCreedy, looking ever older, berated her defeatist and pessimistic attitudes, and in a short time the oppressive atmosphere lifted and I felt the excitement that McCreedy felt, the sensation of hovering at the edge of something greater than imagination.

With the passing months we became a little slack again....

Then things began to happen and it was like an injection of life, both into us and into the hulks that peered at us from the environment.

On the morning of his two hundred and twentieth year (and three months) Martin, having remained virtually immobile for the past eighty years of his life, rose and walked swiftly—on legs that barely faltered—towards the edge of the environment. His heartbeat doubled and his blood pressure rose, and there seemed to be great surges of adrenalin passing through his body at thirty-five-second intervals.

He began to shout, in a language strange to my ears:

"Sibaraku makkura na yoru ni te de mono o saguru ... yoo ni site ... aruite ikimasita ga ... tootoo hutaritomo sukkari ... tukarete nanimo iwanaide kosi o orosite ... simaimasita ...."

"My God," shouted McCreedy, ecstatic. "Listen to that. Listen to *that*!"

"Sosite soko ni ... taoreta ...." Martin seemed to be finding difficulty speaking these strange words, "... mama inoti ga naku-narun' d'ya nai ... ka to omou to kyuu ... ni ... taihen osoro-siku natte ... simaimasita ...."

He fell silent, but continued to stand at the edge of the environ-ment and stare through at that part that was projection.

McCreedy was shaking his head, almost in disbelief. "The lan-guage of angels . . ." he said softly. "It has finally happened . . . it has finally happened."

"Actually it was very poorly pronounced Japanese," said one of the technicians, a young girl and a member of the Life Plan team.

McCreedy stared at her for a moment while the rest of us tried to hide our smiles. "The point is," he said slowly, "Martin never *knew* Japanese." His face beamed again. "He never *knew* it, don't you see? So how could he have learned it? We have our first mystery . . . Lipman, we have our first mystery!" He was obviously delighted. The same technician, looking as if she hardly dared speak, said, "Well, not exactly. We programmed him to take an elementary course in Japanese when he was thirty. The only mystery is how his pronunciation could be so bad. . . ."

McCreedy was completely deflated. The rest of us could hardly hide our mirth, but that was so unfair. We had all lost.

When McCreedy had gone—back to his small office to recover from his disappointment, I asked the technician what Martin had said.

"For a while we were groping our way along as if it was in the deep of night, but eventually we sat down without saying a word, completely exhausted. Then we suddenly felt . . . frightened, wondering if we were going to die, there where we had fallen."

I looked at Martin, who was still standing at the edge of the park, staring into nowhere. "Beautiful," I said.

"Page 233," she said. "Check it up."

One day, when I arrived a little early for my shift, I found McCreedy seated in his small office, holding an alcohol swab to his lower left arm. An ampoule of *Chronon* lay empty on his desk. Immediately I understood why he had begun to look so old these last two years. Immediately the true dedication of the man to his own beliefs was apparent. Immediately his hypocrisy was crystal clear—expect nothing, he had said, and here he was, already modi-

fying his own life on the basis of what he believed would occur—
McCreedy, searching for a place in the kingdom of the Gods,
wearing his age without regret or apprehension. Was he oblivious
to the fact that, having never been screened against disease, his
destiny was a natural death in an unnatural period of time? I
didn't ask. His dreams were his reality now, and I couldn't help
but remember Josephine's parting words to me.

McCreedy just stared at me and I stared back. I left his office
without saying a word.

The changes began shortly afterwards. An initial report of
slight increase in girth of the crowns of their heads, was followed
rapidly by bizarre growth patterns in both subjects. Their heads
grew to almost twice their original volumes, the increase being
not in the brain but the amount of fluid in which the brain was
cushioned. Their eyes became sunken and tiny. Martin's arms
lengthened and the fingers stretched from his hands like tendrils,
flexing and touching all that they contacted, moving almost inde-
pendently.

His height increased and he began to walk with an exaggerated
stoop. He found Yvonne again.

The changes that Yvonne had experienced were not the same.
Her gross flabbiness became packed with fat. She became huge, a
mound of flesh, and her limbs, by contrast with Martin's, shrank
until they seemed mere protrusions from the bulk of her torso.
Her hair fell out and the great shining dome of her head shook
constantly. She remained on her bed, slightly propped up by
pillows so that her tiny eyes could continue to watch the monitor.
Martin fed her and cared for her, kept her covered with blankets
now that she could wear no clothes.

They regained an element of their earlier sexual ability; there
was a certain revulsion in watching the reconsummation of their
life together, but equally there was a certain fascination about
the event. We watched silently, and in great discomfort, and drew
no immediate conclusions.

"We are seeing the beginning of the metamorphosis," said
McCreedy eventually. He was consumed by his dreams, and yet, as

the days passed and the bizarre features of the subjects became more bizarre, and their copulation became more frequent and more incomprehensible, so we all began to wonder what was to be the end-result.

The monitors filled our files with information, the rocketing, fluctuating chemical levels, the unprecedented hormonal changes, the degradation and rebuilding of body parts.

In February of '02, just seven years after the experiment had begun, Martin and Yvonne copulated for the last time, Yvonne not moving from her position, almost flowing across her bed, bearing the weight of her husband. Her great head turned to stare at the monitor and then turned back and looked at the ceiling. Martin slipped off her and crouched by her, staring into the distance. They began to tremble.

The trembling, a violent shaking of their entire bodies, persisted through the day.

McCreedy was bright-eyed and full of excitement. "It's happening," he said. "It may take days, but it's happening, the change, the final metamorphosis."

He made copious notes, and in the environment the trembling persisted, a persistent whole-body muscular spasm.

After a few hours their heartbeats began to slow and the electrical output from their brains began to lessen. By evening the hearts had stopped and the brains showed no activity at all.

The monitor screens became quiet, all except one small panel, a red panel that lighted up with black words on red background. "Subjects are dead."

We entered the environment and approached the bodies. McCreedy stared down at the corpses for a moment. He was shaking his head. "I can't believe this," he said finally, thoughtfully. "Keep a brain activity watch . . . it may be that the whole metabolic rate has slowed to a phenomenally low tick-over level. We may be witnessing some sort of stasis prior to a major change."

I said, "Ray—there will be no change. The subjects are dead. Completely dead."

"Nonsense," snapped McCreedy. "To take that attitude at this stage would be disastrous." He began to examine the bodies, apparently oblivious of the fact that he might be contracting or spreading disease.

I left the environment and sat, for a while, among the silent technicians who watched McCreedy on the monitors. I felt the quietness, the emptiness of the place. I stared at the white walls and the meticulously clean equipment and benches. The atmosphere was heavy, dull. One corner of the laboratory was filled with neatly stacked print-outs representing the last fifty years of the subject's life, and staring at that pile of information I realized that nowhere in its bulk could I put my finger on a single statement of feeling, of awareness. Even the sheets on which were recorded the last living moments of Martin and Yvonne were bare, sterile accounts of failing physiology and murmurings and alpha waves; there would be no account of what they thought, what they felt as death unfurled its protective wings about them.

We had concerned ourselves with two lives and had studied everything but life itself. It had all been wasted. In the end, bizarre hormonal changes had captured our attention with their effects upon the physical forms of the two subjects, and we had sunk without trace into chemical formulae and physical law. Perhaps the inevitability of such a conclusion should have been a personal vindication, but I felt a deep sense of guilt as I left the Institute, a powerful sense of failure.

I returned five days later to collect my few belongings and to draw my pay cheque. I visited the laboratory and was surprised to find everything still in operation, although there was no one there. The sealed door to the environment was open and I called through. There was a peculiar smell in the air.

"Who's there?"

It was McCreedy's voice. I walked to a monitor screen and stared at him. He stared towards the camera, obviously not seeing me. "Who's that? Lipman?"

"Yes."

"You couldn't see it through, eh? Well . . . I can't say I blame you. But I don't give up so easily."

He returned to the subjects, both of which were now in a bad

state of decomposition. Yvonne's body had liquefied quite phenomenally and the distended, distorted bones protruded through
stretched skin.

"Something will happen," he shouted. "This is the most abnormal decomposition I have ever seen."

His sleeves were rolled up and a thick, green slime coated his
arms—he was feeling around among the bloated viscera of the
dead woman, and the body seemed to writhe beneath his touch.

I turned away. Behind me McCreedy shouted, "Look—Lipman,
look!"

I closed the door against his madness.

The Graveyard Cross

He had been the first to go, but he knew he would not be the first to return. He would not be a hero, but he had no need of that; after twenty years in space he wanted nothing but home.

It would not be his home, either. There would be none of the old gang, the happy group who had watched him leave, nearly three centuries before. But that was not important. There would be greenness beneath his feet and coolness on his face, and his past would be there, inscribed in the very genes of the people whom he would get to know.

He would have lost very little.

He switched on the transceiver with a rising sense of excitement.

"This is Deep Space Probe Orion. Commander Summerson. . . ."

And after a few moments: "Welcome, Summerson. It's been a long time."

It was the first human voice he had heard in twenty years. He requested landing permission on Earth, asked for the correct co-ordinates for touchdown.

"This is Littrow City—on the Moon. You'll have to land at Serenitatis Base, Commander Summerson. You'll have to check in here before anything."

"No thank you, Littrow—I've waited twenty years for a sight of Earth and I can't wait a second longer. I want to go straight down."

"Impossible. I repeat, impossible. Commander Summerson, you must *not* attempt to make any such landing. Please bring your ship down at Serenitatis."

Argument was useless. He complied, reluctantly, complaining all the time that since he had never left the ship in the whole of his mission, there could be no possibility of his having acquired a strange disease. Why did he need quarantine?

"It isn't quarantine, Commander. But you've been gone three centuries and things have changed on Earth. You may not want to go. . . ."

"Oh I'll want to go ! And nothing is going to stop me."

He snapped off the transceiver, and swallowed his disappointment, but he landed at the huge unmanned base in the Mare Serenitatis, and waited to be picked up.

Decontamination. Then de-robing.

Summerson was small, less than five feet five inches, and his body was thin. To look at him was to think: emaciation. But he was very fit. And something within him drove him towards Earth, something irrational, perhaps, but something strong.

Debriefing, and an account of stars and worlds that set alight the minds of those who listened. Those sessions were quiet indeed save for the voice of Summerson as he told of *Cyberon* and *Vax Sinester*, of worlds passing silently below, searched and then ignored as he went deeper into the deep, watching for a second Earth that he would never find.

When the sessions were finished Summerson packed his belongings together and went to Base Commander Wolfe to say Good-bye. His job was done; now at last he could go back to Earth.

Wolfe said No, and Summerson sat quietly and watched the younger man.

"Explain that." Icy.

"Earth has changed."

"Of course. I'm expecting to be the alone-est man on Earth for a while. But the things I want most of all won't have changed."

"Everything has changed," said Wolfe. "Everything down to the smallest leaf. Summerson, that isn't Earth any more. Earth died a long time ago; after you left, before I was born. It died of a cancer that had begun hundreds of years ago. Small and unnoticed in those days, it eventually took hold and Earth died. It's a different planet, Summerson. Totally."

Summerson shook his head and his fists clenched. "War? Are you telling me that there was——"

Wolfe laughed. "Not war, never war. War maims—it never destroys. Let me rephrase what I said. Earth *evolved*."

"Let me ask some questions," said Summerson, and inside he was breaking up because there was something wrong, something very wrong, and it was going to stop him; he knew it and he could not face it.

"Are there humans on Earth?" Wolfe smiled, nodded his head. "Are there two sexes of humans? Do they have arms and legs, a single head and a heart on the left side of their chest cavities?" All affirmative.

"Is there air on Earth? Is there water? Is there food? Life? Cities?"

"Certainly there are."

"Can I live on Earth?"

"You can. You can live there like any of us could live there. It wouldn't be much of a life—at the outside probably a day. Long enough to see a few sights before you choke up so much blood you drown, and find yourself being consumed before you've fully died."

Summerson stared at Wolfe and shook his head.

"Your Earth is dead, Summerson. Face the facts."

"Not dead," cried Summerson. "Only hidden. It's there, beneath, disguised, distorted perhaps, but there just the same. I must see it."

"Fine. We'll fly you across it. As many times as you like."

"I must *stand* on it."

"Wear a suit and we'll take you to the desert areas."

"Oh Christ, Wolfe, don't you understand? I must *be* there, I must feel it in my body like it was in my body twenty years ago!"

"Three hundred years ago!" shouted Wolfe, and they glared at each other, softened and fell back into sullen silence.

"You can't go back," said Wolfe.

"I'm going back," said Summerson.

"You won't survive."

"I'm going back at any cost. You can't stop me, Wolfe, not you, not anyone. I'm going back at any cost."

"The cost will be very great."

"I'm a rich man. My investments at the time I left were——"

"Not the money cost. You'll never need money at Littrow, or

Tycho, or Clavius, or Mars . . . you are a lifelong guest if you care to stay."

"I don't. I don't care to stay, I care to go. What cost?"

Lafayette, in white, with deep-set brown eyes that never seemed capable of meeting Summerson's gaze, fixed him down on a bed of steel, and began to push electrodes. He worked with an intensity that negated conversation and Summerson was glad because he was thinking of Oxford Street and a park (with a lake) that was called Hyde Park and had vanished a long time ago, Wolfe had said.

The electrodes aggravated and there were so many of them, and a computer burbled self-indulgently and planned and plotted Summerson's body and designed the frame that could be built upon the frame he already had.

Lafayette, talking with a slightly French accent (he was from French Imbrium where the French tradition was maintained) told Summerson that he was to sleep, now, and he would wake in twenty hours. Nothing would have changed, but over the weeks he would grow.

Summerson grew, and from five five he reached six six, and that was where he stopped because the computer said to stop. His long bones had lengthened and widened, his ribs had expanded, his shoulders broadened, the overall calcium content of his frame was increased (with no noticeable effect on his increased weight) and a para-parathyroid stopped his body correcting the fault. He was skeletal to look at and his head was small, but only because his body was so large.

He looked at himself in the mirror and felt sick. But it would get him back to earth.

He was fed, and nourished, and the skeletal display vanished and thick muscle appeared at a noticeable rate and eventually he was heavy set and a monstrous-looking man, and only two months had passed since he had insisted on the treatment.

Wolfe came to see him.

"How does it feel to be tall?"

"Why did they do it? Why is it necessary?"

They sat facing each other and Wolfe grinned. "It gives you a competitive advantage. Or put it this way, it deletes the competitive *dis*advantage of your short height."

"And there's more? Yes, I can see there's more."

"It was your choice."

It had been his choice and there was no denying it. To get back to Earth he would have to adapt to Earth. So Summerson tried to forget about being six foot six when he had lived a lifetime as a short man among men, and he tried to think of Earth, which was easy to do.

Wolfe sent him a woman and when he didn't express absolute delight, he sent a second, and a third. Summerson rejected them all.

Wolfe was upset and made the fact plain in no uncertain terms. Summerson accepted the anger and when Wolfe was calm again he pointed out that blind dates went out with the Ark.

"We could make your life on the Moon—or Mars—one long, lingering holiday. Summerson, I appeal to you. Don't risk your life, don't waste your experience by going down to Earth. If you want work, there is masses of it. Anywhere in the System, Summerson, anywhere. Name it and you'll go there and you'll never want, never need."

Summerson clenched his fists. "You don't—you *won't*—understand. Sure, in a year, maybe two, I'll come back, I might *beg* you to take me back. But only after I've been Home, Wolfe. I must go home first. I must survive and I must feel Earth again. *Then* send me beautiful women and the keys to the Solar System. . . ."

Wolfe sighed. "Earth will chew you up and spit you out, even with the changes we can make in you. Once down you'll never find peace, you'll never be able to return. Think, Summerson, think man. The solar system is buzzing with life. It's all new, it's all fresh, clean. It's frontier work, the sort of work a man like you would find second nature. You're a leader, Summerson, a man to place on a pedestal. Think about it."

"I've thought all I need. Earth, Wolfe, Earth is where I'm going, and *then* I'll think about your offers."

He was a frantic scrambling shape, sending up clouds of dust as he flailed across the crater bed beneath bigger and heavier loads: Earth watched.

In time he could move as fluently as a sprinter in track gear, and he could dodge and duck, and reverse direction on a thin and unexpected line. All this on Luna, and when they placed him in the IG simulator he did as well. He became fast and powerful; he could run. He could escape.

Lafayette began to thicken his skin.

"Why?" said Summerson. And Lafayette just smiled. "Your choice," he said.

"You sound like Wolfe. Why? Why thicken my skin?"

"Radiation," said Lafayette. "There's less oxygen on Earth, now, but more supersonic air vessels. The ozone layer has been reduced to an ozone smear. The UV reaching the surface would fry you in a week."

"My God," said Summerson as his skin thickened across the days. "The effect on evolution!" He sat up. Already his brain was learning to cope with new surface sensations. Heat he never felt. He could blister himself before he felt the pain. But his body was aware of heat and his reflexes remained fast. Pain came slowly. Damage was less likely because of his almost chitinous pelt.

"Exactly," said Lafayette, "what exactly will happen is anybody's guess. Over the next few generations we should start to see an effect."

They tanned him then, and he emerged as brown as oak. "Is everybody this colour?"

"Getting that way," said Lafayette.

There was a day when they took out his lungs and placed them in a machine. The machine cycled its strange body fluids through the veins and arteries of Summerson's gas-bags, and the walls, the linings of the air sacs, thickened. They became more resistant as the chemicals in the machine blood stimulated them and coaxed them. The mucous glands multiplied and spread about, and the cilia tracts in the bronchi became as dense as forests.

For several days the lungs wheezed on the machine and Summerson breathed not at all, his blood cycling through the body of a volunteer who lay, with Summerson, in a coma, breathing high oxy atmosphere and keeping their resting bodies alive and nourished.

The lungs found their way back to the body, and then there was his heart, which they removed and enlarged, made it into a three times as powerful squeeze-bag of muscle and sinew, and the bundle of *His* was removed and replaced with an artificial cable that was ten times as fast and twenty times as efficient, and would remain so for a thousand years thanks to the way that Lafayette had designed it.

One day Summerson awoke after sleeping for twenty days and found himself hung like Goliath. "Why? For whose benefit?"

"Sexual prowess is very important. It can save your neck."

"To impress women?"

"To quiesce dominant males."

"How bloody stupid."

"Earth has changed," said Wolfe simply. "Oh my God," said Summerson, and crept away to hide.

They strengthened his fingers and thickened his nails until he carried five spears at the end of each arm, and could dent hardboard with a single prod. They toughened the edge of each hand until the nerve endings had gone and the horny layer was thick and strong as iron.

As Summerson slept Lafayette removed the scalp and the skin around his eyes; down to his mouth the living bone was exposed and for twenty days a grinning skull watched as Lafayette softened the bone, and then thickened it, and as the calcium and phosphate lay down in crystal lattices so he inserted a criss-cross of non-irritating steel rods, and Summerson's skull became as strong as a helmet, and the brain below it was not the least affected.

Lafayette built a new cornea and fixed it to Summerson's so that the join could not be seen. The new cornea was a biological material that joined at the edge of the eye with the old cornea and formed a tough and deflective barrier against a normally blinding stab.

When Summerson looked into a mirror he could no longer see himself. But since he knew he was there he could take the shock and sublimate it into mere uneasiness.

If Summerson ever had doubts he walked to the edge of the enclosed city; there, standing dark and unreal, he would stare at the planet Earth. When the planet was in full bloom he felt something inside him stir and cry, and he knew that whatever was happening to him, he was right to go through with it, for it meant survival on that beautiful world.

When the Earth was in quarter phase then, as the months went by, he would feel uncertainty. He would look at himself and remember how he had been, and only the knowledge that no one down there was going to recognize him anyway kept him from screaming to Lafayette to "take it all off".

Monitoring his frustration, Wolfe arranged for a visit by Roz Steele.

There was a time when Summerson would have gasped. Women as large as Roz were circus exhibits, not lovers. And yet, standing inches taller than her, he found her magnificent.

She was black skinned and when he touched her she hardly felt the touch, and when he kissed her she hardly felt the kiss, and when he took her hand he found the callouses and stiffened fingers and he knew, then, that....

Roz said, "Don't look so surprised. You knew that other starmen had been arriving back before you."

"And you wanted to go to Earth . . . and this is what they did to you."

Roz nodded. "I'm a damn sight better looking than I was when I left."

"And you went back to Earth."

"No. I never made it. I gave up wanting to go down towards the end of my adaptation. I've lived the fullest life possible since then."

For a moment Summerson found himself nodding, then he realized. "Wolfe sent you to work on me."

"He sent me to lie with you. As simple as that. You will work on yourself. I hope you *do* go down to Earth. You'll be the first one that did."

"And the others?"

"Scattered through the solar system, mostly on Mars. That's a world and a half. I spent ten years there. I'm going back soon. Why don't you come with me?"

Summerson smiled. "How do you know we'll get along?"

She reached over and unbuttoned his tunic. Summerson stood motionless with his heart hammering and the excitement of the moment causing him to rise to his full gargantuan extent. When he was naked she unbuttoned her own robe and let it slip from her shoulders.

It was a passion that Summerson might never have known, for he was not, in his original form, a passionate man. An attitude to love depends largely on confidence in one's physical appearance, and now Summerson felt powerful, and he was a powerful lover.

Lafayette, seeming to relish his task, called for Summerson for one last time and while Summerson slept he made him into a high-tension man. He altered the threshold level of the feedback loop that governed the adrenalin flow into Summerson's vascular system, and when Summerson emerged he found that the slightest sensation of unease precipitated him into a state of complete mental and physical alertness. He began to bristle, he began to twist and turn as he walked as if some shadow haunted him and, should it creep up on him, would overcome him.

Likewise his temper suffered and he snapped and jumped, and his eyes became the eyes of a searching man, never still, always restive.

Except when they gazed at Earth.

Roz took her leave and Summerson watched her go with regret. She shipped for Mars and inside him Summerson knew that should he ever leave Earth he would head after her.

He had lost his taste for food and Lafayette explained that his stomach was changed. It would now break down alcohol in a matter of seconds. No drunks for Summerson. At the slightest sign of poison or infected food the stomach would void its contents and flush the chamber with acid which would also be voided. Much of the food on Earth was unfit to eat because of high phosphorous and chlorine contamination. It would be poison to Summerson. A tiny bio-sensor in the wall of his stomach was his guardian.

"Food is not so important to you now," said Lafayette. "You're a walking storehouse of all the vital amino-acids, vitamins and elements you need. Only a few weeks' supply, of course, but no doubt you will eat and these are just back-ups. There are bio-monitors in the hepatic portal and right brachial veins and they're reading your blood composition all the time. Any ingredient falling below the necessary level you can rectify at once. Prolonged deficit will be made known to you by a skin itch over your right arm. A timing mechanism—a unit of monkey liver cells actually, designed to accumulate whatever your stores are secreting; critical level reached—reflex loop to histamine-loaded cells in your skin, and you are warned."

"Monkey cells," said Summerson, almost in disbelief.

"Your body thinks they're you. We tagged them with your identity factor. Settling in nicely I should imagine.

"We've done much the same thing to some highly educated lymphocytes—they've been exposed to every disease organism we know about. They'll be your watch-dogs. Instead of the delay to produce primary immunity, during which time you'd die of many of these diseases, you can now react with secondary immunity which appears very fast."

"And I won't reject the cells?"

"Not if I've done my job properly. Those, by the way, are human lymphocytes, but like the monkey cells they've been tagged with your own identity-factor. You'll greet them like friends. They're also very long-lived cells—just a lysosome stabilizing gimmick that was developed about a hundred years ago."

"When I die my white cells will live on, is that it? Roaming the wastelands of Earth searching for a host."

For a few hours, as Summerson basked in Earthlight on the rim of a small crater, south-west of the colony at Littrow, he imagined that the preparations were finished. His body had been rebuilt and he could no longer call himself Summerson with quite the same meaning as before.

But now it seemed worthwhile, the waiting, the delaying, the endless sleeps while Lafayette had probed and changed and strengthened and destroyed.

Lafayette had enjoyed his task. He was the Base surgeon but the few travellers who returned and who needed the engineering job for their return to Earth were his real interest.

And yet, when it was finished, none ever returned. It was as if their changed bodies caused their minds to change, made them find Earth as repulsive as Wolfe found it.

Summerson felt no such repulsion. He was a hideous being by his own standards, and if he reflected the needs of Earth, then Earth was probably a hideous world. But beauty, as the saying went, is only skin deep. Summerson was interested in a deeper level of Earth. And the longing was still with him; the desire to return, whilst not now voiced as often as it had been voiced by his newly returned (shorter, whiter, less perfect) self, was just as strong.

He returned to Littrow and to his solex, and though Roz was gone and the room was cold and empty, he found comfort there.

And D'Quiss.

"I'm Felix D'Quiss," he said, rising from the couch. A tall, thin man; sparse blond hair over a nordic head; eyes blue, quite intense. A firm shake of ugly hands, the big meeting the grotesquely big. Smart, in a white protex suit, the telltale signs of medical status scattered across the pockets—a watch, a pen, a probe, a contact unit unobtrusively lodged behind his ear.

"Summerson," said Summerson. "Mark II."

"I know. You have taken the changes with remarkable complacency."

"I want to get down to Earth. I'd change anything for that."

"I'm glad to hear it."

Summerson shivered and crossed to the ice box. He fetched out two mash cans and proffered one to D'Quiss who declined it. Summerson opened his own and sipped the drink. "Let me guess," he said, crossing to the wall window and watching as Earth seemed to twist away again, just out of reach. "My mind."

"Yes."

"You're going to change it. You're going to remove Summerson from my head like you removed him from my body."

"Part of the sacrifice," said D'Quiss, smiling. "You said when they started on you that no cost was too great. You will have to have meant it if you want to get to Earth."

"I certainly want to do that!" Summerson said loudly. "With the emphasis on the *I*. If you alter my mind out of all proportion, if you take the little Summerson in my skull and change him into a para-Summerson, then it isn't *me* any longer. The man who goes down to Earth might not give a damn about the planet. . . . Is that what you want? Is that what happened to Roz and the others? After all this anatomical change you then 'make' us not want to return? Because in fact you've been adapting us to conditions on Mars. . . ? Well, I'm sorry to disappoint you, Mr. D'Quiss, but I've taken all the change I intend to take. And I *still* intend to go down to Earth."

D'Quiss nodded, smiling in a self-assured way. "Is this the rational and calm Summerson that came to Littrow?"

"I'm losing my identity, D'Quiss. That's enough to make any man jumpy."

"You're not losing your identity, merely your appearance, your inadequacies."

"I've lost all the inadequacies I intend to lose. Tell Wolfe I'm leaving right now."

D'Quiss sat quietly and stared at Summerson. He told him, then, that there would be no more change. That the adaptation by engineering was over, finished. The mind, however, was a delicate organ, dependent for it function on environment, both social and physical, and Summerson's mind could not tolerate the environment, both social and physical, of Earth.

"So you want to change it. Like I said, chop here, replace there, Mark III Summerson, grinning idiot, oblivious, non-existent."

Nothing of the sort, said D'Quiss. A few emplacements to help Summerson fight the mental pressures.

"Look at it this way. You've already manifested several neuroses."

"For example?"

"Your shame, embarrassment when Lafayette expanded your sex organ."

"Oh . . . that."

"Yes, that. A small enough point on its own, but on Earth do you realize how destructive any sort of sexual embarrassment is? You would not survive to walk down the street. But we can mask, condition, certain facets of your personality that might be embarrassing to you."

"No. Positively no."

"Or we can place artificial connections between several areas of your brain that will allow you to see exactly when a dangerous mood, feeling, response is approaching, and you can then say to yourself, *careful Summerson, pretend* . . . you see? It will give you the ability to conquer your mental inadequacies without losing the power of choice. Well?"

Summerson was silent.

D'Quiss went on. "Let me put it this way. Earth is totally hostile. Not hostile by its own standards—it has the same range from extreme to extreme within the population with the bulk of the population filling the centre of the curve. But in the three hundred years you have been away that curve has shifted towards the hostile extreme. What was extreme in your day is now matter of fact. Violence, death, attitude to privacy, of body and home, all these things are set within different parameters. You wouldn't last five minutes."

"So you keep telling me. So Wolfe and Lafayette keep telling me."

"All right, so it's a figurative expression. You might survive a week, a month, a year, but it would be fighting all the time, a terrible struggle for survival."

D'Quiss was watching him very intently, but his face showed complete calm, unlike Wolfe who had seemed almost exasperated by Summerson's doggedness. "And with a few electrodes in my head I would find it easier to survive. Is that what you're saying?"

D'Quiss nodded. "The most essential thing is that you keep your wits about you, that you remain even tempered. Stable. When your heart breaks your mind has got to be oblivious to it; when your heart sings, the same thing goes. When your temper flares you can calm at a moment's thought, but the cause of your anger will not be obliterated so you can still act on it."

"A few electrodes . . . no invisible conditioning, no twisting of a paranoia here and moving it slightly so I can't feel persecuted?"

"Not unless you want it."

"I don't want it! I want Summerson—me!—to see Earth as he saw it when he left. I want to see the change, feel the difference, seek out the unchanged elements. I want to feel the sadness or the horror as Summerson, *this* Summerson, would have felt it three hundred years ago." He turned to stare up at the Crescent Earth. "When I was twenty years younger," he said softly.

D'Quiss watched him impassively. After a while Summerson moved from the window and sprawled out in an armchair, staring at the other man.

D'Quiss showed no discomfiture. "Why do you want to go back? What's the real reason?"

Summerson laughed. "Does there have to be a *real* reason? Isn't it possible that I was telling the truth?" D'Quiss said nothing. After a moment Summerson went on, his eyes focused nowhere in particular. "It's funny you know. I can remember standing on the ramp at Southend, looking at the shuttle. Such a tiny ship. I wanted nothing else but to get away from Earth. Since I was a kid I wanted to be a probepilot. My parents did everything they could to discourage me, but I was too determined. They came to Southend when I was launched and watched me leave, and I didn't even say good-bye to them. Twenty years in space and I couldn't stop thinking about them. I really came to understand them, to love them. Can you imagine that? Twenty years, and no way back. . . ."

"It must be an intolerable thought."

"Thanks," said Summerson dully. "But no, nothing is intolerable. It's just . . . the emptiness."

"The emptiness of space?"

"Of everything. A man is much more than just a mind in a body. That's just a small part of him. He's everything that relates to him and which he relates to in turn, and that part of me has gone and I feel just . . . just a shard. There's only one place I know where I can come to terms with that emptiness."

"Earth?"

"Earth."

"What do you plan on doing once you get there?"

"Oh, explore. Remember. Write. Talk to people."

"What if they regard you as a freak?"

"Why should they?"

"Why shouldn't they? An off-worlder, *the* off-worlder to many of them. You will be the first to set foot on Earth for more than two generations. They will react to you, I'm sure of that, but that reaction could well be hostile; and if not hostile to begin with, then later certainly. When the novelty wears off. . . ."

"Will they leave me alone? Will they let me search for the things I want to search for?"

"I don't know," said D'Quiss. "You'll have to find yourself employment which could be difficult. And if you feel that you might want to leave for the Moon, then we'll have to arrange a method of communication so we can come and pick you up."

"You'd do that? After I've declined your every offer for help whilst I was here?"

"We're not barbarians," said D'Quiss.

Summerson slept.

After five days he awoke looking the same, feeling the same, but weighing slightly more—the weight of the bio-lam electrodes and miniature power pack embedded partly in his skull and partly in the substance of his brain.

They tried a simple test involving the arousal of his anger and he became angry. They explained that he had merely to think about *not* getting angry and it would pass. They tried the test again and he felt anger rise in him, and then he thought it away and he saw the test for what it was. He tried to think away the remorse at losing Roz, but he couldn't.

It only worked for the future. And when he eventually left Earth he would be able to lose the electrodes, the power pack and the influence of D'Quiss.

He packed his bags and, almost fatalistically, walked towards Wolfe's office. Wolfe was there, and Lafayette. And D'Quiss sitting relaxedly in a corner and smoking a non-inhalant cigarette.

"Are you ready to go?"

"You mean no more changes? I can hardly believe it."

Wolfe smiled. "You'll survive unless there's something we've overlooked, something important."

"Which we don't know about," said Lafayette, almost as if he were justifying a certain failure.

"But which we will know about after your decline," said D'Quiss from the side of the room.

Now at last Summerson took his grateful leave and went to the base airlock. A 'bus took him to Serenitatis, to a small ship, now long disused, that would take him down to Earth.

He had been on the Moon for over a year. And as he walked across the metal ramp to the waiting ship he suddenly felt all the excitement at going home he had felt as he had arrived in the solar system, all those months before.

With a yell and a laugh he jumped high in the vacuum and bounded to the ship, to take his place (the only passenger) in the small cabin. Wolfe was a black shape in the brightly lit 'bus, parked half a mile from the ramp.

The sea, the ocean, heaving, white flecked (but somehow . . . duller than he remembered), Summerson's eyes trying to leave his head to see down to the Earth. Asia, drifting below, and China, and the China Sea, scattered islands, the buzz of high-flying planes, eyes peering at the ship as it glided slowly round the world.

The coast of California sliding below like some huge projection —more buzzing, a swarm of high-flying sightseers, klaxon blasts rending the high atmosphere, the swarms dropping away in front to reassemble behind.

The Atlantic, darker, more sombre than the Pacific, and England, then, and down.

Home.

He was an island. There was dust and shadows. There was no moon. The sun shone through clouds. There was movement, and the cries of the dying. There was dying, and the roar of movement. There was the barking of dogs and the straying of cats.

He was an island and he stopped in the middle of the world and there was nothing to see but the shadows that moved by, and the walls that enclosed him, brick fingers pointing to the sky. He went to where he had once lived.

It was now a slag tip, the waste of centuries poured across an area of several square miles. Bomb waste, desolation, with driverless machines calmly chewing their way through the sea of junk.

There was a girder twisted into the shape of a cross, a single cross, a graveyard cross. He walked through ghosts and filth and picked up a handful of ash and stared at it for a long time.

He saw no people, just dark, hard faces. He heard them, he touched them physically, but they moved so fast, they lived so distant. He tried to move fast to match velocities, but they changed direction and he could never keep up. He drifted through streets, cities, towns, breathing the dust, choking up his food, waking up with his face a bloody mess, registering the attack of screaming gangs, feeling the delayed pain, conscious of his own ferocity . . . everything moved around him, never with him. Everything seemed so fast. He spoke words and the words were heard, and he heard words back, but there was never any . . .

Communication.

There was no communication. He was a perfectly adapted man, but they could not have known about communication. They had prepared him for poison, fumes, attack and flight, but they had not prepared him for the indifference.

He died a hundred times—hit, spin, shattered—left naked to die and he crept away and found himself and . . .

Hit, spin, slugged, and woman's laughter, and an insane and blind achievement of sexual satisfaction and . . .

Crawled away.

There was the filth of alleyways, the smell of faeces, the pain of broken bones that healed so quickly. . . .

The fierceness of dogs, the fastness of movement, the stench of air, the burning of sun, the coldness of children, the emptiness of thought. Confusion, starvation of emotion.

No communication.

He could not identify. He was planes apart, worlds away, points out of focus, miles off target. He was so alien that he hardly registered, and his body was a fragment of litter and it blew away. . . .

Something went wrong and his anger became uncontrollable. He was hit on the head and something dislodged, and he lost control. And there were armed men and he was hustled away at right angles to the human flow, and he found himself :

In peace. There was peace. A small room, a barred window, the distant grating of metal locks. A filthy pit in the floor, a hard bed. Rats, roaches, sweat, tears. . . . Light from the window— sounds so distant they were almost familiar. Peace—and Earth.

He had found Earth again.

Sitting in the stillness he knew he was home at last.

Robin Douglas

Agapé

Sfiff remained motionless and watched. The creature was in trouble, he could see that, but wild beings in pain or terror should not be approached rashly, and this was a creature the like of which he had never seen before. Its limbs—at first Sfiff was confused as to how many of them there were—appeared, some of them at any rate, to be involved in locomotion. Two of them proceeded by being lifted and placed on the ground alternately one in front of the other, and on these the bulk of the creature was supported, swaying about in a precarious manner which suggested that forward movement was a matter of toil, a thing of great effort and concentration. Two more limbs, Sfiff noticed, were attached one on each side of the tubular middle section, about halfway up, and these were held close to the creature's sides, both of them bent at a joint so that half their length was tucked away somewhere at the creature's back. Besides these, he could make out a further four limbs that apparently sprouted out of the creature's back in pairs, one pair kept dangling forwards about its middle, and the other around what Sfiff could only presume was the creature's neck. In a structure so unlike his own, he couldn't be sure, but considering the forms of other species known to him, it did seem to be a neck : at least, two things very much like heads rose from it. One of these appeared to be injured : it lolled and tossed below the other which was held more or less steady, and in which two dark round holes swivelled about, showing flashes of curious white (smelling organs? sight organs? hearing organs?). But perhaps the other head wasn't injured. It was just possible that the creature habitually used only one head at a time, holding the other in reserve for emergencies or so as to be able to dispense with sleep. . . . Sfiff could not decide on the point, and his thoughts shifted to another mystery. He tried to understand the creature's covering, a silvery, fitting membrane in which there were gaps indicating that it was not an integral part of its wearer. This disturbed him more than anything else. He had never heard of any being other than the Raider-birds purposefully skinning its prey, and even Raider-birds only lined their nests with such gruesome trophies, never pulled them onto their own backs. But this . . . Sfiff stared hard at the macabre spectacle before him. He thought the beast must be particularly savage and brutish to carry around on its body the skin of its victim, and hoped his camouflage would prove adequate. As his fear mounted, he made a point of reminding himself that his conclusions were not necessarily correct. There were things unaccounted for. From what kind of animal, for instance, could this eight-limbed monster have originally stripped such a skin? Sfiff could not think of one. The species of the victim was no more familiar to him than that of the predator, whose appearance was utterly alien. Not even in his race's myths was there mention of such a being in its shiny, acquired skin . . . and casting around for other explanations, he suddenly filled with hope: maybe this secondary coating was not a predatory trophy but the animal's own growth after all, a worn-out pelt, about to be discarded in favour of the seasonal new one growing underneath. That would explain the gaps in it. The idea calmed Sfiff, and at that moment he would not have moved even if it had seemed safe to do so; richly endowed with the passion for fairmindedness native to his race, his fear was matched by his intense interest. Staining the enigmatic silver coat he observed blemishes in a bright colour, something vaguely akin to his idea of red or brown, and instinctively he knew that these were signs of damage, moisture seeping out from the creature's internal organs. In spite of his apprehension he longed to move closer to investigate. Could he help in some way?

Wisely he did not move. There was too much strangeness, and the strangeness, Sfiff sensed, extended to depths he dared not permit himself to realize. . . .

Cosgrave eyed the boulders ahead of him with misgivings. He was panting hard in the acidic air, while his blood hammered and whined through his brain. That attack a while ago by the bird-like monstrosities had been vicious, really vicious; at one point he had been obliged to drop Vernon like an old sack, standing astride him while he fought them off. Poor bastard, Vernon. He heaved the unconscious man a little higher on his back, movement which sent stinging pains across his shoulder-blades. Yes, he was much too tired to go further. And where, in God's name, should he go in any case? It all amounted to the same. Despairingly he thought of *The Panegyric*, and saw again the mind-splitting explosion which he had so narrowly escaped. He, and Vernon. The unlucky ones. Their eighteen colleagues, dead or unconscious on impact and quickly blown to bits—clearly that had been payment for their virtues, not their vices. Cleanly wiped out in the blast of a moment . . . Cosgrave, who had never been a traditionalist in religious matters nor cared for the latest scientific hypotheses on the subject of after-life, noted to himself wryly that he envied the eighteen dead their freedom: Earth, Alpha Centauri—any damned spot they cared for now lay within their reach if anywhere did, whereas he and Vernon . . . what hope was there for them, stranded here, which was precisely nowhere, without the means of living? Despite his exhaustion, Cosgrave glowed with energetic bitterness. It would not have been so bad if *The Panegyric's* crash could conceivably have been an accident, but in such a sophisticated craft, with the very latest in computers and fail-safe devices, only ingenious sabotage could have flung her so far off-course and crashed her in such a manner that the chain reactions got out of hand. And genius of that calibre (not to mention ruthlessness and resources) was the possession of only one terrorist movement: AGAPÉ—damn the irony of that obsolete word—the Action Group Against Planetary Exploitation. These were high-minded fanatics; horrified by the rapid expansion of human colonies across the galaxy, wasting and abusing new worlds' natural resources, they were committed to hindering it by any means that proved effective. Cosgrave was familiar with the reasoning of such men: "What are the twenty lives in this ship we destroy," they'd argue, "compared with the millions still living at subsistence level on Old Terra, or those trapped in the degenerate conditions of the commercial colonies? What's the use of expansion in any case before we've learned to distribute resources justly? And what right have we to pillage other worlds? What if we should encounter intelligent life? Are we showing any moral readiness for that? Of course not. . . . This criminal expansion must be halted. Mankind must be given time . . . consolidate. . . . And for a noble cause, there's always a price."

Cosgrave was part of the price. He continued staring at the boulders. Almost without noticing it he had come to a standstill, daunted by an unnerving impression that something was watching him. There was also a scent hovering about the rocks, faint and so alien that he could hardly detect it. Were the boulders alive? They looked solid enough, inanimate. Would they shelter himself and Vernon from the hellish winged things? Or was this exactly the kind of terrain in which they made their lairs? Cosgrave felt clownishly vulnerable, standing in the open, bowed under his burden and debating with himself. He coughed uncomfortably, noting the furry sensation in his throat. There was another irony. The furry throat was a symptom of Colonial Fever, a mutation of an old terrestrial 'flu strain, and only during the previous Terra-day-cycle the ship's medic had warned him that it was potentially serious. Cosgrave smiled without humour. Where was the medic now? Blasted specks of protoplasm fused into alien rock. Cosgrave felt desperately lonely.

"Well, Vernon, old man," he spoke jauntily to the silent load on his shoulders, "can't stand here all day. Reckon I'll put you down among those rocks under the cliff face over there. Then I gotta find us some water. . . ."

Vernon naturally said nothing. His face hung grey and empty beside the other man's neck. He seemed more than half dead already. Maybe he was dead. Maybe Cosgrave had made the wrong choice when he'd pulled him out of the tangled mass of bodies, just because he was so young and freshfaced, and this had been his first trip. Maybe Vernon's crack on the head had been fatal, and Cosgrave had wasted the only thing he'd had to offer his nineteen shipmates—strong arms with which to carry clear one of them. "To hell with it," he muttered. As if there had been time to work out the respective merits of nineteen men and each one's chances of survival. He'd reckoned on less than sixteen Terra-mins to get out of the blast area, and that hadn't left him much margin for fine estimations. . . . He stopped studying Vernon's face and turned his gaze back to the boulders. As he did so—didn't something move? He thought something moved. Among the boulders. His breathing almost stopped; he suffered a momentary paralysis in which there flashed through his mind a vivid image of *The Panegyric's* arms cabinet, every weapon neatly locked away inside it. A beamer, a sonar-pistol, anything would have been a comfort. . . . As it was, he stood defenceless confronting the rocks, and hoped he was hallucinating. The strange atmosphere, perhaps, or the Colonial Fever: a touch of delirium. For a complete Terra-min he waited, sweating wretchedly, but when at the end of that time nothing had happened, he began to move again, slowly edging towards the nearest boulders. He laid down Vernon in the first sizeable gap he found amongst them.

"There you are, son-of-a-gun, sleep it off!"

His voice sounded very small, almost meaningless, in all the uncharted desolation that surrounded him, and Cosgrave hated hearing it. Still, he felt compelled to speak occasionally—a natural, decent thing, talking to another human being . . . his fingers explored Vernon's chest in a controlled flurry of panic. The unconscious man felt cold, deadly cold, but that was shock, it had to be shock. . . . He stared at Vernon's ashen face stupidly. Beneath his fingers, inside the silence, he could feel a meagre, unrhythmical something—a cardiac whimper, a child crying . . . his last contact with his own kind, with someone to talk to. There had to be someone to talk to, or he would go mad.

"My God, don't you die!" whispered Cosgrave desperately, "don't you run out on me, you bastard!"

He withdrew his hand and closed up Vernon's jacket with helpless gentleness; and after that he sat resting his head on his bent knees, peering out between the boulders at the plain he had just struggled across. He had to look in that direction because something made him reluctant to stare too long at the boulders and the cliff rising behind him, as though he feared catching sight of

c

another movement. He didn't want to see. He was simply too tired, and preferred to rely upon his ignorance.

The nearer portion of the plain was nothing more than a series of cracked dust-slabs, baked hard and ungiving, but beyond these lay the shadow of a vast area covered with tall, feather-like plants, and quite a way beyond these again, mercifully concealed by them, must lie the charred crater fringed with molten fragments of humans and human inventions—the place where *The Panegyric* had exploded.

"I won't think about that."

He drew his eyes away and wrestled with his nerves until he could peer round at the cliff face. It rose almost sheer to a great height with the boulders crowding up against its base in a tumbled pyramid. There were plenty of dark holes and crevices among the boulders themselves and on the lower stretches of the cliff where something sinister might be lurking. Cosgrave felt he had been mad to come here. He had been drawn toward the high land in the hope of finding water, a stream running down from the plateau, or at the worst some slight trace dampening the rocks; but now that he had reached it, the rocky outcrop seemed as dry as the flat desert, nothing more than a collection of bleached bones splitting with age and aridity.

"An ungiving world all over," he told himself, "no promises, no water, no way out...."

He moved his larynx with tender caution, noting how the fur-like sensation in his throat turned to one of burning as he did so. He couldn't fight this fever without water. Those feather-plants he had pushed through on the plain—he had hopefully (and rashly) snapped their stems by treading them down with well-aimed steps, but if he hadn't paid for this foolhardiness by being splattered with toxic sap, neither had he found any kind of moisture. The stems were hollow, utterly brittle, and slowly Cosgrave had realized that the plants were so feather-like because they were desiccated, only the fragile skeletons of their living selves.

"Must be the dry season."

He wondered feebly whether one of those winged monsters

could be snared. Would it be nutritious if he managed it? Would it have anything like blood that he could drink?

"Should have followed them, not run from them," he muttered, "damn things must eat something. . . ."

A novel idea came to him, and he eyed Vernon with a strained, inquisitive expression, desirous—but it was only for a second, before he hid his face in his hands.

It took Sfiff time to recover from the shock. First, the unnerving creature had stopped advancing, and focussed its dark headholes directly on him. Next, it had twisted one of its heads towards the other, apparently to communicate with it, and the sounds it had made had interested Sfiff so much that he'd risked a quick movement to realign his second auditory centre. The creature appeared not to notice, because shortly afterwards it began to advance again and came as far as the first boulders. There it had made another halt, and by flexing its limbs in various directions, bending low with a contortion of its body—it had come apart. Split. One half had arranged the other half on the ground and become completely detached from it, taking up a strange posture by its side. Sfiff was so taken aback that he had almost turned and fled, but instead he managed a logical thought : reproduction ! He had just witnessed a birth ! The creature developed its large, cumbersome embryo externally, swathed for protection in a secondary skin like its own, and now it had just completed the act of separation. Yes, yes, a birth . . . and yet. . . .

As he watched the parent creature examining the other's body, he was struck by an unwelcome impression that this behaviour was not parental at all. It was more like the concern of a friend. A friend's concern for a friend. Nonsense ! He made a determined effort to discipline his thoughts : if he carried on in this vein, he'd have to believe that what he had taken for one animal had always been two, the strong one carrying the injured ! Which was impossible. On Sfiff's world no savage animal would do such a thing, life was too hard. Even among his own kind incidents of that nature were uncommon, because no individual would allow himself to be a burden to others—suicide was preferable. So how in the world? But here Sfiff's thoughts shuddered into a dark wall.

He knew now with unavoidable certainty that these strange beings among the rocks—they were nothing in his world: they had come from outside it.

Outsiders!—From where? Was there anything outside to come from? Sfiff felt a panic urgency to escape, to inflate his underbelly and glide over the rocks to the cliff face, attach himself, and struggle up it onto the plateau. He longed for his own kind, the togetherness of the Community. Besides his fear, his hormonal condition was urging him in that direction, because now the Hibernation was over and soon—he could feel it on his skin—the rains would come, it was time for grooming and courting rituals. But how to move away without attracting attention? Now that he saw them for what they were, the creatures seemed doubly dangerous, possessed of powers his world knew nothing about. Perhaps they could kill him with a thought. . . . Sfiff kept boulder-still and wished he had not come down the cliff for Hibernation in the first place. It was rare for his kind to do so, because the cliff face was in parts maliciously sheer and smooth so that one could not be sure of getting up again. When the plateau's one pool silted up at the approach of the dry season and the Community scattered to hibernate, most chose nooks and crannies on the exposed plateau itself where several would be lost, picked off by the marauding winged Raiders. Others chose the far side of the plateau, where hot gases seeped out of the ground and kept the Raiders at bay; but this site was also unsatisfactory because each season several hibernators were poisoned by the fumes and would die in their sleep. So Sfiff had taken it upon himself to make a daring experiment. Often he had peered over the cliff edge and considered the shadowy gaps between the boulders far below, an ideal area of camouflage and shelter, lying cool in the shade of the overhanging cliff, and he had decided to spend a Hibernation down there. If the experiment proved successful, if—as he thought—it proved within one's powers to clamber up the face again, he would recommend the site for consideration by all the Community. It had been a courageous and eminently worthwhile enterprise, but as Sfiff stared at the Outsiders he was sufficiently weak to regret having undertaken it.

Something about the atmosphere was also adding to his discomfort. Apart from the tingling symptoms of imminent rain, a light dust had been falling on his skin and the sky seemed strangely dense and brilliant, especially across the plain beyond the feather-plants. True, long hibernation could play tricks on one's senses, but he thought he had been aware of an eerie flash on the horizon just as he had woken from his sleep. Was that how these Outsiders travelled? Down out of the stars on streaks of dazzling light? If so, they were, they were ... but Sfiff's racial concepts did not include one of divinity.

Suddenly his coiled tentacles stiffened with alarm. One of the creatures had risen on two of its limbs and was flourishing the other two at the sky, whilst out of its head poured a desperate sound of misery. Sfiff did not doubt for a second that it was misery.

Vernon had just died.

"Bastards!" croaked Cosgrave, "murdering, pious bastards!"

He stared madly into the yellowish expanse of nothing that arched over him: in fact he wasn't shouting for Vernon's sake at all, but for his own, out of pity for himself caged alive at the end of nowhere with no purpose left to human speech. He flung his hatred for the AGAPÉ agents out into space, directing it to wherever they lurked in hideouts on Old Terra or the Colonies, plotting their next sabotage, and the next.... Perhaps what gave his hatred its sharpest edge was his awareness of AGAPÉ's futility. Even if they sabotaged half the commercial fleets, they'd never stop expansion. At best they could only delay it, add to its costs, and make the competition between rival companies even more vicious. This would mean even greater exploitation of the masses AGAPÉ thought they championed. What fools! How could they hope ever to control human greed just by damaging its implements? Senseless, naïve murderers. . . . Exhausted with horror at his own situation, Cosgrave crumpled into a heap beside Vernon's body. His heart was banging wildly and he felt sticky with heat. His throat had constricted into a tight ball of fluff and he found breathing painful—a constant reminder that the planet's atmosphere probably contained toxic gases. There had been no time to analyse its contents before *The Panegyric's* crash landing, and no point in any case. Yes, most likely he was being slowly poisoned by something in the atmosphere, and that, helped along by the fever, would soon finish him off. Good . . . good . . . the idea brought him only profound relief.

Now the Outsiders lay side by side, one very still, the other moving its limbs at intervals, turning its head this way and that, vulnerably. . . . It was an appropriate time in which to escape, and Sfiff ached to do it; but, painful as it was for him, his thoughts began to give ground to a new problem: he saw that it remained true, what he had first noticed: these creatures were in some kind of distress. And who would help them if Sfiff did not? Something unheard of, wonderful, beings from Outside—how could he just make off and neglect them? Sfiff made his decision.

If he'd been human, he might have scuttled away to rally support among his own kind before approaching the aliens, but belonging to a species hard pressed for survival, it was his moral duty not to involve others in any risk, and he was fully conscious that the first approach must be made by himself alone. Ideally, of course, he should have found a way of letting others know what he was about to do before he did it, in case the beings killed him, and could therefore be considered a threat to the Community; but as Sfiff debated this point, instinct warned him that the Outsiders were dying. If he delayed, clambered up the cliff face to the Community and came back later, by that time they might both be dead. Already they were behaving as if they were dangerously weakened, and Sfiff, in his logic, thought of food. Perhaps they were starving. Sfiff had food; not much, after the Hibernation, but the remains of his store; all that he had refrained from eating before the long sleep he had gathered up and crammed into his feed-pouch on waking in order to prepare himself for the gruelling climb that lay ahead. It would be quite a simple matter to remove this still undigested food from his pouch and lay it before the Outsiders. Cautiously he began to inflate his underbelly, gradually swelling to twice his bulk until with one last hesitation to scan the sky for Raiders, he dilated the underbelly's valves; his upper muscles contracted with a downward pumping motion while his intake valves stretched wide as they sucked in the air; then his tentacles uncoiled, and Sfiff began to move.

Cosgrave sensed the movement. Sick as he was, some mental alertness returned, enough to prevent him from jerking his head up suddenly. He kept his cheek low, resting against his arm on the ground, but slowly, opening his eyes by careful fractions, he turned his head towards the disturbance—a disturbance of sound and smell, a rasping noise as of gas being forced out through tubes, and a stench like bad breath or a fart, warm and personal. . . .

"Dear God!"

It seemed as if a massive boulder had dislodged itself from the pile at the base of the cliff; grey and oval, it half bounced, half rolled towards him over the others, semi-buoyant, and aided by three muscular protuberances . . . a compromise technique of locomotion, a kind of inefficient hover-beast that used its squid-like extensions alternately to support its central bulk in an upright position and to grab hold of some crevice ahead by means of which to drag the central part forward. A ludicrous monstrosity of a thing . . . utterly hideous.

Halfway down its otherwise featureless body yawned a gap, dark and unequivocal. Some kind of mouth. Cosgrave had no doubt of it.

"Going to make a bloody meal of me!" he thought; "not if I can help it!"

He managed to clamber to his feet like an ungainly animal emerging from water, tottering and shaking. The monstrosity stopped. Perhaps it was watching him. He couldn't tell: he could see nothing that looked like eyes in it. Only the horizontal slit in its middle opened wider.

"Go away! Get away!" he whined, backing off.

It remained where it was, resting its body on a boulder, but one of its tentacles slowly looped round and thrust itself into the gross cavity of its mouth. That was too much for Cosgrave: the damned thing seemed to be asking permission to eat him. . . .

"Eat Vernon! Leave me alone!"

He stumbled a few paces out into the plain, but his legs no longer felt his own and the horizon lurched crazily up at right angles to the sky. . . . The fever was having its heyday. Cosgrave collapsed, panting, a bundle of terrified anticipation. Perhaps the monster would eat Vernon. . . . Or perhaps it didn't like its food dead. . . . Or perhaps it didn't exist, and he was hallucinating. No: this thing was real enough . . . and now it was inspecting the corpse, hissing over the boulders between which the dead man lay, poking about with its tentacles. . . . At the thought of contact between that hideous flesh and human flesh, even dead human flesh, Cosgrave filled with nausea. He buried his face in his arms to be rid of the sight of it, and heard the thing's deep sighs, the brushing of its belly over the rocks as it began to move again. So it was rejecting Vernon, hover-dragging closer. . . .

He was terrified by an abrupt silence: expecting to find the beast almost on top of him and about to strike, he raised his head with a gasp of protest, only to check himself, amazed. It had stopped several metres off. It had lowered its bulk onto the plain, and now all three tentacles were delving about in its mouth, coming out at times to lay down lumps of something in the space between itself and Cosgrave. Lumps of what? Was it defecating? Laying eggs? Maybe it hadn't noticed the second man at all . . . maybe it was blind, not interested. . . . Cosgrave stared at the moist greyish lumps, and then back at the silent bulk of the creature. He could not believe it wasn't interested: he had the strongest impression that in some way all the antics of this thing were related to himself; they seemed calculated, almost rational.

"Easy, easy!" he told himself, "you're not mad yet!"

Now the beast had closed its mouth, and was resting, completely motionless, apparently waiting. Cosgrave made no move. At last, after a long, tense duel of silences, the beast swung out a tentacle and pushed one of the foul lumps closer to Cosgrave, so close that its odour made the man turn his head away.

But in the same instant, he understood. Food! He was being

offered food ! For one moment after the realization, his mind
fell blank, and then laughter, raw with irony, banged about inside his head. Was this it? The longed for encounter with another
intelligence? Had AGAPÉ, desperate to prevent such a thing,
actually precipitated it here on a planet off all the records, and
in the person of a man who for all human purposes had already
ceased to exist?

"It need not be intelligence. . . ."

Insistently one tentacle was nudging food towards him, whilst
another picked up one of the remaining lumps and deposited it
back in the horizontal slit. A demonstration to help him understand? Cosgrave marvelled at the non-human patience of the
beast, and in spite of himself, felt some of his fear subsiding. He
could actually feel his mind arranging to trust the monster; sick
and defenceless, he desperately wanted to; and then, inexplicably,
it was as if some rarely used instinct in him recognized
benevolence in the beast's behaviour. He struggled to counteract
these impressions, remain alert. He reminded himself that the
odds were overwhelmingly against its being intelligent. The so-
called food was probably drugged, a method of paralyzing its
victims before devouring them. . . . Again a tentacle was nudging
the sticky mass towards him, whilst the other two repeatedly
demonstrated where it should be placed, and Cosgrave, as he
watched, saw that all his thinking was pointless. He had no
choice but to trust the beast. It might be dangerously offended
if he refused to eat, and even if it were intelligent, who could tell
how it might behave when angry? The thought of those tentacles
lashing out and tearing him to pieces, or thrusting him alive and
squealing into that great mouth to be slowly digested made up
his mind for him. Hesitantly, without taking his eyes off his
solicitous host, he stretched one arm along the ground until his
fingers could curl round and sink into the nearest clammy bolus.
The beast made no move to interfere. Cosgrave sweated. Half
expecting to be pounced upon as he did so, he began slowly to
draw his arm back, dragging the sticky mess with it.

His nostrils flared at the stench rising through his gummed
fingers.

"Sweet mercy ! I can't eat this !"

He stared at the beast in hopeless misery and as if by way of response, it went through a series of rapid gestures, darting its tentacles back and forth around its mouth with great eagerness— or was it with impatience this time?

"In any case, what am I worrying for?" Cosgrave wondered, "don't I want to die? Don't I want a way out?" He made himself concentrate on that argument, and ignore the fact that even a man in love with death prefers one method to another. Resignedly he raised the bolus to his mouth and brushed his lips with it. The monster wasn't satisfied. (Clearly it had eyes, and sharp ones, somewhere.) Not amused by the pretence, it pepped up its demonstrations, stretching and snapping shut its mouth and flashing its tentacles about so fast that Cosgrave could only interpret the behaviour as anger. Alarmed, he lifted the mass to his lips again, and this time allowed it to rest for a second against his tongue in his open mouth before hastily pulling it out. Thanks to the fever, he had lost all sense of taste if not of smell. Laboriously he began to chew in a slow, emphatic manner, nodding appreciatively at the beast as he did so. He felt unspeakably ill. Consciousness, he sensed, was slipping from him : an indication that the fever, taking advantage of his exhaustion and shocked state, was entering into its critical phase. Already the beast's globular body was turning into a murky tremble before his eyes and his thoughts were becoming confused.

"Drugged food," he smiled to himself vaguely, "I knew it . . . not intelligent at all. . . . Hope I poison the bastard."—To finish his life as a monster's meal struck him as grotesquely appropriate. The galaxy had swallowed him completely. . . .

He slumped into a coma, and the smile fell from his face.

Sfiff waited anxiously. Now and then he scanned the horizon for Raiders, but though he saw one a long way off, they seemed singularly absent for the most part, as if something had disturbed them—perhaps the strange flash which had set the air glowing and brought the thin coating of dust down out of nowhere onto Sfiff's skin. He waited for the Outsider to move, experiencing as

he did so agonizing pains in his cerebral area caused by the harsh
dictation of hormones urging him towards the courting rituals
and the deep reassurance of the grooming sessions. Determinedly
he ignored this agony: his first duty was here. What was wrong
with the Outsider? It lay deathly still—just like the other one
which he had turned over with his tentacles among the rocks
and sensed was no longer living. Had Sfiff's food killed this one,
poisoned it? The thought made him wretched. He had persuaded
the Outsider to eat only with great difficulty, and no sooner had
it tasted the food than it had apparently collapsed, lost awareness. . . . Desperately Sfiff hoped it would move, indicate it only
rested. He waited, suffered, and waited, until he could bear the
silence and his own craving to get away no longer. Uncertainly
he edged towards the prostrate figure, dragging himself to its side
in a timid, reluctant manner. . . .

It lived. Noises rose from it: the slow thump of some muscular
organ inside its body, and the rasping intake and output of air.
Sfiff sweated with relief; but he also stiffened with dislike. The
creature's odour was unpleasantly tainted, as if it were not entirely
in its original form but had been tampered with in some way. It
made the body difficult to touch, but in spite of his abhorrence,
Sfiff's concern for its life prompted him to wrap a tentacle round
the upper part of the Outsider's form and pull it over onto its
other side, so that the head part of it lay with its orifices pointing
up at the sky. Down the sides of these orifices shone traces of
moisture which he wiped away with a careful brushing motion of
one tentacle, while from deep within their protective folds of skin,
his many eyes scanned every portion of this strange being for some
sign of how best he could help it.

He had never felt so useless. The Outsider's structure was
excessively fragile—anything he did to it might prove damaging—
so he sat in a quandary by its side, and listened to the sounds it
made, observing how the muscular thump grew fainter,
slower. . . . To soothe himself, he gesticulated with his tentacles
the entire ceremonial tribute to the dying, reaching the end before
he realized that the muscular thump inside the Outsider had
already stopped. The creature had joined with silence. Its strange

head pointed at the sky with all its secrets locked up in it, or fled out of it, for ever. . . . Sfiff's tentacles folded elaborately around each other in a token of respectful farewell.

And then he was free. It was difficult, in spite of a deep sense of guilt for the Outsider's death, not to feel released, react buoyantly. He had fulfilled his duty in so far as he could towards the creatures, without jeopardizing any of his own kind, and this knowledge helped console him as he began to scale the cliff. It proved a hard struggle, but not impossible, not quite the desperate task it had looked; and Sfiff's original intention of proving that Hibernation off the plateau might be the saving of the Community came rushing back into his thoughts, filling him with triumph. But when at last he reached the high ground, he paused to look back for a second, making out far below him two dots of silvery white, one among the rocks, the other at the edge of the plain, and again he gesticulated his farewell before hurrying off to the courting rituals.

The Colonial Fever which Sfiff contracted from Cosgrave made short work of the Community—wiped it out in a matter of Terra-days. It could have wiped out the entire species but for the fact that even though they did not understand what was happening to them, Sfiff's people remained loyal to their first moral law— never jeopardize the lives of others. They therefore remained together, sealed off on their plateau, and resisted the temptation to disperse in search of other settlements in which to shelter from their incomprehensible misfortune. We now know, of course, that these other settlements survived unharmed, to be visited in the following century by the great explorer Velikov when he discovered the planet, and on whose report this reconstruction of early events has been based. As Velikov himself said, we are left with a series of ironies to consider—not least in regard to AGAPÉ, the organization that sought to protect not only humans, but also aliens from human abuse. One is compelled to ask, how could such talented men have been so mindless? How could they have failed to see the consequences of even one man surviving the crash of a space craft? With all decontaminating facilities inoperative, what could such a man do but spread contagion on the planet with his every move?

So it is that a high ideal can be sabotaged by its own fanatics—for all fanaticism is blind.

SUBMITTED TO CENTRAL CENSORCOMMITTEE TWELFTH-DAY TENTHMONTH YEAR COLONIAL FOUNDATION 376.

Findings:

Imaginary reconstruction of Sfiffian character subversive and grossly sentimentalized. Recommend withdrawal writer's licence. Corrected version possibly acceptable, omitting references to "greed," "abuse" and also closing sentence. Following to be added as final paragraph:

It was this kind of flaw in AGAPÉ's logic which doomed the movement to failure, allowing us to step forward into the Golden Age of Development. Let us be grateful for that failure. The resources of the galaxy lie within our grasp in all their rich variety, with all their promise of expanding horizons. And in whose hands should these riches lie if not in those of responsible, progressive beings of advanced intelligence? Who else understands their potential? Even on the unspectacular planet of this narrative, as every well-informed man knows, the oils produced by a Sfiffian skin in certain states of tension have been found to possess important properties as chemical catalysts, highly valuable in certain areas of industry. The farming of these oils on a viable commercial basis is even now being perfected by ASUU the Alien Species Utilization Unit. Thus yet one more world has made its own unique contribution towards mankind's technological progress.

Night Out

Kelly had no intention of turning back. He heard the scream—but what of it? Looking out for other people's interests wasn't the way to survive. Almost silent on his bare feet, he ran hard, intent on putting as many streets as possible between himself and the scream in the shortest possible time.

Blocks of offices glittered in the moonlight: they were pocked with areas of black where vast holes gaped in their sides. As he ran, Kelly's eyes darted from one to another of these holes in a quick, methodical survey. Speed was essential. So was remembering his way. One slip of his memory, one slip of his luck come to that, and he'd come face to face with a 'Trol. Kelly both cursed and blessed the moon. It picked him out with its cold eye, the sole thing moving among the debris, but it also helped him identify the streets.

"Wellington St.", he read on a wall plaque, and the information made him glance at his watch. By now the East Sector 'Trol would be turning into Lord Street. He had five minutes in which to beat it to Dock. That was tight. Even so Kelly knew he ought to stop and check the wind. He had been running now for over six minutes without a check and that was dangerous. With a costly effort, he forced his feet to stand still. It went against instinct to stand motionless in the open street. His heart banged against his ribs fiercely. Kelly ignored it. He brought all his acumen, his every nerve to bear on the question of the wind, and to aid concentration he even licked a finger and held it up in the leisurely old pioneer fashion. Then part of his mind began to consider a row of one-storey buildings just a little way ahead to the right. He paid particular attention to the roofs. Nothing dark crouched up there; too much moonlight. That was something at any rate. And the wind was still on his side. Cautiously he shifted the pack strapped across his shoulders to make sure nothing clinked. No sound. Each tin snugly wrapped in its rags lay muffled against its neighbours. So far, so good. And if those buildings were really as innocent as they looked, he might make it.

Up to now, of course, Kelly had always made it. You did until you didn't. Until you didn't, you did, which is why you went on being a Forager. That ration bonus it brought in meant something—power, if you like. Any woman you wanted. A measure of respect. Not that Kelly was entirely satisfied. He had heard that the Blue Gang, for instance, gave a Forager double rations, whereas the Green, to which he belonged, awarded only an extra half-ration. Kelly thought he might consider changing allegiance one day, if he lived long enough.

His eyes jerking from ground level to roof and down again, he sped past the one-storey buildings. In front of one of the entrances a car lay on its side. His quick eyes took that into account, too. Nothing inside except a picked-clean skeleton which was half toppled out through the window and stretched one ivory arm out onto the street. Kelly sprang over it. On his left, two roads would shortly be coming in to join the main road. Running as close to the wall on the right as he could, he read the name plaques as he passed both junctions. "Surrey Rd.", "Devon Rd." The next one should be Somerset Road if he'd done his homework right, and he'd have to turn down that one, wind or no wind. Dock lay at the end of a semicircle and Somerset Road was the latest turn toward it he dared take. If he was not off Wellington Street in another minute he'd find himself staring at the South Sector Sub-'Trol; but if he turned eastwards too early the East Sector 'Trol would be sure to pick up his scent. So Somerset Road it had to be.

And the main trouble with that was the Blue Gang, who claimed it as the first road in their territory. The reason was manifestly obvious. Middle Western Garment Bank loomed large in it, and although no one had yet worked out a way to blow its vaults with its priceless deposits of textiles, a store like that was a considerable asset, and—Kelly stopped. Something was rising out of a crater in the road. It had a bulbous head on a stalk. Great eyes staring wildly. Kelly made out two bony, hooked arms, something like a leg. It had a plank in its hand; but it looked pretty well done for. Slop. Kelly calculated it had no strength left. Was it one of their own, the Greens? He ran past with scarcely a glance. He didn't recognize it, although it might conceivably be Moorhead who had been slopped for filching two consecutive sleep periods without forgoing his day's food ration. A Capital offence. Still, Moorhead had been slopped four days ago, and they rarely lasted that long. Blue Slop, more like. Kelly assiduously didn't hear the half human things it said. He was past and turning into Somerset Road. Again his moist finger checked the wind, but this time he couldn't bring himself to slow down as he did it.

There was a boarded-up nursery school on the right, he noticed, still looking much as it had done on Evacuation Day when he'd not been more than a kid himself. But boarded-up buildings were no safer than any others. Appearances were deceptive. A 'Trol could gnaw through just about anything. Lower down on the right, a gas station, raided and gutted long ago. Then a black patch of rubble, ash, and nothing. But Kelly was more worried about the left-hand side with its jumble of ravaged cars and torn-about filing cabinets littering the pavement. And on this side rose the bulk of the garment bank, a blasted giant of a structure. Its vaults might still be intact, but apparently little else about it was. The moonlight fragmented off twisted girders and contorted sheets of perspex. A jagged tear five or six storeys tall darkened its centre. At street level, the great glass doors had been bashed in. On the roof over the porchway lay a heap of mangled 'Copters. This was the sort of place, thought Kelly, where you ran into Guards, set up either by the Blues or—far worse and far more likely—by the South Sector Sub-'Trol, who had no use for garments themselves, but knew that their quarry did.

By this time Kelly was experiencing sharp pains across his chest. He was struggling for breath. Running that far, that fast. The Blues were right to give Foragers a whole extra food ration. Greens were nuts. You couldn't do this sort of thing three-quarters starved. Half starved, you just might. In direct contradiction of his own argument, three-quarters starved, Kelly ran on.

Then he stumbled over something he had not even noticed— a dangerous failing in a Forager. As he started away from it, he saw it was a naked pink plastic doll. One of its legs had been chewed. The 'Trols would have a go at anything. Kelly thought of the kids back in Dock. Savage, alien little things, devious and grasping. Wizen old men.

"There won't be many of us left soon," he was thinking, "who can remember what a doll was."

Momentarily a face drifted towards him along the road. It was Tib, his first woman. Dead now. The East Sector 'Trol got her on a fuel forage in the early days. During the Ecoloclast when Kelly and she had both been kids, their families had been neighbours. Then Kelly's people had taken Tib in when her parents were interned for their business connections with China. Right through the Food Riots and the Privation Program, Kelly's family had fed Tib along with themselves, even though, by law, they could have thrown her out. It was understood that the children of Internees would be among the first "economy cuts". The Government said so. But it never had come to that, because the International Food War intervened, and when that was over, Tib along with Kelly had survived and found themselves a safe Dock. Which was more than any Government managed.

Kelly still missed Tib's round, stubbornly gentle, yesterday's face. Even in the years she lived in Dock, scratching and starving like the rest of them, her face had never quite got the knack of expressing, "Me first. I'm going to have that." The way the others did. The way the damned awful others did. . . .

He checked himself. Lack of food did this; mind wandering on a forage. As he ran past the ash patch, he thought, "Kelly, this is the way to get nailed. Got to get your mind sharp. More food. Have to trade Joy for it." Joy was his new woman. She should fetch a can of beans at least. He smiled. In the early days in Dock, you still traded a woman for her sex. Now a woman was what you covered yourself with while you slept to wake you up if a paranoiac got ideas, showed a knife. . . . She watched your interests in Dock when you were out on a forage. She grabbed your share of anything going if you weren't around. And if you came home from a forage empty handed, forfeiting your own food ration, well then, the woman gave you most of hers. These were women's jobs; on how well they did them depended their value. No one wanted a woman he couldn't trade in a tight moment, and a woman no one wanted—she lived under the constant threat of being slopped. Why not? What was she contributing? So they did their jobs well, the women, and Joy was an especially good watchdog and scrounger. She'd trade high, and those beans would put Kelly back on form.

He was nearly out of the street. Just one more office block. It was a charred skeleton on the sides of which a few scorched insults and slogans still showed brown and bitter in the moonlight.

"Black M—ket Punks !"

"Food Now ! —lk Later !"

"Fascist H.Q."

The place must have been a Ration Distribution Centre, thought Kelly, though he had time to make out only one of the angry splashes of words clearly : "Who eats who?" in blistering paint over the doorway. That question really struck home. It brought up the notion that haunted Kelly and everyone else in Dock. A very presentable solution to the problem, viewed in one light—cannibalism. There was even a rumour that over the other end of town, two groups, the Darts and the Quills, actually kept up a murderous feud for the specific purpose. . . .

Something hurled itself at Kelly's legs. He went over like a bowled skittle, and groaned as his pack of tins bit into his shoulder-blade. Then he lay still and made no attempt to struggle. A Forager never panicked. Right up to the end he kept his mind sharp, assessing his situation and means of getting out of it. He already knew it wasn't a 'Trol. This enemy was human; one of the Blues. And where there was one, there must be at least two. These days no one attacked in ratios of less than two to one because malnutrition played funny tricks, and man to man, you couldn't calculate who'd have the advantage. A man of skin and bone was sometimes weak as an infant, sometimes had the strength of a maniac. Attackers didn't take chances.

Kelly felt his forage bag ripped off his back, and then he was turned over to lie face upwards, staring into a taut negroid face. He expected a knife flash. The Blues were vicious. But instead of killing him outright, the negro held his knife point up against Kelly's jugular vein and stared at him. The other Blue, Kelly could see, was kneeling on the road close by with his ear pressed into the dirt, listening.

"Green scum!" snarled Kelly's attacker, "this is our beat, and you know it."

Kelly's face was sardonically calm.

"You going to sit out here and let me argue about it?" he asked. "We've got about two minutes till the E.S. 'Trol pass by that corner. You want to wait for them?"

At that moment the other negro got up and came to join his companion.

"Jeez, Don," he whispered, "I heard them that close, it hurts!" and he plucked at Don's sleeve nervously as he eyed the booty of tin cans, "We've got the eats so let's get the hell out of here."

Don apparently fancied himself a leader. He contemplated. The moon caught at the whites of his eyes—they had a jaundiced yellow look, noticeable even in a negro's face.

"Okay."

He put away his knife decisively and stood up, releasing Kelly's chest from the pressure of his knee. Kelly made no move. When you were in a hurry, you didn't mess things up by being over hasty. He watched Don slipping his arms through the straps of the forage bag.

"Can I stand?"

Don nodded. The two Blues were already turning to run for it.

"And you tell that Green Boss it's no deal!" hissed Don over his shoulder, "you buggers are cleaned out, and we're not, so what's to share?"

Kelly only half heard. He was up and moving faster than he had though himself capable of. He ran like a primed athlete. Time was just about dead. At this stage he was glad to be rid of his heavy forage bag. Never mind eating—what mattered now was life. He turned out of Somerset Road and into the last few kilometres towards Dock. He could actually see it, a stained, re-

inforced concrete door, the first of many successive barricades
that lay between the city and, far underground, the old fall-out
shelter of Physicare International, where seven hundred and
thirty-two human beings lived packed together. Up to now, Kelly
had been one of them.

The moonlight indicated the door with bland impartiality. The
wind had changed. As he ran, Kelly involuntarily visualized the
'Trol, how it would pause, raising every one of its muzzles to
detect scent, and orientate, before co-ordinating approaches and
finally surrounding. . . .

He covered the last stretch to the door breathless with fright.
Was it only his blood that drummed like that, or the East Sector
'Trol on his heels? The Dock guard wouldn't open the door if
when he looked out through the eye-hole he saw anything too
close behind Kelly. The Forager pulled frantically on a chain that
threaded its way from the interior out through a small fissure high
up in the concrete. Inside, although he could not hear it, Kelly
imagined the bell jangling. Fearfully he glanced over his shoulder
at the wide, empty street. They would come at any second. Then
he stared in earnest at the tiny disc of the eye hole on which his
life depended. Sometimes at this moment he'd think of treachery
in Dock. Someone bribing someone to keep him out. Such things
had been known. His eye met the guard's eye through the small
round hole.

"Kelly."

An infinite pause.

Then, noises inside, very faint, scraping of iron.

The door opened outwards just enough to admit Kelly exhausted into the comparative safety of Dock. He leaned against
the concrete wall of the passage-way, panting, taking care to listen
to the dull thud of the door as it closed, the rough clang of the
lock, and the sound of bolts falling back into their deep slots.
It always calmed him to hear these things. As he regained his
breath and became accustomed to the darkness, he watched the
shadowy form of the guard going through his check-up routines,
with something like impersonal affection. The guard, used to the
way of Foragers, especially when they'd only just made it—how

they needed a few words at this point to release the tension—
slung a scornful touch of sympathy over his shoulder.

"No doings, eh?"

"Lost it to a couple of –**– Blues," explained Kelly. He was
glad to communicate.

The guard leaned against the door, folded his arms, and grinned.

"Boss'll love you."

"Yeah. And they gave me a message for him, too."

"No deal, eh?"

"No deal."

The guard spat disgustedly.

"What can you expect?" he sneered, "they know we're about
cleaned out. No damn good a coalition unless you've got something to offer."

Kelly shrugged and moved away.

"It's not that simple," he muttered.

Sure it wasn't. The 'Trols were picking off the groups one at a
time. What the groups needed was to get together, all of them,
Blues, Greens, Quills, Darts . . . pool resources. . . . Kelly had to
stop and leaned against the wall again. He was dizzy with fatigue
and hunger. Joy would have to give up her whole ration, and to
hell with her. Now the Blues, they used another system. They
guaranteed all Foragers a basic minimum in the case of their
coming back empty-handed, providing they didn't do it twice in
succession. Not for the first time that night, Kelly contemplated
changing teams.

Outside in the city, the East Sector 'Trol, having analyzed the
scents the change of wind brought into their area, made their
choice. Ignoring the one man, an Aryan scent, no doubt a Green
making towards his Dock, they had swung in a great wave down
a side street and into Church Row, which the other two men, the
Negroid scent, would have to cross in order to reach the Blues'
Dock.

So in Church Row, the 'Trol massed waiting, eyes bright and
attentive, ears flattened against their thin heads, their dark bodies
glistening where the moon stroked their sides. Occasionally their

tails twitched in small spasms of anticipation. And their fangs were ready.

Running hard out of a side door in the Middle Western Garment Bank, the two negroes with Kelly's confiscated forage bag had headed down an alley for Church Row. They found the alley obstructed with debris from a collapsing roof which recent bad gales had been helping to finish off. This unexpected barrier took precious moments to negotiate. They longed to get across Church Row. It was their only hope. If they had chanced it back up Somerset Road to a higher turn, the South Sector Sub-'Trol would certainly have picked up their scent as it swept along Wellington Street. . . .

Crouched in wait, the rats of the East Sector heard the men coming. They listened to the rasping of tired lungs, the desperate speed of the naked human feet, and as they listened, their dark forms quivered both with appetite and hate-filled contempt. Would these humans never learn? A remarkably stupid species, whose groups preferred to bicker among themselves and starve in isolation rather than co-operate, co-ordinate. . . .

Though they farmed their dwindling stocks with scrupulous care, the rats were concerned about their main source of food: they feared the humans' extinction.

The Tunkun

Visiting diplomat Konrad screwed up his nose. He held the brown, whiskered thing between finger and thumb, as if it were extremely filthy. Their ceremony concluded, the Ogans hovered about the human party in evident anxiety. The Tunkun had not been well received. Konrad turned to the lean, austere-looking man who stood next to him.

"You sure you got that right?" he demanded. "You sure they called this thing a token of love? You know, I expect to be protected from political demonstrations."

Interpreter Faraqhui exercised his trained smile. He despised ignorant peacocks like Konrad.

"You must remember, Konrad Sir," he explained soothingly, "that here on Oga very little can still grow. A world first scorched, and then subjected to fierce erosion. The least scrap of lichen is considered precious. To keep in existence such a plant as that you hold in such a place as this—only the Ogans could do it. And even *their* extraordinary talents—which are the outcome of millennia of a garden culture—are taxed to the utmost. To understand what it means to them, this thing they've given you, try to imagine all this"—he waved his arm at the barren plain—"as a garden, famous for its beauty through two solar systems. In those days, one could almost have said the entire world of Oga was a garden, and the Ogans the most skilful of gardeners."

Konrad stared round at the seemingly endless expanse of dust and rock, and grunted. He was not gifted with superfluities of imagination. Faraqhui had paused to consider stone knuckles that thrust up through the ground by his feet.

"What the Ogans have given you, Konrad Sir, is a symbol of all they value. Their entire philosophy is based on a relationship with plant life. Their moral code is based on an aesthetic response to Oga's flora, and on their understanding of its ecology. They evolved mental disciplines out of gardening activities, and acquired much wisdom. But now, as you see, the unfortunate side-effects

of those solar probes conducted by neighbouring Lampas 3 have
stripped Oga of her assets. And the surviving Ogans struggle to
keep alive the few remnants. However, owing to the thinning
atmosphere, they will soon have to leave, and. . . ."

"Yes, yes, I'm aware of the situation," interrupted Konrad.
Mention of Lampas 3 had roused his impatience. He'd done his
best to avoid this diversion to Oga—the backyard of the solar
system—and was anxious to get on to the main world. There at
least he might expect a human welcome. Besides, he found these
"conscience-calls" to places like Oga mawkish and unhealthy.
Wanting to get away, he tried to hurry things along by the
hearty approach.

"All right, Faraqhui," he bantered, "a planet of gardeners. But
what am I supposed to do with this thing? Chop it up, and
stew it? Maybe they'd like to give me a recipe to go with it, eh?"

Faraqhui winced. He hoped not one Ogan present had understood what had just been said. He glanced at them. Their swart,
khaki faces were puckered with unhappiness. They'd understood
enough, at any rate, to be concerned for their Tunkun's welfare.

Faraqhui tried again.

"With respect, Konrad Sir," he said quietly, "you haven't
understood. What you have there is a Tunkun root. You plant
it in this bag of dirt they gave you—dirt which is worth riches
here now, you appreciate—and very soon, with correct treatment,
the Tunkun will sprout, grow and flower. A most beautiful,
perfumed flower."

Konrad squinted sceptically at the shrivelled thing he held.

"More precious, even, than the Orchid of Lampas 3," Faraqhui
added, "being, of course, so much rarer."

Konrad's interest sharpened. His well-groomed face suddenly
assumed some intelligence.

Why are these diplomats so predictable? wondered the interpreter contemptuously.

"By precious, you mean—worth money?"

There was no telling with these interpreters.

"I believe one might say so," replied Faraqhui, suddenly looking
strained.

"Well then," Konrad handled the Tunkun more carefully, "you tell them I'm very glad to have it. Much appreciated. A most appropriate token of goodwill. You know the sort of thing, Faraqhui; get the message across, but don't go on so long we fall behind schedule, eh?"

The interpreter nodded. Turning to their apprehensive hosts, in a steady, deliberate manner, he began to offer the visiting diplomat's sincere thanks and assurance of appreciation. Konrad in the meantime beamed round on the cluster of Ogans, all false benevolence. Mentally he was already back on *The Orient Star*, and heading out towards Lampas 3.

Mira Konrad assessed her husband's trophies with a practised eye. There were beads of genuine Scilicot, a table of Orrago fibre, a mechanical device for reproduction of dream experiences in a waking consciousness, put together by convicts on Ceres β, and there was a bag of dirt with a bluish shoot of vegetable matter sprouting out of it.

"Not a very good trip!" called Konrad from his dressing room. He knew what she was doing. "That sector really is the backwoods. Low production level, and the quality's downright embarrassing."

Mira appeared at the door, holding the string of Scilicot beads round her throat.

"Pretty," he commented.

She smiled with the indulgence of a disappointed woman.

"Do the catch for me, will you?"

She lowered her head for him to do so and thought out her next words carefully.

"You know, Micha, these beads can only be Standard Two. If you look close, you can see several of them are flawed. Are you sure they—value you at your worth?"

Konrad frowned. He had often wondered that himself. In fact, he was far more concerned with that question than Mira was. Coming from her, the enquiry was in part a reminder that in two years' time, at the age of forty-five, Konrad would be retired, and the standard of living they might then expect depended on what he had amassed in the way of trophies during his diplomatic tours. So he merely shrugged.

"Is that plant out there a Lampas 3 Orchid?" she asked hopefully. That, at least, would be an indication of his prestige.

"Oh, that! Afraid not." He flicked a switch, and bathed his mirror in ultra-violet light, peering gloomily at his facial blemishes. Hovering by his shoulder, his wife's reflection looked piqued.

"Well, what is it?"

"Something the little things on Oga gave me."

He spoke with light good humour, although Mira's insinuations about his professional status always nettled him.

"The Ogans live in a terrible place. Apparently their world used to be famous for its gardens, but now it's a miserable desert. Got blasted when those Lampas 3 solar probes got out of hand in the thirties, you remember? Now it's even losing its atmosphere, and only a few moss-like things can grow there. Plus that plant they gave me. I wasn't going to bother with it, but Faraqhui—that's the interpreter—he dropped a few hints about it being worth something. So I pushed it into the bag of dirt during the hop over to Lampas."

Konrad fiddled with his tight neck-band, and turned to his wife.

"Will I do?"

She scrutinized him, and as usual, let her pride show. His years had hardly touched him. But then, she and he—they both took good care of themselves.

"You'll do. Come and see if we've all the right drinks. You know what the Benns are for catching people out."

"Damn the Benns," grunted Konrad, "my first night home. Anyhow," he resumed, padding obediently after her, "Faraqhui seemed to get obsessed with the thing. All during our stay on Lampas 3 and on to—wherever it was. . . ."

"Kelpha must have come next, dear."

"Yes, Kelpha. Well, all the way, I'd catch Faraqhui at odd moments in my quarters—when I hadn't sent him in there, mind —whispering away like a madman. I wasn't sure what he was up to at first. He always stopped dead just as I came in, and he'd never be at a loss for a pretext. It would be—'Oh, I just needed a look at the schedule, Konrad Sir, and I've lent my copy to So-and-so,' or, 'I was feeding the reports you asked for into the Recorder, Konrad Sir, there is so much noise in the Relay Room. . . .' Always some bloody excuse. He was quite clever."

"Yes, but what was he being clever about, Micha?"

She was looking round for somewhere to stand the Tunkun. It was an ugly thing in its synthetic bag. She placed the bag in a large bowl brought back from some primitive place where they still hand-made such items, and parked the bowl in an obscure corner of the room, behind some effective house-ferns.

Konrad watched with approval.

"About his whispering of course. And what he was really doing in my quarters. In the end, the whole business got on my nerves so much, I put it to him:

'Faraqhui,' I said, 'you can deny it if you like, but I think you creep in here to talk to that grubbed up bit of root in its bag. And that gibberish I hear you whispering, that's Ogan, isn't it? Speak up,' I told him, 'or I'll have you classified as mentally unstable.'"

He checked the 'Puter-Bar perfunctorily. All its lights were twinkling.

"Drinks O.K. Well, Faraqhui confessed I was right. He said Tunkuns needed talking to."

"Quite a lot of plants are responsive, dear."

Mira was checking the dinner table.

Konrad frowned.

"Yes, but I got the impression he meant more than that. Something like, if you don't give them love, they won't grow. At one time, I even thought he was implying they were intelligent."

"Like the water-weeds on Lampas?"

"They're not really plants, they're more like animals, a kind of hybrid. And anyway, Faraqhui said intelligence wasn't—how did he put it?—a relevant factor. He got quite heated about it. In fact, he stepped out of line—more or less told me I wasn't the right sort to have a Tunkun."

"Oh." Konrad's wife was genuinely offended. "And what did you say to that?"

"I stood firm, don't worry. Told him to keep out of my quarters in future, or I'd see to it he lost his licence. Faraqhui's an odd fellow. All that interest in the thing, but when it came to the crunch he wasn't prepared to argue. Just walked away without a word, and there were no more chats with the Tunkun after that!"

Mira Konrad was mollified. She nodded.

"He was obviously testing your authority. They're far too arrogant, these linguistic drifters."

The truth was, Mira didn't like interpreters. They had travelled so far, and seen so much, they made her feel inferior.

Konrad looked doubtful.

"Oh, I was right, all right," he said, "but I've got to admit the Tunkun hasn't grown at all since."

The guests arrived. First and foremost, the Benns. Raymond Benn was an ageing diplomat who had spent the greater part of his mediocre career among slow-witted Kelphans. His wife, Anna, was a manically bored and garrulous woman. The Konrads cultured their friendship for the same reason that everyone did, and it was not a good one: Raymond Benn's brother, a considerably more dynamic type than himself, was chairman of the Tax Alleviation Committee. The other guest, Carrogan, was something of a tamed ruffian, a Speculator in primitive crafts wherever he found them. The Benns had once expressed a wish to be introduced to this—in their eyes—half-wild individual, and Mira Konrad had seen fit to oblige, her husband's first night home seeming an appropriate occasion: there would be plenty of material for conversation, and, she knew, although Micha grumbled, he actually preferred to set the seal on his home-coming by playing the host.

Still, the Benns and Carrogan turned out, as Mira had feared, to be an unfortunate combination. The Benns, doggedly conventional, prided themselves on the accuracy of their observations, tenderly correcting each other when guilty of a minor slip. ("Oh, no, dear, you mean turquoise, surely: I'd never call Kelphan Phase 2 pottery green. That's so misleading.") Carrogan, on the other hand, was provocatively outspoken and given to having his facts not quite wrong enough to undermine his opinions, but not altogether accurate either. A fault brought about, he claimed, by "going too many places too fast". The result was a series of aborted conversations, the Benns glowering and anxious to correct Carrogan's clever but imprecise arguments, Carrogan mischievously goading them on, and the Konrads heading off every attack before their dinner party exploded.

"I really don't see, Carrogan, how you can possibly draw parallels between the two cultures," rumbled Benn, all ponderous sincerity, "the similarities are, to say the least, superficial."

"Oh, come on!" Carrogan laughed; he enjoyed baiting people, and Ray Benn was easy game; "surely all similarities are superficial in one sense or another. At least that's what I've found in my experience."

Benn's wife looked suddenly interested. She cast a quick glance at her husband who was imitating a thunder cloud, and interposed,

"Excuse me, but I'm sure that can't be true at all, you know.'

Carrogan raised his eyebrows at Benn enquiringly, and smiled with great charm. At that moment, Mira Konrad remembered the old diplomat had just brought out a tape on "Kelpha and Andana: Analogous Cultures", and she decided to intervene before Carrogan managed to make his attack personal—as he obviously intended. She suggested liqueurs. An awkward silence settled over her dinner table as the 'Puter-Bar moved stealthily from guest to guest, serving the drinks. She caught a desperate look from Konrad: the Benns sat ruffled and offended, Carrogan impolitely smug. Light diversion was called for. A much experienced hostess, Mira Konrad cast hastily about in her mind, and came up with the answer. She smiled round at everyone breezily.

"Incidentally," she chirruped, "you'll never guess what Micha brought back from his trip. Something quite out of the ordinary, isn't it, Micha?"

She appealed to Konrad with a cunning touch of feminine idiocy. Benn, all tensed to launch into his thesis on similarities in unrelated cultures, was suitably silenced by the dictates of etiquette, being, as he was, so conventional. Konrad noticed that, and was relieved.

"Uh, yes," he responded dully; he had no idea what his wife was referring to.

"Oh, do show ! I can't abide secrets !" cried Benn's wife, roused by any promise of the extraordinary.

"It'll be a rodent from Ceres β, I'll bet you," said Carrogan. He leaned back in his chair with sardonic resignation. It sometimes nettled as much as it amused him, being headed off.

Mira Konrad gave an artificial laugh to cover up Carrogan's bad manners.

"Oh, something much more interesting. Just you wait !"

Getting up, she went over to a corner of the room and shifted aside a display of house-ferns. In a moment she came back with a girlish air of triumph, holding a bowl, over the rim of which a bluish plant shoot was just visible.

Konrad admired her. He had to admit it : Mira really knew how to manipulate these dreadful parties. She cleared a space among the dinner plates, and set her prize down.

"There now, what do you think ?"

The Benns, especially the wife, looked disappointed.

"Most unusual," was their comment, "I really couldn't say what it is, could you, dear ?"

"No, I don't think I know that species, dear."

"There you are, you see !" said Mira Konrad gleefully, "if you two don't know, it *must* be unusual !"

The Benns grunted, a little consoled.

But Carrogan stared at the thing. His face had become pinched and animated with excitement; and the intensity of his silence slowly brought the eyes of the others to bear on him.

"Well, Carrogan," challenged Konrad brusquely, "any guesses ?"

The Speculator didn't take his eyes off the thing.

"A Tunkun," he said at last, and his voice was gentle with desire. Suddenly he turned on his host.

"Tell you what, Konrad. Name your price. I'll meet it."

Amazed, Konrad's lips parted slightly, but no sound came out. He couldn't think of anything to say. As he stalled, he ran a finger along his uncomfortable neck-band. Carrogan was known as a hard bargainer, even for a Speculator. And here the man was, not only telling Konrad to name his price but obviously unable to conceal how badly he wanted to make the purchase—an unheard of failing in a Speculator. It made Konrad cautious. Mira gaped. This turn of events was outside the realm of her expectations and she had no clear notion how to react.

Konrad took care with his words.

"Well, you know," he said slowly, "I hadn't meant to sell it."

For a second Carrogan looked merely exasperated. Then some taken-for-granted restraint inside him apparently broke.

"But you can ask what you like !" he cried, "twenty-five credits, thirty, thirty-two—that's all I've got—just think what you could do with that sort of money !"

Beneath its alcoholic flush, his skin had turned white, and the combination of high colouring and sickly pallor gave him a fevered, fanatical air. His hands were actually trembling, although he had the presence of mind not to keep them long enough in one place for anyone to see. Mira Konrad got nervous. This strained confrontation in the middle of a dinner party was not to her liking, and yet she was fascinated by the prospect of such a windfall. She protested feebly,

"But it couldn't be worth all that—could it?"

Konrad frowned at her.

"Surely not," said the Benns, aggrieved at not being able to judge for themselves. They were inclined to suspect Carrogan of playing a vulgar joke. But Konrad, meeting the Speculator's eyes, could not doubt Carrogan's sincerity, and he smiled. By this time he was inwardly delighted; and he worked at appearing calm, as if he knew all about the market value of Tunkuns.

Carrogan was in real distress. He had completely forgotten that he was a guest at a dinner party, circumscribed by social etiquette, and he launched into a new, more aggressive attack.

"Look, Konrad," he began in harsh tones, "I bet you don't know how to rear that thing. And if you can't get it to grow—well, potential that comes to nothing isn't worth anything, is it? Now I know how to rear it, and I'm telling you to name your price. You can't have it fairer than that, damn you!"

Konrad's smile developed barbs.

"Oh, but I do know how to rear it. An interpreter called Faraqhui told me all about that. We intend to talk to this thing morning, noon, and night—don't we, Mira?"

A diminutive white spot was glinting under his right cheek-bone. Mira noticed this sign of tension, and was alarmed.

"Yes, yes, of course we do, darling."

Taken aback, the Speculator stared at Konrad hard; and then, on reflection, appeared to consider his case not hopelessly lost. He even rallied enough to manage a short laugh.

"All right, Konrad." He forced himself back in the chair, as if relaxing; "all right, I wish you joy of it. I won't press. But if you change your mind, let me have first bid, will you? And don't go round quoting thirty-two credits as my ceiling, eh?" He stared lividly at Konrad's diplomatic mask, and cursed himself for having lost control. The surprise, the absurd unexpectedness of the challenge had been too much, and now bitter regret for having betrayed his usual wily self was working in him like knives. His breath came and went irregularly.

"Goddammit," he thought, "I'll be weeping next!"

Konrad clearly had no real ideas about the Tunkun's worth. If only Carrogan hadn't made such a scene. Somehow the Speculator managed to keep smiling.

Konrad considered. Carrogan's proposal seemed sound. If he could rear the Tunkun, well and good; he'd put it on the open market. If not—well, he'd always have one buyer. Under the circumstances, he could afford a magnanimous gesture.

"All right, Carrogan," he said at last, "if I decide to sell, you get first option."

They shook hands on it.

Bitter, scorching winds swept across Oga, lifting dust in clouds, shaping the clouds into whips that fell stinging across the Ogans' hunched forms, except where, behind their great windbreak of imported Einicon, a select few placidly tended the Tunkun plantation. The metal shield thundered, heaved and billowed with the impact of the wind. Now and then there was a loud crash as gravel and dust were flung up against it with all the force of a gigantic clenched fist. But in the narrow strip between this shield and the cliff wall, the Tunkun of Oga continued to grow, quietly, insistently, the last reminder of a world's annihilated beauty. There were less than a dozen. Three were in full bloom, their great trumpet-heads glowing with bluish luminescence. Their perfume swayed in a mist over the Ogans, safe from dispersal by the wind, and as it touched their olfactory centre, the Ogans would pause in their work, exchange words of benediction, gestures of brotherhood and harmony, before bending again over those plants less advanced in growth. They stroked these young shoots with sensitive, taper-like fingers, and their facial muscles ruffled with mental exertion as they murmured back into the ground such expressions of goodwill as the mature Tunkuns' perfume inspired in them.

Konrad stared at the bluish shoot in despair. No doubt about it. The wretched thing not only was not growing; it was actually withering slightly at the tip. He was in a good way toward losing a fortune. Should he call in Carrogan now, before it was too late? Or might the thing recover? Konrad's idea had been to bring the plant into bud, and then market it. He'd expected a higher price that way. But now, four months and a lot of inane Tunkun chatter later, he feared his chance might be slipping by. He eyed his wife suspiciously.

"Mira, have you been over-watering this thing?"

"Of course I haven't," she looked up at him from her romance-tape, annoyed, "you said yourself there's hardly a drop of water on Oga. Too much would kill it."

"Well something *is* killing it!" Konrad stroked the shoot unhappily. It felt dangerously limp. His wife pursed her lips. It was like Micha to blame her.

"You can't be speaking to it right," she said acidly, "and didn't

D

Faraqhui say it needs love? All you do is stand and growl and
say 'Grow, damn you !' I don't think I'd respond to that."

"I don't stand here growling. That's Ogan. I've learned twenty
expressions of the hideous language, and the one that sounds
like a growl means 'I love you'."

"Oh, does it." In spite of herself, Mira looked amused. "Well
it doesn't sound very convincing to me."

"It's not you I'm trying to convince !"

Mira bowed her head to this graceless remark. Konrad decided
to telecom Carrogan.

The Speculator had kept himself—at some considerable inconvenience and expense—squarely on Konrad's world since he had
seen the Tunkun. His subordinate, Louis, was amazed to find
himself sent out on prize assignments, reaping magnificent
commissions, whilst his boss volunteered for the donkey work at
home. Carrogan couldn't risk not being available if Konrad had
a change of heart. There was a fabulous commercial empire to be
built on that plant, if he could only get hold of it. . . .

Once, as a young man, Carrogan had been duped by a rival
Speculator. This individual had painstakingly sown a crop of false
rumours in the junior's path to divert him from a cache of
primitive "reflectors" or hand-mirrors on Kelpha. On Oga, so the
stories ran, several wall-carvings from the Classical Period still
lay hidden in secret places known only to the Ogans themselves;
and for a price—the smuggling of an Ogan Rights Speaker to one
of the more sympathetic colonies—the guardians of these treasures
might be persuaded to part with one. Such an artefact, with its
curious depiction of now extinct Ogan shrubs and flowers, would
raise a fabulous price on the Colonies market. To his endless
embarrassment, Carrogan fell for the ruse. At once he abandoned
the hunt for "reflectors"—items of middling value—and made all
speed to the scorched little world of the gardeners. He should have
known better, as he muttered to himself for the next twenty years,
because as their world had died, the Ogans had been forced to
strip it of every saleable commodity in exchange for the goods and
technology which enabled them to cling to their barren home a
little longer. Carrogan had just not been thinking clearly. He

believed in his own luck, and had a young man's hunch that the Golden Chance every Speculator watches for would come to him early in life. His hunch appeared to have been mistaken. The trip to Oga was mortifying, if not entirely fruitless. And yet—no, it was not entirely fruitless. Whilst there, his interpreter-escort had taken Carrogan to visit the Tunkun Plantation. Entrance to all but specially honoured aliens was forbidden, but the two men had gazed at the full-bloomed plants through the transparent Einicon windbreak, and the interpreter had made some noteworthy observations.

"You notice how the Ogans pause in their work to salute each other?"

"Is that what they're doing? I thought they were scratching their fleas."

"They are responding to the scent of the mature Tunkun flower. It has an extraordinary pacifying effect; one is filled with a joyous sense of well-being and goodwill towards one's fellow creatures."

"That's what it does for the Ogans."

"Oh," replied the interpreter innocently, "it has a similar effect on humans. I had the honour of escorting the High Councillor of Lampas 3 on his last conciliation visit here when he toured the Tunkun Plantation, and so I know. . . ."

These words were not lost on the Speculator.

What would a desperate world not pay for a Tunkun? Ceres β, for example, with its settlement of mutinous convicts, or Purila, with its unfortunate mutations? They had only to analyze the chemistry of its perfume, manufacture the stuff by the tank-full, and any government could reduce even its most hostile citizens to states of benign docility. Out of the wizen root of the Tunkun grew potential power that was almost limitless. Was that why the Ogans guarded these last plants so fiercely, never permitting one to leave their planet? Carrogan had turned his back on the Einicon windbreak like a man who is leaving behind a priceless jewel sealed off in another dimension. Over the years various incidents brought the Tunkun back to mind, if only because in that moment, staring at the great trumpet flowers, the young man had finally attained the true speculator's mentality. It had stood him in good

stead ever since. As for the Tunkun project itself, until Mira
Konrad set that blue shoot down on her dinner table Carrogan had
assumed it was a mere dream, a tantalizer, a toy of the abstract
world. The Ogans would never part with one.

But now, incredibly. . . . As he thought of Konrad's Tunkun,
Carrogan experienced twinges of panic. Why had the diplomat
not got in touch? The fool would never get the thing to grow,
Carrogan was sure of that. But had Konrad stumbled onto the
same idea as himself? What a fool Carrogan had been at that
dinner party, letting himself get so excited ! Then the Speculator's
mind would race to other worries. If he could raise more capital,
shouldn't he sponsor the research rather than sell the Tunkun
outright? Carrogan, sole possessor of the Tunkun's secret. Yes,
but if the project failed, if the scent proved impossible to manufacture, he would stand to lose everything.

So Carrogan bit his nails and watched the calendar until the
momentous day when a blurred and agitated Konrad flickered onto
his telecom screen.

Konrad didn't stop for niceties.

"Carrogan," he blurted out, "do you still want this—Tunkun
thing?"

Carrogan's heart gave a mild bleat, but he set his face, and
looked cagey.

"Why?"

"Because you can have it—for a price." Konrad noticed with
alarm that Carrogan had got his wits back, and was not display-
ing any enthusiasm.

"The truth is," he went on with a forced show of candour, "it's
not quite so easy to rear as I'd imagined. Mind you, if I could get
in touch with Faraqhui, I wouldn't sell. He'd put me right in a
second. But, well, I'm a busy man, Carrogan, with another trip
coming up shortly, and I don't want to leave this thing for Mira
to look after, you understand." He coughed to hide his embarrassment. He had no intention of referring to the shrivelling at
the plant's tip: why should he? In his position, would
Carrogan?

The Speculator suspected nothing. He was too close to a once-in-a-lifetime goal to be able to, but he managed to maintain a little business acumen, and pretend that he could.

"Well," he havered, "if it's so difficult to grow, maybe it's damaged. Or maybe the change of atmosphere. . . . Look here, Konrad, this makes the deal a bit of a risk. . . ."

Konrad looked scared.

"Under the circumstances, we'll say twenty credits, and call it done," announced Carrogan crisply. His heart pounded. Was even Konrad such a fool that he'd accept a drop like that? To his astonished relief Konrad's voice came back immediately.

"Done."

At a conference on Vraskos the following month, Konrad, a well-contented man with a new fortune of twenty credits to his name, encountered the interpreter Faraqhui. That is to say, he went out of his way to encounter Faraqhui whose back he recognized far down a corridor in the Conference Complex. Konrad acted like a schoolboy and ran after him shouting,

"Faraqhui, hey, Faraqhui!"

The Interpreter stopped and turned. Konrad caught up with him, panting. Faraqhui, remembering the presentation ceremony on Oga, smiled with controlled acidity. He had an idea what was on Konrad's mind.

"I didn't think you'd be at this affair, Faraqhui," Konrad said, suddenly feeling stupid. The knowing smile on the other man's face made him uncomfortable. The Interpreter wryly inclined his head.

"I am here with the Kelphan Delegate."

"Oh."

Faraqhui's eyes watched him satirically.

"How is your Tunkun getting along?" he enquired after a pause, "has it flowered yet?"

Guilelessly Konrad swallowed the bait. He was consumed with curiosity, and involuntarily ignored the scorn in the other man's voice.

"That's just it. That's what I wanted to talk to you about."

"I thought you might."

"Just how did you get that damned thing to grow?" demanded Konrad, taking hold of Faraqhui's arm, and trying to walk him down the corridor in a confidential chummy manner. The Interpreter did not exactly respond. He withdrew his arm discreetly, and his features remained rigidly formal.

"You know that yourself, Konrad Sir. I talked to it."

Konrad got the strongest impression that he was being teased, but all he could do was pursue his enquiry earnestly.

"Yes, yes, I know that. But I talked to it, too, you know, and it wouldn't grow for me. So what's the secret eh?"

His fingers bit again into Faraqhui's lean arm.

"Perhaps it didn't like you, Konrad Sir."

Offended, Konrad just managed the necessary laugh.

"Be serious, Faraqhui. You can't fool me!"

At this the Interpreter gave him a sidelong glance that was remarkably stern. "Konrad", he was thinking, "is a poor sort of clown."

He stopped walking.

"Very well. Very well, Konrad Sir, I will tell you how to grow a Tunkun. You talk to it, yes, because that helps to build up the rapport, but what is vital is—that you anticipate it."

"Anticipate it," repeated Konrad woodenly. He groped for meaning. "Listen to me, Faraqhui, at one time I had a deal of thirty credits on that thing. I hoped it would fetch even more if I got it to bud. If anticipating would have done the trick, I'd have been smothered in Tunkun flowers. . . ."

Faraqhui dismissed this protest with a cursory gesture.

"You misunderstand, Konrad Sir. By 'anticipate' I mean visualize, step by step, cell by cell, fibre by fibre, from the first sprouting of the root to the final uncurling of each petal. And also the perfume," Faraqhui smiled, "you must also anticipate the perfume. Or else, of course, you are sure to obtain only negative results."

Konrad stood braced between angry disbelief and dismayed credulity.

Faraqhui's smile was complacent. He nodded.

"Yes," he went on calmly, "imagine the discipline, the patience, the desire for the thing in itself entailed in such a process. You will recall I told you, Konrad Sir, that in their day the Ogans were Civilization's most accomplished gardeners. Did you not ask yourself what that implied? The true art of gardening is not a mechanical practice, but a skill of mind and matter working in harmony. Would you not agree? The Ogans achieved many sophisticated extensions of this principle. They learnt how to create new forms of communication between conscious intelligence and its environment. They learnt how to transfer some of their own psychic energy into organic matter and so create living forms which would illustrate by their actual existence the Ogans' highest ideals." Faraqhui paused. The diplomat stood before him pale and dumbfounded. "You must understand," resumed the Interpreter evenly, "that the Ogans had no wish to dominate organic matter, only to work creatively in partnership with it. For this reason they never sought by further research to make the processes easier. The arduous mental discipline necessary to produce such a plant as the Tunkun, for example, is a most efficient safeguard against abuse."

Faraqhui paused again, uncertain whether Konrad had grasped the kernel of so much fine talk. He decided to use a simple image.

"If you like, Konrad Sir, you could say the Tunkun is a delicate organic computer. It is programmed to produce certain aesthetic, moral and emotional formulae, but to function it requires external agency of a highly skilled order."

"So it was useless," muttered Konrad, "because I've never seen a Tunkun flower, never smelt one . . . I couldn't possibly have grown it. . . ."

"On a crude level, that is more or less the sum of it," agreed Faraqhui with undisguised callousness.

"Then why did they give me it?"

Faraqhui shrugged.

"I suspect they were ashamed. They had nothing else left to give—so distinguished a visitor."

Konrad wasn't listening.

"I sold it to Carrogan—Faraqhui, do you think Carrogan ever saw a Tunkun?"

The Interpreter repeated his shrug.

"It is possible. Not since my time on Oga—I would have heard—but before that, who knows? You mean the Speculator, Carrogan?"

"Yes."

"Ah. Then he will have no success, in any case. Even if he has seen a flowering Tunkun, I doubt whether he has smelt one. Why should they let a mere trader—and he must have been very young if it was before I ever went to Oga—why should they let such an individual into the Plantation? I can't believe he has experienced the perfume."

"You have, though," suggested Konrad, suddenly aggressive.

Faraqhui almost smirked.

"Interpreters accompany V.I.Ps.: V.I.Ps. visit such places."

"Of course," Konrad's voice was cold with annoyance, and, if he could have recognized it, with jealousy. None of this was missed by the Interpreter who relished seeing the diplomat trimmed to size. However, Faraqhui's triumph was not yet complete.

"But I wished to point out, Konrad Sir," he continued, "that even if your Speculator friend has smelt a Tunkun flower—even then he could not hope to grow one."

Konrad felt bitter joy inside his vexation.

"And why's that?"

Faraqhui looked mildly exasperated.

"Because he would be interested in it primarily for commercial reasons. Now I ask you, Konrad Sir, how can you possibly visualize anything accurately unless you are seeing the thing for its own sake? Ulterior motives warp our perceptions. You simply don't see a thing unless you see it for itself."

This argument made sense; but Konrad found himself trembling at Faraqhui's self-righteous tone.

"And you," his lip curled, "it grew for you, of course, whose mind is so pure...."

"So disciplined," corrected Faraqhui, not in the least offended, "but since I appreciated the Tunkun cannot be exploited, I was, in any case, interested only in the plant itself."

They had come to a door marked with Faraqhui's name. The Interpreter spoke a number and the door opened. He crossed the threshold without extending an invitation to Konrad.

"Yes," he added, as a parting shot, "—in the plant itself. Having once smelt the Tunkun flower, how could I feel otherwise?"

And as the door closed, Konrad, if he had been less angry, might have detected a wounded expression, almost resentment, lurking deep down in Faraqhui's eyes.

On the same day on another world, Carrogan's fingers pulled away the dirt. The Speculator was shaking. Five weeks almost sleepless, channelling all his forces into visualizing this thing cell by cell—oh yes, he knew what the fool Konrad hadn't known about anticipation—and all he was left with was a shrivelled shoot and a foul stench. He had no idea what had gone wrong. The smell had started up overnight. Until then he'd refused to believe the evidence of his eyes, had held on day by day, savagely willing a resurrection. But now his one thought was to save the root. Perhaps that alone would be sufficient for analysis. . . . His fingers tore through the bag and scattered the dirt on the floor. Then his hand sank into a black, treacly mess that gave off an outraged and outraging odour. The root had putrefied right through. Carrogan's first reactions were of nausea and shock. He flung the disgusting thing on the carpet, and leaned against the wall feeling sick.

Then, after a little while, he began to mutter between clenched teeth.

"Twenty credits. Twenty stinking credits. . . ."

Martin Ricketts

A Matter of
Life and Death

Cooper and Lansdale were glad to stretch their legs on the planet.
At the outermost limit of the elliptical orbit that took them beyond
the known sector of the galaxy, they had come upon it unex-
pectedly, a final reward for the months of fruitless exploration
spent cramped in the tiny cabin of their FTL module.

Each morning, as the tiny robot machines that they carried
with them gathered as much ecological data on the planet as they
were equipped to assimilate, the two men stood outside the module
and breathed the rich clean air. They were camped on a grassy
hill, and below them the wide coniferous forest stretched to the
horizon in every direction, interrupted only by an occasional hill
similar to the one they were on. Their automatic data-compilers
advised them of little fauna on the planet. There were a few
species of small insect, and these were the staple diet of the
thousands of white grub-like creatures that littered the forest
floor. These grubs were eaten in turn by the small monkey-like
creatures that moved in hordes through the uppermost branches
of the trees.

Cooper, a naïve and sentimental man, was enchanted by the
peace and apparent order. He called the planet idyllic. Lansdale
was tougher and more practical. He made them both wait until
the machines pronounced the forest reasonably safe to enter and
then together they went down the hill to take a closer look at
the trees and the creatures which inhabited them. Under their
heavy boots they couldn't help crushing some of the grub-like
creatures, while overhead the monkey-like creatures scurried away
at their approach cawing in alarm.

Lansdale bent to pick up one of the grubs. He was a slim man,
shorter and less muscular than Cooper, yet there was an air of
authority about him that the other man did not possess. He showed

the animal to Cooper. It was fat and greasy looking, resembling an Earth caterpillar.

"What do you think, Joe?" he said. "An insect larva?"

Cooper shook his head. "There are no insects here large enough to have developed from things like this. And there's something else. . . ." He gestured around them. Criss-crossing everywhere across the ground and the rough grey bark of the thin trees were narrow lines of some moist silvery substance. "They leave tracks. They're probably some kind of slug."

Lansdale nodded uncertainly. "Maybe. Let's take a handful back for analysis. We'd better take one of the monkeys too."

Lansdale unbuttoned his hip-holster and took out his stun-pistol. From what they evidently thought was a safe distance several of the monkey-like creatures were sitting in the trees watching the two men curiously. Lansdale sighted his pistol on one of them and pulled the trigger. There was no sound, but the monkey fell to the ground unconscious. The other monkeys instantly scuttled away once more shrieking in renewed panic.

"It's strange," Cooper said as he read the print-out from the first analysis machine. "This creature has no reproductive organs whatsoever."

He glanced down curiously at the monkey strapped still unconscious inside a metal sample-cage, electrodes connected to its head and limbs, and then at Lansdale.

Lansdale put down the supply pack he was opening and came across to Cooper. He looked at the print-out and then at the monkey. It was a strange animal, covered in a soft white coat and possessing prehensile fingers and toes, its head more like that of a long-jawed cat than a monkey. It was no larger than a small chimpanzee.

Cooper passed more print-out to Lansdale. "It's absolutely sexless—no ovaries, no sperm and no genitals. How do they reproduce?"

Lansdale shrugged. "Maybe they're parthenogenetic."

"Maybe." The big man looked thoughtful. He pointed across to where another machine was analyzing the grubs. "Or maybe those white grubs *are* larvae; maybe they turn into monkeys."

As he spoke a print-out came from this other machine. Lansdale tore it off, read it and then passed it across to him, smiling.

"You're right. Larvae. No doubt about it."

Cooper looked down at the monkey. "And all that these things spend their time doing is eating their young." He shook his head sorrowfully.

"That's not unheard-of," said Lansdale. "Lots of animals do that—even on Earth."

Next day the two men took their module on a low-level tour of the surrounding area. As they flew Cooper sat with his large blond head pressed against the module's curved view-port watching the monkeys swarming among the trees a hundred feet below. He had come rapidly to terms with the apparent fact that the monkeys' young were also their staple diet; to him it now held a certain poetry. As he remarked to Lansdale, the planet had an ecology that was so simple it was beautiful.

Ahead of them the sky was a clear blue and to the east the planet's small sun was rising, casting its soft light down on to the endless forest. The long shadows of the frequent low hills stabbed across the tops of the trees like exclamation marks.

"This is just up your street, isn't it?" Lansdale said. "Utopia."

Cooper nodded. "It's beautiful and it's uncorrupt. Innocent."

"But the grubs eat the insects and the monkeys eat the grubs—it still has the universal law of the jungle about it."

"But there's no cruelty in it," Cooper told him. "The animals eat merely to survive. They *need* each other. . . ."

Lansdale smiled and said nothing. A moment later he frowned. He gripped the control column and put the module into a slow descent. "Joe, down there on that hillside."

Cooper followed his gaze. Then he saw it too: on the grassy slope of one of the hills was the decaying corpse of a large creature.

Lansdale brought the module down on the flat summit of the hill. Warily they made their way down to the carcase.

"The data-compilers gave us a complete list of the planet's fauna," Cooper said. "This wasn't on it. What's happened? Have the machines gone on the blink?"

"I don't know." Lansdale looked puzzled.

It was a large four-legged lizard-like creature, its purple flesh leathery, hard and scaled. Its head was long and thick with two curving white tusks set on either side of its wide mouth. Its empty eyes were large and colourless. And then suddenly the two men stopped—in place of the creature's stomach hundreds of the white grub-like creatures were tumbling and wriggling over each other like giant maggots as they slowly devoured its intestines.

Cooper winced. Cautiously they began to walk round the carcase. Lansdale looked down the hill. The grass of the hill was dry and healthy in the gentle heat and soft light from the planet's sun, no different from the grass of the hill on which their camp was, save that in places this grass was pressed down flat and stained with blood.

"So much for your planet of innocence," Lansdale said. "This creature has had its stomach ripped out in a fight."

Cooper turned away from the dead creature in disgust. "Let's get back to the camp," he said quietly.

They flew back towards the camp in silence. They had almost completed the journey when Cooper said:

"Abe, have you noticed anything?"

Cooper was looking down at the forest. Lansdale followed his gaze, then looked back at him in puzzlement.

"No. Should I?"

"The monkeys," Cooper said. "There aren't any."

Lansdale looked down again at the forest. Sure enough there was no movement among the trees. Quickly he put the module into a sweeping dive. They banked towards the north-west, accelerating. And then suddenly, on the horizon ahead of them, they saw movement. In a moment they were swooping low over a horde of monkeys.

Lansdale laughed. "Nothing to worry about—we just misplaced them." He brought the module round in a steep turn and they headed once more back to the camp.

"There can't be as many of them as we thought," Cooper said quietly. He shifted uncomfortably. He looked out over the forest stretching endlessly beneath them and could not account for the vague feeling of unease he suddenly felt.

For the rest of the day and most of that night the trees around their camp were silent. Just before dawn they were awakened by the chatter of swarming monkeys. Before breakfast as the sun rose, they sat in the warm scented air eating their cereals and watching the monkeys swinging past through the trees. Afterwards Cooper went to see the monkey in the sample cage. It was awake now and began to chirp with pleasure at seeing the big man. It moved up and down slowly on its thick hind legs, its large eyes blinking at Cooper. It seemed to be expecting another bowl of the hot protein soup that they had been feeding it on since it regained consciousness. Cooper obliged.

"Lap it up, Bert," he told it gently. "It's better than eating babies."

He looked down the hill at the other monkeys moving quickly through the trees. Utopia, Lansdale had said. Cooper smiled; he knew that the other man had been chiding him. He had never made a secret of the fact that the only reason he had joined the Frontier Corps was in order to escape what he called the vicious double values of Earth, where love was supposed to be one of the great virtues yet was all but obliterated by hate and violence, and to find a better world. When the two of them first landed here he thought they'd found it, but since seeing that dead mutilated creature he wasn't so sure. And there was something else now that disturbed him, something he couldn't quite put his finger on. Although the other man had said nothing, Cooper knew that Lansdale felt it too. Before they left this place they would have to find out what it was, for Frontiersmen were obliged to make reports that were wholly accurate as far as a planet's human colonization prospects were concerned. Earth Emigration Control were forbidden to disturb a planet's ecology too much, and it was on the Frontier Corps' report that they judged a planet's potential. The smallest error therefore could well prove expensive or fatal—or both.

The monkey finished eating. Cooper was about to put the bowl in the automatic cleaner when there was a shout from Lansdale.

"Joe ! For Christ's sake, Joe !"

Cooper dropped the bowl and ran to where Lansdale was leaping to his feet and running up the hill towards him, hands to his face. For a moment Cooper was puzzled—and then the nauseating smell hit him too.

"Sweet Christmas !"

Holding their noses, both men ran back up the hill towards the module. They fumbled in through the air-lock, gagging and coughing and cursing each other's obstructing bulk and lack of agility. At last they had the lock shut and Cooper punched the button of the air-recycler.

"What in the hell caused that ?"

"I've smelt some smells in my time," Lansdale said, "but . . . Jesus !"

They went to the cabin window. The trees below them at the bottom of the hill were suddenly devoid of monkeys. On the left of the module they could see Bert huddling himself as flat as he could to the bottom of the sample cage.

Then suddenly they saw movement at the edge of the forest. As they watched, a huge animal of the same species as the corpse they had found came crashing into view. It charged up the hill, its big double-tusked mouth open in a great baying roar. Halfway up the hill it turned. And then they saw that it was pursued by another, larger creature. This was a long green quadruped, its clawed forelegs longer than those of the first creature. Its huge mouth was open, revealing double rows of sharp pointed teeth.

It came up the hill and paused in front of the first creature. For a moment the two creatures confronted each other without moving. Then, with a growl of unmistakable fury, the second animal threw itself at the first. They fell to the ground, stabbing and tearing at each other mercilessly again and again with tooth and claw.

Heaving, Cooper turned from the window. Hands to his mouth, he collapsed into the navigator's chair and closed his eyes. Lansdale continued to watch the struggle. At last the creature which had been the pursuer lay inert in the bright stained grass. The first, smaller creature pushed itself upright over the corpse, raised its tusked snout to give a soft baying roar of triumph, and then plunged down the hill and disappeared among the trees.

Ten minutes later the two men emerged from the module. The smell had gone. Below them the trees were filling with monkeys once more as if nothing had happened. Bert was chirping excitedly inside his cage, his white fur bristling.

Cooper looked at Lansdale. "What do you make of that?"

The smaller man shook his head, wholly at a loss.

"That smell was undoubtedly an attempt by that first creature to defend itself—although the closer it got the more incensed the other creature seemed to be." He looked at the other man worriedly. "There's something odd about everything in this place. We've now seen *two* distinctly separate breeds of large animal that didn't show up on the data-compilers' lists. Why not? Surely *all* the data-compilers can't be malfunctioning at once?" He started down the hill towards the corpse. "Come on, let's get the analysis machines working on this—maybe then we'll have a few more answers."

"Is there any point?" Cooper said. "They'll never allow colonization of this place—not with violent and savage creatures like this roaming around."

"I don't know." Lansdale stopped. He looked down at the forest and at the chattering swarm of monkeys. Then he turned thoughtfully to the other man. "We'll get the machines fixed up and then we'll take the module up again. It may or may not have something to do with it, but I've just had an idea about the monkeys."

Thirty minutes later they were hovering a hundred feet above the swarming monkeys. Lansdale was leaning over the dials of the control console taking a reading. He sat back and looked at the other man.

"The monkeys are all moving in the same direction," he said.

Cooper shrugged. "So what? They live in tribes—tribes always move together."

"It's more than that." Lansdale shook his head. "These are a different group from the ones we saw miles away yesterday—yet that other group were heading in the same direction too."

He unlocked the control column and took the module into a sweeping turn towards the north.

Ten minutes later they had left the swarm of monkeys behind. Lansdale accelerated, the two men scanning the empty sunlit tops of the trees below. Presently Cooper gave a shout.

"There! Another swarm."

Lansdale decelerated the module. He brought it to a halt and kept it hovering as they took another reading. They fed both readings into the auto-navigator. A second later it chattered out a result.

Lansdale tore off the print-out and gave it to Cooper. He grinned in triumph. "That's it—if those two swarms keep moving in the same direction they'll meet some seven hundred miles west of here."

He gripped the control column and swivelled the hovering machine. He pushed the column forwards and both men were pressed back into their couch seats as the module accelerated rapidly towards the west.

The hill was much larger than any of the others. It thrust steeply out of the endless forest, and unlike the other hills was almost completely devoid of grass. From the module the two men could see several dark spots on it that could only have been cave entrances. Its lower slopes were swarming with monkeys.

"I think that's where we'll find our answer," Lansdale said.

He took the module down. They landed gently on a flat area near the summit of the hill.

They made their way carefully down to the nearest of the caves. As they approached it they could see that hundreds of monkeys were coming up out of the forest and entering the cave; they noticed too that none were coming out.

Cooper felt an odd cold prickle of fear travel the length of his spine. All around there was a strange silence, and he suddenly realized that the monkeys were not making their usual endless chatter.

They reached the cave. None of the monkeys seemed to notice them. The two men took their pistols from their holsters, switched on their chest-lamps and went in among the silent scampering creatures.

The tunnel was damp and hot, the smooth uneven rocks of its walls and low ceiling covered with a glistening film of slime. The two men followed the tunnel as it wound into the mountain, the monkeys all around apparently oblivious of them. Presently the tunnel became narrower, forcing the men to crouch, and then suddenly it widened.

The two men stood up, gazing around in amazement. They were in a vast dark chamber inside the hill. From the dripping rocks overhead hung bulbous, brightly coloured stalactites. Their lamps sent odd shadows plunging across the walls and ceiling of the chamber between them, overlayed by the criss-crossing shadows of the scurrying monkeys. More stalactites hung from ledges around the chamber wall, and bulging up from the floor were hundreds of stalagmites.

The two men were standing ankle-deep in guano and wet fungus. Around them several of the monkeys were beginning to chatter as if in excitement.

Cooper looked at Lansdale and shrugged. "Okay, where's the answer?"

The small man frowned and said nothing. In the beam from his chest-lamp he watched one of the monkeys lean against a stalagmite. Its surface yielded slightly to the monkey's touch—and suddenly Lansdale realized that it wasn't a stalagmite at all.

"Joe!" he said. "Chrysalids—you were right!"

Cooper gaped around the cave. And then they both saw why the monkeys had come here. The creatures were climbing the rocks now, finding suitable positions for themselves and then pressing their small bodies against the slime. There was a single-mindedness about the monkeys as they climbed and pulled themselves over each other, breaking off some of the chrysalids as they did so. As they fell on to the rocks several of the chrysalids burst open, revealing what was inside them.

"Monkeys!" Cooper stepped back involuntarily. "It's not the grubs that go through a metamorphosis—it's the *monkeys!*"

"Okay, Joe." Lansdale turned back to the tunnel. "There's your answer."

"But what the hell do they turn into?" Cooper asked as they flew back to the camp. "And the analysis machines told us that the grubs were larvae—what do *they* turn into?"

"It's obvious," Lansdale told him. "The monkeys metamorphose into one or other of those big creatures we saw fighting today— which one no doubt determined by some kind of chromosome inside the monkey. As for the grubs, we know they can't be insect larvae—they probably don't develop into anything at all; they're just an ecological dead-end."

"But there are thousands of the monkeys. Why have we seen only three of the bigger creatures?"

"How tall would you say the average tree was, Joe?" Lansdale said. "We've seen so many monkeys simply because they move among the tops of the trees; there are probably hundreds of those big lizards down on the forest floor where we can't see them. And you saw what was happening in that cave: probably hundreds of the chrysalids are smashed by the arriving monkeys. Maybe only a small percentage actually complete the metamorphosis. It explains too why the data-compilers didn't list the big creatures. Those machines aren't as sophisticated as we'd like them to be: they couldn't see beyond the fact that the lizards and the monkeys are the same species."

They approached the camp. The sun had passed its zenith now, but the trees and hills were still wavering in the hot air.

"But there's something else," Cooper said. "Something we've missed—I'm *sure* there is."

The carcase of the huge beast was exactly as they had left it. The analysis machines had chattered out their findings and fallen silent.

"Sexless," Cooper said. "The same as the monkeys." He looked at Lansdale. "Don't tell me these things metamorphose into something else again." He passed the print-out to the other man.

"You're wrong," Lansdale said when he had read it. "Agreed, it has no sexual organs, but there is an indication here of a latent potential for bearing young." He frowned. "Or maybe it's an atrophied ability. . . . I don't understand it, Joe. Somewhere we've got it all wrong. If in their final adult stage the monkeys become these beasts, and these beasts are sexless and do not bear young, where do the monkeys come from in the first place?"

Cooper shrugged. "The grubs? Maybe there's a double metamorphosis—maybe the grubs become the monkeys and the monkeys become these creatures."

"But that merely replaces one question with another," Lansdale said. He looked down at the carcase. "It still doesn't tell us where the *grubs* come from." Shaking his head in bewilderment, he began to walk up the hill towards the analysis machines. As he reached the one that had analyzed the grubs he saw that some of them had escaped from the samples tray and were crawling over the camp leaving their silvery tracks everywhere across the grass and equipment—and then the realization hit him. "The grubs! My God, that's it!" He turned to look at Cooper coming up the hill after him. "Joe, we're a couple of unobservant fools— the grubs *are* the key to this whole thing!"

Cooper frowned. "What do you mean?"

"It was staring us straight in the face when we found that first dead creature! Its stomach was a squirming mass of the grubs, but where did those grubs come from? They couldn't have come up from the forest."

"Why not?"

"Joe, the grubs leave their sticky tracks everywhere they go, *but there were no tracks anywhere on that hill!*"

Cooper's eyes involuntarily sought the carcase below them. Suddenly he began to understand. He felt sick. "Abe, you mean. . . ."

"Yes, Joe! As soon as it was killed grubs began to form from cells *inside* its corpse, no doubt feeding on its putrefying flesh until they were strong enough to make their own way down into the forest. And this creature here—if we wait long enough I'm willing to bet that we'll see little monkeys emerging from inside its decaying body!"

Cooper shook his head. "Abe, I don't think. . . ." But Lansdale gripped his arm.

"Joe, there's no other possible explanation! Think about it. The two types of lizard-creature die, and in so doing produce either grubs or monkeys. The monkeys eat the grubs, and once inside the monkeys the grubs act like enzymes to start the physiological reactions that make the monkeys eventually change themselves into chrysalids. And inside these chrysalids the big lizard-creatures are formed." He began to laugh.

"What's so funny?" Cooper said.

"The reason why these two large creatures fight! That smell wasn't a defence at all—it was an enticement, something ejected by one of the creatures in order to arouse the hatred and fury of the other—hatred and fury enough to make it want to fight to the death. Because only in death can they procreate! You see what it means, Joe?"

Cooper saw only too well. He shook away Lansdale's restraining hand and began to walk up the hill towards the module. Lansdale came after him.

" 'An ecology so simple it's beautiful,' " Lansdale said. "That's what you said it was—and it is! Joe, how many life-supporting worlds have an ecology like this, with, apart from the insects, just one species of animal with a three-stage life-cycle, each stage no doubt with its own purpose in that ecology? And how many life-cycles are so tidy, and so exemptive of waste with the new generation forming itself from the remains of the old?"

In silence Cooper began to reprogramme the machines methodically for repacking the equipment back inside the module.

"Joe, I don't think you'll *ever* find what you're looking for," Lansdale told him. "No goodness exists without corresponding evil because goodness by itself is a neutral thing; it's only in the presence of evil that good can *be* good. Pure love can't exist without hatred and cruelty in some degree, Joe; and I think this is the nearest to pure love you'll ever get—here where the sex-act is a fight to the death !"

Cooper stopped and looked at Lansdale. Since they had teamed up he had taken Lansdale's constant chiding in good part. Now, with surprise, he realized that during the months they had been working together Lansdale had been waiting for such a moment as this : in the small man's eyes now was something close to a look of triumph.

For the rest of that day Cooper continued to reprogramme the machines for winding up their operations. Their job here now was finished. All that remained was to find out whether the lizard-creatures would react adversely to human intrusion. If not, this place would have to be reported as suitable for colonization.

He couldn't bring himself to look again at the corpse at the bottom of the hill. As the day wore on he was aware of an intensifying of the scent that rose from the forest all around, and he wondered how only a short while before he could have possibly considered that smell pleasant.

It wasn't until the equipment was all but packed away and he was ready to enter the module himself that he collapsed and was violently ill on the soft grass in front of the hatchway.

Limbo Girl on the Flat She Walked

Picture me a red.

You ask: a red what?

But here is where the difficulty begins. Here is something beyond the mind to imagine or words to describe. It is something felt, and once felt never forgotten. An indelible crimson stamp that furrows through the brain and leaves its mark there for ever, a subliminal fossil of thought and memory that can never leave the mind it touches once it has touched.

And its colour is red.

You all know your history, don't you? You remember the first unmanned probes which were sent to Proxima Centauri. That was way back. It took them fifteen years to get there, which in those days was pretty damn fast: caused quite a sensation. But those little blue and silver machines never once travelled Faster Than Light. How could they? The Sabini-drive didn't come until nearly half a century later, and by that time the probes were manned. Ten years out and ten years back those manned probes were going then; still less than the speed of light but still quite a rate. And for what? For a couple of arid dust-bowl planets and five or six spheres of ice. It nearly destroyed the sanity of some of the ones who went; a twenty-year round trip for *that*? Oh brother!

And then the Sabini-drive.

The first automatic probes made the round trip in about four months. They came back intact and shiny, even more shiny than when they left, having been polished by the smooth imperceptible friction of Sabini-space. The instruments chattered out their reports: all's well, all's well. Oiled smoothness and humming efficiency. Everything as it should be. But of course machines don't have minds, do they? How could they have known?

The first manned FTL ship left in 2102. A crew of three were on board—Chambers, Took and Henneweil. You can still see movies of their departure: smiling and waving, standing at the top of the slender gantry against a sky being emptied of colour by the roaring heat of a Florida afternoon. And then lift-off and that's the end, the last the world ever saw, or will ever see, of three happy intelligent men.

They came back all right. Oh yes. They came back, but they weren't the same men, were they?

Three wooden dummies. Breathing and sleeping and still accepting their intravenous nourishments. But their minds were gone, drained away into the unknown limbo somewhere between here and Proxima.

Not surprisingly there was an uproar about that. Yet three years later two more volunteers, Stephens and McKrae, took another ship to Proxima Centauri.

They came back the same way: living corpses.

For a quarter of a century no one tried FTL. They sent animals, and there were no ill-effects. But still they wouldn't send a man.

Eventually they sent me.

Myself:

I'm no ordinary man. My mother was the daughter of a politician, an adviser to the President, and my father was Controller-in-Chief of the whole Sabini project. That had some bearing on my future, but that's not all: you see, there was something missing inside me when I was born; I grew up slowly and painfully, and they told my parents I would deteriorate rapidly beyond my twenty-fifth year. I was mentally different. The actual word they used was retarded.

So what had they—or I—to lose? I was twenty-five years old already. Sane men had come back as vegetables. What would happen if they sent someone like me?

They tell me it was a black night when they took me out to the ship. Clouds obscured the stars and moonlight spilled intermittently across the pads. Not many of them knew: only those whose participation was absolutely necessary. They say my mother cried for two weeks afterwards, but she showed her face to no one but my father.

Next day, when the ship actually lifted off, everyone not involved in the plot assumed that it was merely another unmanned probe.

I have now no recollection of my life until then. Or, to be more accurate, until I was out between the stellar systems on the way to Proxima and the relays clicked the Sabini-motor into operation and I became FTL. . . .

"What is your name?"

The girl was slightly taller than me, fine blonde hair framing a slender pink face. Her intelligent eyes watched me with an almost circumspect shrewdness and I felt uncomfortable.

"Danye," I told her. "Danye Allison.'

"How old are you, Danye?"

"Twenty-five years and four months."

"Years? Months?" She seemed puzzled. "What are those?"

I frowned. "Look, if you're kidding me. . . ."

She shook her head. "Danye, believe me I'm not."

My frown deepened. "You *really* don't know what a year is?"

"Yes. No. I mean that's right, I *don't* know."

"A year is the full cycle of all the four seasons," I told her. "The time it takes the earth to complete one revolution of its orbit around the sun; the time it takes the earth to spin on its axis 365 times, except every fourth year when——"

"What's 'the earth'?" she asked suddenly.

Then I became angry. "Now you *are* kidding me!"

"What's 'the earth'?" she repeated, genuinely puzzled. "What's 'the sun'?"

"Boy, are you stupid!" My anger turned to laughter and I lifted my arm to gesture at the sky—and then I stopped. For the first time I realized I was somewhere I had never been before. Beyond the girl's shoulder the land stretched towards a distant, perfectly flat horizon. There were no trees or hills. Sunlight streamed from the sky and that was the whole trouble.

There was no sun.

The sky was a pale blue, merging to turquoise. As if affected by gravity, the colour seemed to drain towards the horizon so that the sky seemed more richly hued there. It was bright warm cloudless daylight, but nowhere in the sky was there a sun.

"Where am I?" I asked in a whisper.

The girl smiled. "You don't know?"

My eyes followed the curves of the white silky garment that hung from the girl's shoulders and swirled at her feet. I suddenly noticed that she cast no shadow. Abruptly, my heart was thudding like a piston and my head was filled with thoughts of ghosts and vampires—and then I noticed that I cast no shadow either.

"The probe?" I asked. "What happened to the probe?"

"Probe?"

Suddenly I felt exasperated, panicky. "I don't remember landing," I said. "I was in a probe, heading from the Solar System to Proxima. As soon as the Sabini-drive cut in I. . . ." I shook my head. I could remember nothing but the glaring unexpected redness that had permeated everything. And the next thing I remembered was that I was standing here and this lovely girl was asking my name.

"Am I in Heaven?" I asked.

"I can speak your language," the girl said, "but I do not understand some of the words. You talk of 'earth', 'sun' and 'Heaven'—but these things are meaningless to me. Are they places?"

I nodded. "Yes, they *are* places. But somehow it's only now that these words hold meaning for me. All my life I've heard them mentioned, but only now—only at this moment—are they more to me than meaningless sounds. What's happened?" My stomach was knotting with fear. "Where *am* I?"

I put my hands to my face. Then the girl touched me and the fear was suddenly not quite so strong. I took my hands away to see her smiling at me.

"Poor boy," she said softly. "You must be a Greel."

"Greel?"

Her hair shook as she nodded. "Perhaps you should speak to my parents."

I watched her doubtfully. All around, stretching into the distance, the land was empty and barren; we were tiny creatures on a flat featureless board. Her parents? We had no transport, it looked as if we had a long walk ahead of us.

"Come." She took my hand.

"What's your name?" I asked as we started to walk.

"Julie," she said. "Do you think that's a pretty name?"

"It's an Earth name," I told her. I shook my head, now more puzzled than frightened. "One moment I'm heading FTL to Proxima, and the next I'm standing in the middle of the strangest place I've ever seen, talking to a strange but lovely girl with an Earth name—and she speaks my language."

"Poor Greel," she said.

Then suddenly I had a thought. "Oh Christ!" I said. "Do you think it's *inside* me?" I put a finger to the side of my temple. "I'm insane . . . I *was* insane . . . but now I feel . . . well, *different*—do you think my mind has gone completely?" Her grip tightened on my hand. "Julie, are you real, or are you just in my imagination? Oh God, what's happening to me?"

"Don't be afraid," she said. "Here, talk to my parents."

I had to look twice. I looked behind me and the flat board stretched interminably to a horizon that was too hazy for me to be certain that it even *was* a horizon. We had taken only two or three steps, I was sure, but there in front of us, suddenly, was a building.

It was squat yet graceful, a delicate construction of pastel-coloured two-dimensional planes, as if someone had created a dwelling from interconnecting sheets of wafer-thin glass that was transparent only when looked at from a certain angle. In the centre was a door with steps leading down to our feet, and at the top of the steps a man and woman : Julie's parents.

He was fairly old, his grey hair long but thinning. He was gnarled and crooked yet rather imperious, eyes like shells, and a shrewd but friendly smile. Slightly taller than her husband, she was a black-haired beauty. High-cheekboned and elegant, yet cordial and welcoming. Wearing similar crinkly creamy dresses, both she and Julie reminded me of angels and again I wondered: Was this Heaven?

Hand in hand, Julie and I reached the top of the steps. The woman leaned forwards slightly, a faint smile hovering at the corners of her lips.

"Are you a Greel?"

"So Julie seems to think," I told her. "But I don't know what a Greel is."

The smile bloomed. The man and woman turned and walked into the house. Julie and I followed. Inside, the house was dark but far from gloomy. Curious points of golden light shone underfoot and speckled the walls like a million freshly minted coins. Julie and I followed the man and woman through a number of rooms, no two of which were the same shape, and all around bizarre lanterns cast pools and bars of pastel light. Set into the walls on each side of us, huge mirrors provided our images with viridescent haloes and echoed distorted perspectives of the rooms through which we walked. What place, I thought again, was this?

"There have only been five Greels before you," the woman said over her shoulder.

"Chambers, Took and Henneweil?" I ventured.

"Those were the first three," she agreed. "Stephens and McKrae came after them. Then there were none for a long time. Now you are the sixth, but you are not the same as the others."

"Not the same?"

"The others could not acknowledge the existence of this place," she said. "Physical experience could not reconcile with mental conditioning. To them we were too much of an enigma, an offence against logic. They could not take us into their minds, so their minds came to us."

"They came back from Proxima," I said, "but they were no longer sane. Are you saying that they lost their minds—literally?"

"Yes."

"Then why haven't I . . ." I began, then stopped. Evidently

this place induced opposites; the five before me had been sane and had become insane. I was *insane* and had become. . . .

"I don't understand," I said, feeling frightened again. I pulled Julie closer to me. Her hair brushed the side of my face and a delicate fragrance drifted to me as she lifted her eyes to mine and smiled.

"Neither do we," said the woman. She stopped walking and turned towards us. "As far as we can remember this place has always existed and we have always lived here: for us it is the only real world. Our parents before us lived here, and after we have gone Julie will live on here.

"But there is this: to you *your* world is the only reality; *your* world has always existed. And that poses many questions."

"I still don't understand."

"Consider," she said. "Consider the fact that we both speak the same language. You know it as your native tongue, yet it is our native tongue also. That is beyond the realm of coincidence, don't you agree?"

"Yes," I said.

"The men who came here—we absorbed their minds, albeit apparently only in part, and each of us in varying degrees. Perhaps we are mere figments of those five men's imaginations. . . ."

"Figments?" I said incredulously.

"Don't be so surprised. There is an entity who is said to have created man—an entity called God. Couldn't it be that man is a figment of *His* imagination?"

"But. . . ."

She smiled and shook her head. "No, Danye, I don't believe that any more than you do. I merely said it in order to plant the questions in your mind. The thoughts of Chambers, Took and Henneweil found homes inside our minds. Perhaps they are now in your mind, Danye. How else can you explain your sudden sanity?"

I was more bewildered than ever. Julie came closer to me and I rested my forehead against her cheek. Her father emerged from the dappled shadows and said with a chuckle, "I do believe the young buck is in love."

His wife threw him a disdainful glance. For a moment we all looked at his dry wrinkled face. Then I looked sideways at Julie and thought: By God, he could be right! Julie suddenly caught my glance and a flush crept up into her cheeks as she smiled.

"Long ago on your world there was a man called Einstein," the woman was saying. "He postulated theories for many things, disregarding reason and using only logic. He believed that gravity, magnetism, electricity, light and time could all be combined into one ultimate theory—the Unified Field theory. But his life came to an end before his work on this colossal concept could really begin."

I lifted my hands in a helpless gesture. "I still don't see. . . ."

"Don't you, Danye? Just imagine for a moment that there was more to it than that. Imagine that time and light and gravity and thought and memory and emotion all tie up together in one huge constitution of reality. . . ."

"Well, don't they?"

"Yes, Danye, they do. And doesn't that take us back to the beginning: What *is* reality?"

A thought suddenly struck me. I pulled myself away from Julie and touched the woman's arm.

"But Leonard Sabini found a way round the Einstein limits, didn't he?" I said triumphantly. "Where does *that* take us?"

She turned slowly and gestured around her, at the shadows and speckled lights and oddly angled doorways. She pointed towards a window through which I could see the immense flat gaming-board of the landscape and the sunlight streaming from the sun-less sky.

"I don't know where it gets *us*," she said, "but it gets *you* right here, doesn't it?"

Abruptly, all three of them were walking away from me. I suddenly had to run to catch up with them. As I came level with Julie, she caught my arm and then we were all heading down a wide flight of steps.

And there—

And there in the centre of a vast room was the probe. Suspended in mid air, yet not suspended, for there was nothing supporting

E

it. It gleamed with a polished Sabini-friction gleam. Light sliced its flanks and spilled across its stubby fins, sparkling down the perspex curve of its canopy. And inside the canopy was a man.

The man was me.

Panic prickled across my neck. Julie, fear flickering into her eyes, turned to her mother. The woman smiled sadly and shook her head. Julie gave a cry and leapt towards me, her hair lifting around her like a halo. I opened my arms to catch her and I was slapped in the eyes by a sudden burning redness, the blood-colour of Sabini-space.

"Julie! . . ."

They took me from the probe as it bobbed in the Pacific.

I remember my father's jubilant face, his slap on his aide's back.

"We did it, by God! The boy's all right!"

Not only my sanity caused a stir, but also my intellect and erudition. What worries me is what would happen if they weren't inside me: gestalt minds: Chambers, Took and Henneweil, and possibly Stephens and McKrae. Am I myself, or am I them?

At night I am smothered by dreams of a girl with blonde hair and a beautiful name and I wake up aching and hollow. It would be impossible for me to find her, for I cannot make the journey a second time. You see, I am too sane. And sane men lose their minds out there in Sabini-space, don't they?

Or am I five minds?

Would these minds disperse, or would they accept the unlogic and unreason this time?

Here is the rub:

I cannot go back because I am sane. I cannot tell them the truth because then I would appear insane, and if I appeared insane they would not let me go because that would prove that their experiment had failed. Yet I cannot go unless I tell them.

I walk out on to my balcony and gaze down the thousand levels to the street below, the city humming and whispering, trundling across the nerve-ends of Time and I wonder: should I jump?

I lean on the balustrade and feel the cool air layering against my hands and wonder about all the people here on this earth and their terrifying unawareness, their constant misunderstandings and misinterpretations, so unsafe in their insularity, and prisoners of their own five senses. I ask myself: Where are we? What is going to happen to us all? When are we going to free ourselves from this abysmal trap?

Julie. . . .

Michael Stall

Gaming

PRELUDE

The year 2130 began with a flurry of freshly minted calendars and much mundane journalistic speculation. No one really thought that it would be much different from the year that had preceded it. There was, or so the story goes, a minor great power dispute over mollusc beds in the Pacific, but peace was well established and hardly likely to be broken over such an issue. But whether by accident or the complex, insane escalation of events, the Break came in late April. It was not complete; some were left to look on from afar; some were left amidst the wreckage; but the Break was complete enough. The game of civilization was over on Earth. Another game began. . . .

FIRST GAME

One

August, 2163

It would have been possible to disembark on the sands just to the south and walk up the beach to the Assembly place that sheltered by the spray-scoured castle, but Marjorie Sollis, the High Commissioner, had been told that the degradation of the seafaring art made it impossible, so they had put ashore from the Grimsby 'cat' just above Blyth and had ridden the rest of the way : a minor but calculated inconvenience.

The tents of the Assembly of the Provinces were impressive, all got up as they were in the colours and devices peculiar to their origin, clustered beneath the western walls of the castle, protected by its grey bulk from the bitter sea winds. But that very proximity was damning : the bastion of ancient and modern stonework pointed up their transience cruelly and their trumpery intentionally.

They had had this scene before them for more than an hour as they rode tiredly up the beach, and had stared at it continually : there had been nothing to draw their eyes seaward; not a sail to be seen, and the North Sea, uncommonly placid, a leaden grey expanse that merged barely perceptibly with the equally dull, heavy sky. Only to Bamburgh castle, its massiveness of form utterly transcending its greyness of texture, was the eye drawn.

"It's ironic, isn't it, Magnate," she said, turning in the saddle to face Bagehot, "a congress of the whole, wide world—in tents !"

That kind of irony could lead on to pity, and was not to be encouraged.

"There are limited precedents, of course, such as the Field of the Cloth of Gold, but as our society is essentially unprecedented, they hardly concern us, but I appreciate that, according to your way of thinking, the castle itself, for instance, would have been more fitting a location; but reflect on the nature of a castle, and you'll come to the conclusion not only is it a redoubt, but also a city in miniature, and to make use of one in this matter would have meant going against the spirit of our ordinances. . . ." He continued in the same vein, in the same pettifogging spirit expressed in wheedling tones, until the nascent spark of sympathy he had suspected had to be well and truly extinguished.

The Commissioner's tent was in gold and green and had two silk shells to cover its many rooms and two medium-sized halls. It was heated by braziers, and the ventilation, while not perfect, was surprisingly good. If she cared to reflect on the work that had gone into all this, considering the reduced facilities of her hosts, she would have been flattered; but she would not, Bagehot was sure, allow herself to be seduced by the barbarian glitter of it; on the contrary, it would be more in the way of a continual reproach.

That was confirmed by the derogatory remarks she couldn't keep herself from making when Bagehot took his leave of her, mildly tempting him to remind her that the bases on Mars consisted of little more than plastic tents pegged down on that scarred, barren surface, but the self-control of a Survivor, augmented by almost forty years of continuous politicking was posed no problem by so minor a containment. He merely made reply that the Assembly would be grateful if she would honour them with a visit at noon on the day following, and promptly abandoned her to the bevy of fawning servants that came with the tent.

He had a tent prepared for himself, the tent of Northumbria, but he didn't go to it: the last thing he could take now was the brashness and lively intelligence of his young staff, and the other magnates (he smiled inwardly at the word) wouldn't expect a courtesy call from him—the job came first. And it might even be done already, or it might need much more than was originally planned; it was his job to know. He made his way to the tent the rest of the party had been assigned. It was a single-shelled affair; inside, John the Ostler and several guards lay sleeping on straw, and Peters, the moodsearcher, another vagrant from the Northumbrian tent, was sitting on a small, folding stool, his legs crossed, and was writing in a large book resting on his lap. He looked up, and Bagehot nodded to assure him that all was well, feeling a sudden urge to ask that most human of questions, What are you writing? but again he restrained himself. He declined Peters' offer of the stool: not only would it be undignified for the 'Magnate' of Northumbria, it also looked uncomfortable. He sat instead on a leather-covered coffer, and tried to think himself inside her skull. She had come from an advanced technological civilization to this, by increasingly primitive stages: after splash-down in the North Sea, she had been picked up by an antiquated Osterby flying boat; after disembarking on North Humberside, she had had to ride across Holderness, come up the coast on an old sailing ship, even then not all the way, and there had been several diversions along the way....

It was hard to judge its effect on her; Peters was monumentally sure that everything was going to plan, but it wasn't his responsibility, and he did have one advantage over him: Peters wasn't old enough to have once lived in a society similar to hers, before the Break; he was. And he tried to imagine himself as he was, forty years back, seeing all that she had seen....

The small party was moving slowly up the hill, over turf straw-bleached and blowzy with leaves in honour of the season; the drab, homespun clothes proclaimed them simple villagers. They were led by a small, pudgy man, wearing a decorative steel chain about his shoulders, the village major. In one hand he held one end of a length of cord, the other being bound about the wrists of the man in the centre of the party who, every now and then, seemed to hold back, and whom the major hurried along with a jerk of the cord. They were making for a wooden structure at the hill's height.

"What's that?" she asked, but before Bagehot could reply, she had slipped down from her horse and was standing, holding the reins loosely. "Is it some kind of ceremony?"

"You might say that."

She maintained a paralyzed silence until the trussed-up wretch had his feet thrust from the retainers and began kicking silently, like a marionette before the curtain of a tin grey sky.

"You must stop it!" she said, as the figure kept kicking. "Aren't you going to stop it?"

"Why should I?"

"But it's barbaric!" She gestured wildly. "Look, it's not right, whoever he murdered. . . ."

"Oh, I doubt that he murdered anyone," Bagehot said, wondering at the childhood that had allowed her not to recognize a gallows when she saw one.

"Then why?"

"I don't know why, but I suppose he's been into a city."

"This is insane." She stood there, her early middle-aged face screwed up unpleasantly, in contrast to its usual appealing plainness.

"On the contrary, it's perfectly sane." It was easy to be ice cold, knowing what was really happening. The figure stopped threshing and hung limply in the air. "I'm sorry you had to see that, though; it really was most clumsy."

She looked up at him fiercely, and then her face set in a mask-like imitation of normality.

"You mustn't let these things upset you too much, my dear Commissioner," Bagehot said patronizingly, "you must remember that you're on Earth now."

She was hiding her disgust and anger with admirable diplomatic skill, but it was a gesture, no more. When they came to the strange stones set by the wayside, it was touch and go whether her annoyance would let her notice them, and ask their significance; her curiosity just won.

"Runes," Bagehot told her.

She repeated the word questioningly.

"An old form of the alphabet, a Germanic variant of the Latin alphabet: the Anglo-Saxons, for instance, used it pretty much as we use, or used to use, the Gothic script. They were revived by a few cultists to give charm to their nonsenses. That transliterates directly to Modern English as:

> 'Stay Traveller
> Do Her Worship
> Immanent
> Eternal
> Spirit That Reigns . . .'

"And so on and so forth. It's an invitation to the worship of the Dianic Cult, of the Earth Mother."

She asked a few questions, the expected ones, and he answered them to the effect that such cults were springing up all over the place, having their basis in old books and a desire, not unnatural considering the turn society had taken, to get back to the soil and primeval beliefs. He hinted, discreetly, that the ceremonies were not delicate, a return of the grosser forms of paganism in fact.

"How can you allow it?" she asked, a question heavy with the tones of the puritan-materialism of the outplanet bases.

In reply, Bagehot simply shrugged.

The Inn was only vaguely attached to its village, being a full quarter-mile down the pack-horse track. Its whitewashed walls were a little less than immaculate, with here and there a shadow of the old brick showing through, but its well rain-washed, red roof tiles were in fine condition, except over the stables, where patches of crudely cut slate showed blackly amongst the red.

Inside, the inn was cosy. There was no other word. There was a fire roaring in the private room—a coal fire, with coal from an old opencast mine to the south, and a couple of logs atop to give a more picturesque effect. She was sitting in one of the hand-carved wooden arm-chairs by the fire, gazing into it, while its glare gave her an almost feral aspect, not softening a single angularity of her face.

Bagehot took the other chair, and smiled visibly at the further harshening of her expression.

"You must remember, Commissioner, that on this world, forty years ago, we saw the death of four and a half thousand million people."

"And that devalues the sacredness of human life. He wasn't even a murderer; he just went into a city."

"Not 'just': that's the worst crime imaginable. Have you ever seen someone die of neo-anthrax? If you had, you wouldn't think it a slight crime to risk bringing that back to your village for the sake of pillaging amongst the city ruins."

There was a tap on the door: the landlord entered, and asked their wants.

"They were hanging a man on Belvoir Hill, landlord; we saw them as we passed. Who would that have been?"

"Now, let me see." The landlord rubbed his chin reflectively. "I suppose that'd 'a' been old Freddie Wheeler. Aye, come to think o' it, I think I did 'ear talk that 'e'd been going into Beverley, or even Hull, poor evil old soul. If they 'anged 'im legal, it must 'a' been that 'e pleaded guilty at t' village court, for we always 'ear tell o' what's been on at t' sessions o' 'Olderness. But now, what can——"

"One more thing, landlord. This lady is a stranger here—perhaps you've heard of her, Dr. Sollis?"

"That we 'ave."

"Well, the hanging upset her; it struck her as barbaric. What do you say to that?"

The old landlord scratched his chin, looking her over carefully.

"Nay, lass," he said finally, "I reckon you don't know as to what tha speaks on. I remember t' bad days, afore tha wert born on anither world, an' I saw t' way folks died then, an' if old

Freddie Wheeler, either through weakness in t' 'ead or whativer, threatened 'is village wi' that, then they'd 'a' been fools and damned fools if they'd a-'tarried a minute afore 'angin' 'im on t' nearest gallows, whether it affronts t'eyes o' pretty lasses like tha sen, or no; and that's a fact!"

"He said something about that poor man being weak in the head, didn't he?" she asked when the landlord had left; "I suppose he meant by that that he was in need of psychiatric treatment."

"Very probably," Bagehot agreed.

Then they waited in silence for the arrival of early supper.

The wind was north-easterly as they carefully tacked up the coast, aware that while the 'cat' was of the same type that regularly traded with the Norse, Northern Baltic and Pomeranian Coasts, and that while it was of the type that Cook had sailed to Australia and through the Pacific, they could just as easily come to grief off a lee shore here, in home waters. In the afternoon, the wind freshened. . . .

Suddenly, the boat began to sway with storm violence; he could feel the salt spray penetrating icily between his teeth, feel its cold force on his forehead. . . . More and appropriate images were conjured up, then rejected as he opened his eyes and stared blearily at Peters, whose face, flickering very slightly in the light of the brazier that was the only light in the tent, was about a foot from his own. Peters' hands were on his shoulders; someone, probably one of the guards, was snoring loudly.

"Enough, I'm awake."

Peters took his hands away. "There's a palliasse of straw for you, sir, in the private section."

Bagehot nodded and muttered a few words of thanks that weren't wholly sincere, for he didn't like to be reminded that he was an old man now, who couldn't be allowed to sleep, sitting on a coffer like a man at arms, but must have a palliasse. It was the justice of Peters' judgement that rankled.

The tents had been arranged in a grid, at the exact centre of which was the great, white single-shelled tent of the Assembly of the Provinces. As one entered it, feeling the soil squelchy under the single layer of tarpaulin, the starkness, in comparison with the other, private tents was striking, and presumably Sollis interpreted that as intended.

There were thirty-one magnates sat about on rickety-looking folding stools, and, one by one, Bagehot introduced them : the Magnate of the United and Cityless Counties of Barcelona and Toulouse; the Magnate of the Province of Hudson's Bay and Environs; the Magnate of the United Province of the Yukon, Alaska and the Southern Rocky Mountain Enclaves; the Magnate of the United Province of the Appalachian Enclaves; the Magnate of the United Scandinavian Provinces and the Livonian and Finnish Enclaves; the Magnate of the United Province of New Rus; the Magnate of the Cityless Enclaves of China; and twenty-four more of them, and not one representing more than three million souls.

It was a melancholy list for Bagehot, and for those whom he named, but she didn't seem to realize that; he could see only her impatience to get the formalities over with.

"Gentlemen," Commissioner Sollis, still unseated, began when they eventually did get down to business, "I take it you all know why I am here, as it is at your request that I am here; originally, all that was necessary could have been handled through Arctic Facility, but I have also been authorized to make a supplementary proposal, an unexpected one, I'm sure, but one that will make you as happy as it made me to hear it; its acceptance will, I hope, mark the maturity of our unfortunate species.

"The ostensible reason for my presence here is for discussions on closer trading and cultural links between the Provinces of Earth and the outplanet Bases. I believe that some of you believe that our intentions merely amount to a desire to milk Earth of her resources, but that is, let me assure you, a misapprehension. We are independent; Earth can offer us nothing but luxuries, while on the other hand, we offer you technology and participation in scientific advance. In the forty years since that murderous war, that almost genocidal war that we term the 'Break', the links between the Bases, the 'Insurance of Mankind', and the Mother World, have not been significantly strengthened. Now, so to speak, we wish to give you back the premium, with substantial interest.

"We offer to amalgamate the Executives of all the Bases and all the Provinces of Earth into one Directorate. We offer, we suggest, we aspire to—Union!"

Bagehot let the word expand to fill his mind with longing, as they all must be doing, but that was only a temporary thing, and not unexpected. The Bases on the Moon, Mars and Ganymede, along with their Rhean and Callistan Stations, were being very generous, if also very naïve. All the same, it was a tempting offer; thirty, even twenty years before, it might even have been acceptable; but not now.

Bagehot was the first, on behalf of his Province, to decline the offer amidst profuse thanks; he was not the last.

"Why?" she asked finally, looking straight at Bagehot.

"We feel it would be better if we both looked after our salvation separately; that decision being made, we will stand by it."

"But will you?" Sollis asked with an anger that was more than rhetorical. "We didn't expect this, but we are thorough, it's the only way to survive out there, and so even such a situation as this was included in the contingency plans. We can't afford another split in the general governance of the race: the last war came as near as anything to wiping us out, and the next one will, so it can't be allowed to happen. You'll either join the Union voluntarily, or be incorporated by force: choose!"

"We do, and we choose neither alternative," Gaston Larbaud, the Magnate of Barcelona and Toulouse answered her. "You know perfectly well that such a war is impossible for you to undertake; look at the difficulty you have getting yourself down, and then back up again! You couldn't land a full company with return tickets in their pockets without exhausting yourselves industrially, and we could eat that number up, even as we are now."

"Could you?" She paused. "Such would never be our intention; it would be idiotic on our part, getting into a ground war with you when it would be the simplest thing imaginable, putting a few bombs in orbit."

"Suppose you do that," Larbaud took her up, "you threaten us, but we don't give in. So you send them down on us. For what? One awful example isn't going to change our minds. You forget, most of us here have lived through the Break, and that was much worse than you're capable of—or capable of even imagining. But you're all bluff in any case. What kind of Union would you get that way? It would be naturally and readily fissile, and worse than no Union at all. And understand, we don't say we'll never agree to unification, just not now; it's a matter of timing, so there's hope for you there." Larbaud smiled, a major concession from that testy Tartarin.

"And what justification would you have," Bagehot said, taking the floor again, "for engaging in war to avoid just that? Are we a threat to you, even potentially, even in the middle distant future? Are our cities preparing for war? Are our ploughshares beaten into swords, or the technological equivalent thereof, or are they slowly rusting in barns, waiting for next year and ploughing time? Just what threat are we to you?"

Commissioner Sollis made no answer, which in itself was an answer. She made to leave, but as she pulled the tent flap aside, she hesitated, then turned and faced them.

"You're right. You are no threat to us, just an insult. You're decaying, degenerating day by day into barbarians, going the long way down—and it's an even longer climb back up, if you ever make it. Soon, you won't even be a potential threat to each other, just dying fragments once on the body of mankind.

"And it's waste, absolute waste. I came to promote Union; you've wasted that option, so I'll recommend instead that the two previous Commissioners' understandings with you on communications be considered ended, in order to isolate you completely in the hope that might make you come to your senses. If you don't, there's nothing more we can do for you, but at least we needn't watch the process of decay!"

She took hold of the flap again, jerked it aside and strode out to her own tent, like a frailer Achilles, of frailer gender, but one who would not be called upon again.

The Minister-Delegates (for they could again call themselves that now) watched from the square, four-towered keep as the Commissioner left, with a small party of guards around her, riding on the wet sands north to where they would pass the Farne Islands in the east and see Lindisfarne with its castle before turning west, keeping just to the north of the Cheviot and riding down through its hills, on the old Border, down Liddisdale to the waiting Osterby flying boat in the Solway Firth and the second stage of her journey to the Arctic Moonbase Facility.

Bagehot saw her turn her head several times and look up at the imposing bulk of the castle, from where, once, the Ancient Kingdom of Northumbria had been ruled, but he doubted that it impressed her. That King Ida had first raised a defensive pile of stones in the dim days of the ninth century, that later generations had augmented, destroyed and finally renovated it, all that could be nothing to her harsh functionalism. What present use had the castle? And yet it had a use. For a short space of time, this old building had been the most important building in the world, for the impression it had helped convey to her mind.

"It would have been embarrassing if it had rained," Minister-Delegate Montagu from the Rocky Mountain Enclaves said. Bagehot turned to face him.

"Not so embarrassing as all that; there's quite a bit of creosote in the camp."

Montagu laughed. Then: "They look so fine, it seems a pity...."

"No doubt, but do you think they're far enough away to see it to its best advantage? It's hard to estimate."

Montagu looked carefully at the party, as if calculating angles in his head.

"Give them another couple of minutes to be on the safe side. How long will it take to start, anyway?"

"Seconds, no more," Bagehot replied, then, abruptly changing the subject: "What did you think of their leather armour, by the way?"

"The guards'? I thought it superb. But it didn't look at all medieval. In fact, it looked like a Renaissance *condottiere*'s flamboyant copy of what he conceived to be the old Roman fashion; and I did think the strips of coloured silk a bit overdone, as well."

"Probably were, but I thought we needed some inconsistency

for everything not to look too suspicious; some of the boys who'll be debriefing her are sharper than razors."

Montagu nodded, rubbing his chin ruefully. "And not hand-stropped ones at that." He paused, and went on, more to himself than to Bagehot. "But they do have a very healthy respect for facts, and such evidence as Sister Sollis will supply them with. Any nagging doubts they might have, they'll be forced by the facts themselves to suppress."

"Now, I think," Bagehot said. Montagu nodded. Bagehot turned to the rest of the Minister-Delegates spaced about the machicolated battlements of the keep.

"Gentlemen, with your permission?"

There was a general murmur of assent. Bagehot raised his right arm slowly, and waved a slow and stately farewell to the departing Commissioner and her party. His hand had no sooner been lowered than the first licks of flame could be seen to rise about the great, white, central tent of the grid.

The party stopped and turned.

The Assembly tent lasted no more than a few seconds: the sheet of flame became a crumbling sheet of fine ash about a black, flame-burgeoning frame; then it was the turn of the gayer, double-shelled tents.

It was a still day in not the brightest of lands: the flickering of the flames as the grid of tents was consumed, from the centre outwards, lit up the walls of the long, sea-backed castle. One by one, the green, the violet, the orange and the purple of the rainbow of tents burnt black, and the torch parties moved outwards, invisible in the smoke.

It was soon over, leaving the latterday Field of the Cloth of Gold nothing but a surrealist collection of blackened, twisted frames, ashes and drifting smoke. The Commissioner's party turned again, and restarted its long, slow journey north.

Two

In the Great Hall, the paintings that had formerly decorated the walls had been taken down, and in their place, like thirty small arrases, were the devices peculiar to the Provinces from which the Minister-Delegates had come. It was three days since the burning and this was their first serious meeting.

They were seated about the room near several small tables, but no one was making any pretence of interest in blotters, pens or pads, or even fiddling with tumblers and water jugs: what had to be decided would be done verbally, and if the hearing of all those assembled wasn't sufficient guarantee of future good faith, a bit of paper would be infinitely less so.

As Minister-Delegate of the Host Province, and thereby Acting Executive Officer for the Assembly, Bagehot spoke first.

"Gentlemen, I have good news: Commissioner Sollis arrived on the Firth at the scheduled hour, and has departed. Mood-searcher Peters, who accompanied her, and who, incidentally, returned cross-country in an Osterby to bring us the news with all possible speed, has offered the preliminary opinion that everything has gone exactly to plan.

"I think, gentlemen," he went on, after accepting their dignified congratulations, "that this is as good a time as any to get down to that other matter on the agenda, the establishment of a Unified Authority."

There were no dissentients.

"Shall we get the minor points settled first. A device, a flag. A canvass has been conducted, and a plain white flag seems to be the favourite; it's hardly aggressive, and the Bourbons would seem to have no further use for it."

There was laughter, and the resolution was carried with it.

"The question of the powers of the Authority, while hardly minor, is not particularly difficult: basically, those now wielded by the Minister-Deputy of the Host Province for the Assembly, with modifications as yet to be agreed upon. But we have a will to agree, so I suggest that we pass over that point for the moment, and come to awarding those as yet undefined powers for the first time. I propose, again on the basis of a canvass, the title of Acting Executive Officer, being innocuous, be retained. Now, we come to the vexed question as to who is to have it——"

Dignity did not prevent them from interrupting at that point,

ready to offer it to him by acclamation. He had expected, intended
that, but he preferred not to be too blatant in his ambition and
requested that the item be put to the end of the agenda. The
result would be the same, and then there would be no taint of
eagerness about his acceptance. Stolidly, he presided over the
routine business.

Had he been dozing? If so, none of them seemed to have noticed
it. He tried to listen to the discussion, but couldn't maintain any
interest in it: in the old days, a meeting would always have held
him, with its clash of temperament and ideas, but there was none
of that here: it was more like the technique of medieval allegory,
with characters that were merely moods personified: for they
seemed no more than that, the mood-shells of a single character,
hived off for the supposed convenience of the narrator—but he
was too bored by it all to narrate, for what did it matter what was
said? It was all decided by their being here, by what they had
just taken part in. All the rest was hot air.

Arrogance, he was getting rather near arrogance, and that was
foolish: it was an emotion that could not be truly concealed. And
yet, hadn't it been his idea to hide the meaning of citylessness by
showing it to her as an irrational development, and counting on
her being too deeply bound up in her city culture to be able to
conceive of any other kind of advanced culture?

Peters, the moodsearcher the Guild of the New Sciences had
assigned him as his aide, had helped, of course, but only with
the details, the fake hanging, finding the dialect enthusiasts and
so forth: the essential idea had been his own, and it had been
necessary. For all the brave words at the Assembly, the outplanet
bases did have the power to establish themselves on Earth, if they
were prepared to be ruthless enough. And if they saw its culture
taking a completely alien tack, who knew what they might do?
A slide into barbarism was another matter, requiring pity but no
action; they were safe now. . . .

If this was a slide into barbarism, it was the most planned one
ever, but there was always the possibility that in the end it would
amount to precisely that: the first few tentative steps in the

New Sciences might yet turn out to be the mere codification of oddities and superstition; the growing apoliticalness of the masses might yet bear evil fruit. . . .

They were still talking and he tried to listen, but it was too dull and staid. He tried, but his mind refused to concentrate on it, leaving him in a queer mental limbo to wander back and forth through a maze of memories and beliefs.

He could remember how cranky the idea had seemed at first, that cities were evil in the sense that they were divisive, and that certain cohesive results could be predicted if cities were excised from human culture.

The proposition that cities were the major source of war seemed trite until one examined it carefully and saw that war was invented with the cities. Essentially it had been no more than large-scale theft and as such had demanded large-scale wealth to inspire and maintain it. In the ancient world cities had been centres not of production but of consumption, treasure-loaded parasites of the countryside. Large-scale slavery had been invented at the same time to create those treasures, those surpluses of food and non-comestible wealth, and had itself been an insidious but very real form of war.

After the fall of the ancient world, cities had for the most part been abandoned, their political and military power being insufficient to maintain their parasitism. They had returned again in medieval and renascence times, parasites still but more and more centres of production now until just before the Break they had achieved a kind of symbiosis with the land, some becoming by means of hydroponics major producers of comestible surpluses. But the mark of their origin lay upon them, and upon their aggregates, the nation states; they destroyed themselves.

To return to them *now* would necessitate a return to the form of social organization they had had at their inception. Other plans could be made; they would fail; it would be so. But this time, apart from the waste of several thousand years of social evolution, the abundant mineral wealth that had lain ready to launch the cities to massive material production would be lacking. The unrequited terror and drudgery would go on and on.

And so would their psychological faults, too: the faults created by their material circumstances, the using of men as machines, then as machine tenders, depersonalizing them, losing them in a maze of man's making until they became little better than machines themselves, but these faults were contingent, engendered of size rather than of essence: the essential fault was the instinctive xenophobia the cities and their aggregates had perpetuated and institutionalized. The world had been made too small for fear of the stranger still to exist. That was the essential burden of city-lessness: unity, and paradoxically, the test of that unity was its willingness to create diversity, in these very special circumstances.

It was hardly a new dream, reshaping human nature, but this time they would succeed; the revolution that was underway was changing the factors that controlled that nature, not relying on exhortation: it was an old aim, and they were not pursuing it with any Rousseauesque misconceptions concerning the nobility of the savage. This was the most dangerous experiment ever conducted, and there would be no going back from it, so there could be no major mistakes.

He tried once more to rejoin the discussion, and, at first, it seemed that he would be able to, but the thought and then the desire were overborne; the press of his thoughts was too insistent. He was thinking too quickly, almost too clearly, as in one of those moments when, waking in the depths of the night, one has the illusory feeling of having fully grasped a splendid new idea, but this was still full day, and there was coming no cold light of dawn to dispel the illusion.

This was the necessary watershed; he had just helped set the seal on the splitting off of the future physical and mental accomplishments of mankind, to the betterment of both, and perhaps that organized dis-unity, which had been the mainspring of Western progress would now be employed by the race as a whole . . . in its disunity . . . such things were never clear cut or simple, though. . . .

And then the chair was being addressed directly. Reluctantly he forced his attention from the maze of the past to the spoken words. It was a question concerning the wine trade. The wine trade! They should not be talking of such things at a time like this; it was ludicrous. He got to his feet. The talking stopped. He was acutely aware of their eyes upon him. He said:

"The wine trade is unimportant." He paused, noting an odd highness of tone in his voice. "We've just set the world to rights and you prattle about the wine trade!"

He didn't sit down, just stood there, and they all kept looking at him.

He wilted under their combined gaze. He felt himself sag, but he didn't fall; just hung there like a rag doll held in the air at one of those demonstrations where distancemovers showed their skill and the public looked in vain for wires. Was he being held? The question crossed his mind, but the answer was of no interest to him. And soon there were hands helping him down to his seat, and faces staring solicitously into his own: they were trying to talk to him, but it was almost as if he were deaf: he heard sounds that conformed with the moving shapes of their lips, and they were loud enough, but he could make no sense of the words.

And then there came Peters, his moodsearcher aide, pushing the Minister-Delegates aside. Bagehot looked at his broad, ugly face with its basalt eyes, and it was, for an instant, just another of the concerned faces. Then, they were all gone, leaving him in a soft darkness, and it was as if he were being stretched out, spread out and pulled to breaking point.

And beyond. . . .

There was a time of dreaming, of golden webs spun fine, and then came a time of half-awareness, when voices were like the droning of bees in the middle distance, and then came consciousness: the droning split itself up into sentences and words he could understand. But he didn't open his eyes: let him hear what they were saying of him. (There was something like a chuckle. Peters? Or imagination?)

There was no contempt: they were praising him. And then, as if it were a memory—though he was surely speaking now—he knew what Peters told them.

"It's nothing, gentlemen, a mere momentary aberration, and

one I've been expecting: it would have happened to anybody having to do what he's done—if they had any imagination at all. Guilt, a vast amount of it. He started thinking about it, and it was too much for him." He paused. "It's often better not to think too much: anything is tolerable, if you don't think about it. But he's perfectly all right now."

Bagehot opened his eyes.

"Aren't you?"

"What?" The word was peculiarly pronounced: he had expected difficulty in speaking which he hadn't found, and the word began in an explosion of air, and tailed off.

"Perfectly all right." Was Peters smiling? It was hard to tell. Then he realized: the face wasn't, but Peters was.

"Oh, that. Yes, of course." He paused. "Gentlemen, I've an apology I owe you...."

"Nothing of the sort . . . you must forget all about this incident.... We certainly will...."

They were kind and understanding, and not especially pitying. But they wouldn't forget. That was the last thing they would do.

Three

"Come in," Bagehot answered the knock, and was not surprised when Peters entered.

"Sit down. I was half expecting you."

"I know."

"Perhaps you do at that." He paused. "I believe I've something to thank you for—my 'attack', for instance."

"How am I to blame if you suffer from a guilt neurosis?" Peters asked, his face hinting at a smile.

"But do I? Even after the Break when I did and saw such things . . . even then, I suffered from nothing like that, and I don't think I've got weaker with age."

"You haven't; you can put your mind at rest; I am culpable."

"It was done solely to discredit me?"

"Yes. They would have confirmed your Acting Executive Officership. We couldn't allow that."

"So the Guild want a weakling they can control."

"No, we want a weakling we needn't bother to control."

Bagehot looked at the young moodsearcher sharply: "Devalue that office and you risk the break-up of the frail union we've created!"

"Not at all; you're still thinking politically: co-operation between Guild members in the various Provinces will be the binding force for the Authority, not the mumblings of a few political cast-offs."

"But——"

Peters interrupted him: "I'm sorry it was necessary to disappoint you. I know you've given your life to the concept of citylessness, but you and all your generation aren't the ones to administer the fruition of that concept. You reject cities intellectually; we've lived our lives without them."

"And just what difference does that make?" Bagehot asked ironically.

"Shall we say that we tend to be more flexible, to see things in relation to each other, and that in relative terms, we do think citylessness is a good thing for us, at this time, but that we must quarrel with your tendency to see things in absolute terms. For instance, you contend that the Guild is a product of citylessness, and in its present form, it is; but the fundamental laws of Nature aren't overmuch affected by the social habits of mankind. Our current conditions do make research easier for us, but our researches could be conducted in cities without too much difficulty. When we judge it the right time for the reunification of the race, and perhaps for cities again, our atechnological, overmentalized culture will complement very well with the psychologically underdeveloped civilization of the outplanet bases. We'll both have something to contribute to, and learn from, the other."

"If your analysis is correct," Bagehot amended soberly. "But to return to matters of current importance: you have the effrontery to have come to ask me to work with the Guild, if I anticipate you correctly."

"Yes."

Bagehot laughed softly, "I admire your confidence."

"Winners are confident; you know that."

"We could still crush the Guild, you know, but of course you do: that's why you're only telling me this now, when I'm half-discredited with the rest of the Assembly."

"Only for executive positions, as I said before, which will be unnecessary for you, as an ally of the Guild. I'll tell you one thing more, you'll accept!"

"You're quite right, because I do have a passion for winners, but I accept with misgivings. The Guild will collect too much power, and having nothing else to do with it, will abuse it, but if that's the price of unity, it had better be paid, for we need it now."

"We're not particularly anxious to rule, sir, but someone has to and the potential second generation at the Assembly could inspire confidence in no one: there's a power vacuum, and if we fill it, it's because somebody has to take the responsibility in the next few years. We won't abuse the power we collect for ourselves, either, because before we can become moodsearchers, mindfeelers or distancemovers, we have to become moodfeelers, so we've every reason to employ that power wisely: the better the society we create, the greater our mental comfort—a practical, not a moral guarantee of good faith."

"You don't have to convince me, I've already agreed, as a matter of practical politics," Bagehot said, before adding cynically, "though I wouldn't be surprised if you eventually decided that duty came before comfort."

INTERLUDE

One

April, 2194

It was early Spring, the Great Season of this Northern land, still half-white and mottled with green, as the party flew above it: four strong young adepts of the Guild Guard, flying the formation of the diamond, Peters cradled in its centre. Their wings flapped vigorously, his languidly, for this was the third day of coast-hopping, lake-hopping and hill-hopping : they had not dared their fragile wings over the treacherous North Sea, but had come from the Guild Main Hall on Mont St. Michel over Normandy, Flanders, Belgium, then over Holstein across the Sound, up the Kalmarsund, then inland over the lakes and hills to Norrland and the Community of destination.

Peters had flown little before : he had been middle-aged before the technique had been perfected, and of sufficient rank to make people come to him but this time he had had to travel, and this, he had been informed, was the most comfortable way—which said nothing for the other methods. He breathed a sigh of relief and stopped beating the foolish wings strapped to his arms when he finally saw it. It was just another Community, like other Communities, the only difference being that while the hall was stone, the out-buildings were wooden; but that was to be expected in this forest land.

Without using his wings, which were little more than aids to concentration, he broke free of the supporting diamond and slid down out of the sky to the hall; his party followed at a careful distance, ready to uphold him if his power broke, but it didn't : he in a cityless, townless, almost idenityless Europe, such trivia had been great, and it hadn't really begun to diminish appreciably yet.

Finally, he was standing with the crisp snow underfoot, and men were coming from the hall to greet him, hands outstretched. This was one of the lands where politeness demanded a hand-shake at every meeting. It was strange, though, he thought, how in a cityless, townless, almost identityless Europe, such trivia had survived, survived even the horror of the holocaust—but he was not so old he could remember that !

"Welcome, sir," said the large, bearded man, currently envelop-ing Peters' hand in one twice its size. "It's good to have you here."

"Thank you," said Peters. "If we may go inside. . . ." Without even the warming action of flapping his wings, he felt the cold at its bitterest.

"I'm sorry," the bearded man said without obvious sincerity, his breath misting: "this way."

The hall was large, its furniture superbly made, finely carved: there was a huge log fire in the centre, with a chimney built directly above it, something Peters hadn't seen before, but it was good to stand nearby and feel the blood flow in his veins again.

"Too old for it," he said to the bearded man.

"We're greatly honoured to have you here, sir."

Peters turned to look at him, without stopping rubbing his still gloved hands together.

"You know I haven't gone to all this trouble just to honour you or your Community, Lundström?"

"I know that, sir, but it's an honour to have you under our roof once again."

Peters ignored the compliment and regarded Lundström intensely:

"Your report of the White Jewel intrigued me."

"I can't think why, sir. Just a variant raving."

"Perhaps," Peters said, then: "How is Ericsson?"

"As well as can be expected."

" 'As well as can be expected,' " Peters echoed the words tonelessly. "Well, shall we go and see just what that means, Lundström?"

Two

Willy greeted them with a vacuous grin. The hut was littered and dirty, pervaded by an animal smell, but Willy's person, despite a vaguely human haphazardness, showed Lundström's diligence to better effect. Willy mumbled something. Peters didn't speak; he sat on the nearest wooden chair and slowly, carefully drifted into Willy's mind. Lundström stood by, entering also, but keeping that entry peripheral.

Peters paid little attention to the ordinary world in which Willy lived; he had long since got over the shock of finding the subnormal mentality embarrassingly like the normal, merely less wrought-up by consciousness. The loneliness of the man would have created guilt in a mind less case hardened than Peters'; he put it aside as a problem to be resolved at a later date and began drawing out mood, searching for the key to the sequence he required. Finally, he found it, and the first of the black jewels, one he had experienced several times before, burst upon him.

There was no pain, just a dull numbness, a stiffness, and greater than both, darkness, the roots of which stretched far back and would stretch further forward: when vision came, it was on a different level, of the mind, and he saw a black jewel, set black on black, with only its facets catching the light, as if it were being moved, though otherwise it seemed perfectly still. Then he realized it was approaching him, slowly at first, then at a dizzying rate, but it wasn't simply moving, it was growing: one of the black, flickering facets slipped over him, and he lost himself in the inner darkness. . . .

Peters withdrew a little way, as Willy's mind continued in a sequence of its own fantasies, modelled on the black jewel input. The sequence was a little different from the last time, but not very much so; the black jewel input identical. Peters hoped Lundström wouldn't notice that; he never had before.

The fantasy sequence was terminating; there were signs, none too subtle, indicating that. Peters chose his moment carefully and plunged again for the next black jewel.

He left the jewel but there was no break in the darkness: there was someone screaming, as if at the end of a long corridor and, acting out of reflex, he tried to reach out, to help, but it was quite useless and at that moment the screaming ended abruptly. He found himself staring at the black jewel once more, only now it had replicated itself and hung before him like a curtain of crystal night. . . .

Knowing what was to follow, Peters hastily cut almost all his moodsearcher links with Willy as a surreally lubricious flood of images followed the second jewel. Lundström was not so quick, since his participation had been peripheral, and Peters saw the Community Master whiten and sicken under the barrage before he broke free. Peters smiled; he might have the white jewel sequence completely to himself. It was odd to wish that, but he did and the prospect of its realization pleased him enormously. It even made him impatient and he interrupted the torrent of pallid obscenities to hasten the advent of the last black jewel. Immediately, he was angry with himself—Willy after all had a right to his thoughts—but the last of the black jewels burst upon both of them, drowning his mild remorse in its vast power.

There was someone screaming again in the omnipresent blackness, a crescendo of screaming that ended to leave him with a feeling of awful emptiness; he was floating then and the jewels expanded to enclose him as the first jewel had but these were green and red and gold and a thousand more colours that no rainbow had ever known. . . .

Suddenly, just as Peters expected the fruits of his long journey, the white jewel, Willy's mind cut off, turned to its own private preoccupations, a washed-out world of brown and dreary green mood qualities. Angered, Peters struck at it, and it quivered, mood whimpered under his power, but held out. Ashamed, Peters relaxed his communion, let it fade to nothing, and turned to Lundström.

Lundström looked squarely back at him. "He's tired."

Peters said nothing.

"He has some rights," Lundström pleaded.

Peters stared him down, letting the inferior moodsearcher know something of the awe-making power he had at his behest. The periphery of Lundström's mind quivered, a mental standing wave of pain.

"Don't !"

Peters' anger and Lundström's anguish died as, startled, they both turned to look at Willy, his doughy face moulded into something akin to pity.

"Don't hurt Lundy !" Willy said slowly and purposefully, "Willy give jewel."

And immediately it burst upon both of them.

It hung in the blackness, a jewel of infinite complexity, radiant in every imaginable colour but seemingly changing by the instant so that before a colour fully impinged on the mind, another had taken its place and the final effect was a blaze of subtly changing white light.

That was only the pseudo-visual effect, and the least important of all. There was also gentle triumph, accomplishment, a redolence of well-being—it was not an end in itself; it was a stage, but a vastly important one. And somehow, this mishmash of emotion arranged itself in pure form, a symphony of emotion played not on one experiencing mind but on a multitude of minds, a progression of them through time, all now united in this achievement.

The jewel grew in the blackness, out of the blackness, blazed forth beyond the capacity of Willy to re-transmit it. . . .

"Pretty jewel," Willy said to the two men who stared blankly in his direction, "Pretty jewel?"

Three

"I'm sorry," Peters said as they walked back from the hut. "I——"

"No matter," Lundström told him. "I understand. It was beautiful. Whoever would think that Willy could. . . ." He stopped, lost for words.

Peters smiled. He didn't understand at all. But that was all to the good; it wasn't safe knowledge for a workaday Guildsman to know that Willy had not dreamed, that that empty mind had only proved a very receptive receiver for the messages generated on a great venture that Peters had indirectly helped launch by a subtle deception years ago. And now he felt at peace with himself, fulfilled; there was much still to be done; unity was now a viable if distant prospect—unity in accepted diversity—but the impulse would have to come from outside. Not in his time, he found himself wishing; he was too old for such changes. He looked around at the white, winter landscape and the dismal wooden hutments. An odd place for such memorable news, but appropriate also.

"Send Willy to Mont St. Michel on the first available transport. Accompany him; shield his mind."

"Sir!"

"Do as I say," Peters said, putting just enough of the tang of command into his voice to cut discussion short. It was necessary there be no loose ends; Willy could be mood shaped into something resembling a normal man. It was a technique used mostly on criminals, but Willy would profit by it, and his black jewels and his white would be lost to him for ever.

Peters left in the early morning, cradled at the centre of the diamond of adepts. As he struggled to use his awkward wings, a suspicion of just what means had been used to attain that bright jewel occurred to him. He smiled as the bitter wind buffeted him, but it was none of his business, nor the Guild's—yet.

He flew on, thinking of another, longer journey.

SECOND GAME

One

June, 2247

Lydia Johnsdaughter landed the shuttle heavily, sighed involuntarily with relief, and waited. It wasn't long before she could see it through the sole porthole—beginning as a tiny, black birdshape in the leaden sky, burgeoning finally into a winged man who hovered with much flapping of strut and canvas wings, watching.

She crawled through the lock and stood for the first time on the softness of the green grass of Earth. She looked up and waved at the flying man, smiling a smile that she was sure could be seen even from fifty feet up. It was then that the winged man began his stoop.

He swerved at the final moment, jabbing a light blow to the head with his foot as he cast about her a loop of leather attached to his harness; then, securing her with his feet, he began flapping his wings at humming-bird rate and they rose, painfully, into the air.

As they began to pick up speed and beneath her the dull panorama of field and hedgerow yielded only to more of the same, as if those features were omnipresent and perhaps eternal, Lydia felt a numbness steal over her, a numbness quite unlike that associated with the shock of the blow, and more akin to sleep. . . .

"You'll come to no harm under this roof," said a distant voice.

Her eyelids felt gummed down, but she succeeded in opening them on the third attempt, and the drowsiness began to dissipate as she stared at the two men who sat by her cot. One was tall and dark—the winged man—and the other was much shorter, a florid-faced young man with eyes that alone seemed to smile at her.

"My name is Thomas," said the florid-faced man. "I was sent for from the Community of Deira to greet you."

Lydia snapped out her own name, lifted herself up with her arms and swung her legs out over the side of the cot. "You are some kind of official?"

"I am the Acting Executive Officer." A short gesture indicated his companion: "This is Jonathan; he brought you here, to the Community of Bye."

Lydia looked at the taller man: "You must tell me sometime how you work those aerodynamically impossible things."

"We give aerodynamics a bit of help," Jonathan answered her in a surprisingly high voice. He hesitated a moment before adding: "I'm sorry about the blow, but it was necessary—if you'd struggled and fallen...."

"I'm quite glad I didn't struggle and fall, Jonathan, but the whole business was hardly necessary: I had a ship to bring me here."

"Something so violently against tradition could hardly be allowed," Thomas interposed quickly.

"I'm not disposed to argue. I came here to contact your government. I would be grateful if you would arrange that."

"Your request will be considered," Thomas replied, his eyes still smiling, and added: "In the meantime, you have the freedom of this little Community. You may be served in the Refectory whenever you wish. For any aid you may require, simply ask anyone you meet. We are all at your service."

Then Thomas's face went suddenly slack. It only lasted for a moment but when the muscle tone returned, it was another, subtly different face. Thereupon, both men got to their feet and left.

Lydia watched them go in silence, a little amazed and not a

F

little disgusted by what she had just seen. She had known that it happened, but seeing it was another matter. She shook her head: this was of the Earth, and strange.

Lydia flew between them, beating her wings in time with theirs; it seemed almost as if the wings were truly holding and moving them through the air, above the brown, stubbly land with its dark hedgerows and copses, and here and there, another community like the one they had left, of a single pattern with it—but with men and women in its streets and fields.

Once, an hour out, she was left without support, and for all her frantic beating of wings so that they almost fell in shards from her arms, she plummeted down, with the bird-shapes of Jonathan and the man who had called himself Thomas wheeling high above her.

It was a test, and she could only let herself pass it; finally, they gently slowed her fall until she hung like a marionette, her wings still, a mere hundred feet above the fields. They let her hang for a while, and she guessed they were waiting for her to try to rise by flapping her foolish wings, but she was in no mood to oblige, and they had to raise her, and when she was near enough, provide her with apologies, which she accepted graciously, but thereafter she kept her wings still, leaving them to provide the full horizontal moment, and soon their weariness enveloped the three like a cloud.

They crossed water for half an hour, land for an hour and then below them was the Community of Deira, the chief Community of the World. To Lydia's untutored eyes, it looked like nothing so much as a small city. She had seen satellite photographs of it, but from six hundred feet it was startlingly different. The tower and wooden landing platform on the Great Hall, even the golden yellow streamer that flew above them, seemed strictly functional. The photograph had given the geometric imprecision of the Community's layout an air of charm; in reality it was undesigned, decrepit and worst of all, tatty. If proof were needed of the rightness of her enterprise, this sight alone would be sufficient.

They were greeted in the ante-room to the Great Hall by a

grey-bearded giant of a man in a homespun tunic; he had smiling eyes.

"We have met before, Executive Officer Thomas," she said, smiling faintly.

"Acting Executive Officer," Thomas corrected automatically, scratching his beard and regarding her quizzically. "So you realized. I thought you might. The outbases are not so ignorant of our ways as some of our . . . older members would like to believe. But it doesn't matter. We have nothing to hide; certainly not the technique of sleeping."

Lydia frowned at the word—sleeping. The technique was named after the passive participant, the adept who 'slept' while another entered his mind and used his body. That was significant.

"In fact," Thomas continued, "it would have had to be explained to you. Most of the Assembly cannot physically be present, so they will express themselves via junior Guildsmen at the Council table. Unexplained, the situation would have appeared odd."

And then, without further ado, he led her into the Great Hall itself, leaving Jonathan and his florid-faced companion behind, and as she entered, she drew her breath sharply, for the Great Hall belied its outward appearance. In the dim light that slid in through the leaded windows carven panelling gleamed darkly; the floor betrayed a vast, abstract mosaic of wood; the Council table glinted with silver, cut glass and mirror-polished mahogany; the Guildsmen about it were dressed for those whose voices used them, in the yellow, gold and scarlet silk of their ranks, a lavishness of colour that by its very contrast pointed out the greater rank of Thomas, the A.E.O., whose office needed no adornment.

Thomas motioned her to a heavy mahogany chair exactly opposite the great chair of the A.E.O.—his own.

"Seat yourself, Commissioner."

"That is not my precise title."

"No matter, Lydia," Thomas said, still smiling with his eyes.

The Assembly began strangely : she was not invited to speak; instead, she had to sit there and listen while they debated whether or not she could be allowed to address them. She did not allow

herself to be annoyed by this: the spectacle of the old and vener
able yielding submissively to the apparent juniority of a young
sleeper was fascinating, bizarre. Finally, under Thomas's quiet
tutelage, the Assembly yielded to the inevitable, and she was
invited to speak.

"Gentlemen," she began, "I get the impression that some of
you believe I am come here simply to lure you back to cities and
machine technology. If I am right in that, then you're just as
surely wrong in that! I don't especially want to lure any of you
anywhere. The vast technological power of the outbases and
outsystems would be only very little augmented by such a change,
and we would have to bear the cost of setting you up with a fully
automated economy in the first place!

"Neither is it our intention or our wish to lure you into tech
nology through trade—what have you to trade? Food? You
might sell luxury items, but you don't seem to have any, and for
the rest, you simply couldn't compete, the economic cost of inter
stellar and interplanetary freightage as it is; and besides which
everybody knows that synthetic protein's better for you. Minerals?
Your world is worked out. People? You have no skills we
need. . . ."

"Then we are to take it," a sleeper began sarcastically, "that
you are here out of pure altruism?"

"Not quite. The fact is, a tree grows better with a root. You are
of Earth, and our roots are from Earth."

"So what do you offer?" Thomas asked, interestedly.

"Contact."

"Cultural contacts," Thomas augmented, as if thinking out
loud.

"Any contact has of necessity a cultural aspect," Lydia said
somewhat tartly. "What objection is there to that? Only the weak
need be isolated."

"We are not weak," asserted a sleeper.

"Then what have you to be afraid of?"

The question seemed almost to die in the ensuing silence, until
after an enduring moment, Thomas, the A.E.O., answered her:
"We are not weak, but we have weaknesses."

A few sleepers began to protest; the A.E.O. stilled them with an imperious gesture, his smiling eyes never leaving her. "You know a great deal about us. Your satellites spy on us, and you probably have spies amongst us. Don't bother to deny it; it's inevitable, and unimportant.

"However, we know little of you. We believe you have reached the stars—we have the speculations in the Testament of A.E.O. Peters, and there are rumours, which you doubtless spread. You have done as much here a few moments ago." He paused. "We are not envious: we are glad for you in that. But here we are tied to the soil. It's the best, but not an easy life, and your civilization could have an unhealthy glamour for the young and the unschooled.

"You know our beliefs. Perhaps you can have cities and not be destroyed by them; perhaps not. But we cannot. The Guild of the New Sciences, acting through this Assembly, has a duty to shield and protect our people, and so it is not from weakness that we would abstain for cultural contacts, but from something very different—a duty of prudent care !"

The Guildsmen of the Assembly tapped the table in muted applause.

"Well answered, but not truly answered," Lydia retorted. "You refuse to permit contact not to shield or protect—citylessness is well entrenched, a prejudice not likely to be destroyed by any glamour of far places. The real reason is weakness, not necessarily of ideas but of yourselves, the adepts, the Guildsmen of the New Sciences !"

Thomas smiled with his full face: "The majority of the population are adepts——"

"No. In a community of three or four hundred, at Bye, I am allowed to meet only two. I was similarly sheltered on my arrival here, in this your chief Community: the streets were empty and I must be brought straight here. The very ineptness of your deceit—I believe I may honestly pay you the compliment of supposing you unused to it—is sufficient confirmation.

"We know the figure: it's less than one per cent. It was simple enough to work out. The proportion of adepts, of the psionically gifted in the population has been on the decline since shortly after the Break, that gratuitous near-destruction of the Earth that left the outplanet bases to seed the stars alone." She tacked. "You believe, I think, that the genetic alteration making for psi capacities was brought on by radiation, in fact a mutation?"

"Logic proves that," the A.E.O. answered her.

"And anything else you care to mention. If you were really serious about your New Science, you would have realized long ago that the mutation theory was untenable. For one thing, the first psis came too soon after the War. What really happened was that in the aftermath of War, evolution in its crudest and quickest form took over: the times were inconceivably hard, and every man's hand was turned against his neighbour, supposing he still had one, so the fittest survived, and the fittest in this case were those who had an edge over the rest—and of all the edges, psi talent was the most effective in procuring physical and genetic survival.

"It grew up in the interstices of the dogmatism of citylessness, which you still venerate—that holds that when men go together in cities for mutual protection, they decrease their antagonism towards their immediate neighbour only at the price of increasing it to all others; thus, war. And hence the idea that having no cities, and taking a little daily mental exercise in brotherly love, we can avoid all that. Rather crude sociology, if you'll forgive me, and now you're stuck with it, but the number of psi talents who hold the crazy non-structure of citylessness together is dwindling: you always were in a minority, for after the War, when conditions got better—were made better—the majority of those without too much of an edge began to catch up again. Without eugenics, there was no way of preventing that, so now there are fewer and fewer of you holding things together, and so the Communities grow larger and larger, so the Guildsmen there can control them: the trend is obvious.

"You fly with wings, you Guildsmen, but the wings are useless: levitation is a Guildsman's art that needs no wings. But you need wings to hide from the reality of the phenomenon, to make it all seem natural.

"You are becoming skilled at hiding from reality, otherwise you would have long realized that the trend I spoke of has only one natural end: the Communities will grow larger until no semantic juggling will be enough to hide the truth from your people or yourselves.

"Your Communities, already cities in embryo, will have become true cities. Without our help, citylessness will die!"

She could say no more: they screamed at her, old and false young alike, even Thomas; and after a while, she was led away, under guard.

Two

The rejection of contact was total, as she had expected it would be; they were very frightened, and for all their peculiar powers, they had reacted as frightened men do. They had begun by restricting her freedom of movement; then kept her in a cell, in which she was occasionally visited by Thomas; then, one morning she was taken out by a guard captain and told she was to be moved back to the "Community of origin".

The journey, this time, was by cart, and took six days, six weary days, with eight guards, dull efficient men, who watched her every move. In the Communities they passed through, and usually spent the nights in, the people were no longer hidden away, but peered at her, in her outlandish costume, as if she were some circus animal: the tale of her passing, with magnifications, would be told for generations, but to these people who leaned from doorways and windows, she showed the same indifference she displayed to her guards: such as these had no political moment, as yet.

After six days on roads that were often worse than no roads at all, she was glad enough to be back at the first Community, where she was kept in the same room that she had used before, but now with a guard outside the door.

The morning after her arrival, Thomas came once again in his florid-faced disguise, and she was led out, through the fields, with two guards trailing them at a respectful distance. After a good hour, they could see the shuttle.

"I'm to be allowed to go?" she asked, a little surprised.

"No. I'm sorry."

As they got nearer, she could see a group of men standing by a pile of stones near the ship. At a signal from Thomas they began laying them about the skiff—which they approached with obvious fear.

"I'm instructed to show you this. You are not to be allowed to leave, and you must accustom yourself to that. We are not destroying your ship, for to do that we would have to risk pollution by touching it, but we can encairn it with stones, and above the stones, we will lay earth, and make a hill of such substance above it that it will be denied to you for ever. So you *must* accustom yourself to that; but as we are aware of the personal injustice done to you by this greater act of justice, we shall endeavour to make your life here as comfortable as possible. . . ."

Lydia stopped listening. Everything was going just as expected: the working conclusions were amply justified. She had been inclined to doubt that they would go so far as this final imbecility of keeping her by force, but she had been wrong, and she was glad of it: the effect would be surer if no modifications proved to be necessary.

"I wish you'd brought wings," she said finally; "it's a long walk back."

And exactly a week after that, she disappeared.

Three

It was pleasant to be back in Moonbase, to sit in decent comfort in this viewing hall dominated by the image of the green Earth. On her first visit she had noticed all Moonbase's faults—its concentration on Earth which had made it seem almost a mirror image of Earth, and though the mirror was distorted and the image reversed, she had recoiled from living amongst images. But with Earth still fixed in her sight and mind, she saw too the virtues of Moonbase, and these were the common virtues of all the outbases: it was a city and a true community: she could sense it about her, both protecting and demanding. And perhaps she was mellowed by the thought of a job well done—for the isolation of Earth was effectively ended.

It would still take time, of course, but the seed was deeply sown. The mystery of her disappearance would fertilize it : they would uncairn the shuttle, see the empty shell of it, see the empty spaces for instrumentation and drive, and see with that how their own Guildsmen's powers were duplicable, and for greater things than flapping on futile wings across an empty sky.

The psi powers, which in their heart of hearts they attributed to citylessness, would one day be shown for what they were : mental manipulations of the sub-quarkian, not fully causal wavicles of ultimate stuff. And this was something better accomplished by an interface between man and machine. Yes, they would learn that, but it was not yet important : the truth of her words was, for it was true that they were in fact sliding towards cities, and that on the rocks of the prejudice they had so carefully nurtured, their fragile society would shatter into a surf of real barbarism. They were not yet so blindly set in their ways that they could not see that, or that they had no real choice of action. They would choose the stars, and to get them, their philosophy of citylessness would suffer a sea change.

The men of Earth were trying to play a game of Community, but the rules they had adopted were wrong; on the outplanet bases, on the new settled planets of new conquered stars, men knew that only too well. Their rules had been painfully relearnt and reforged in bitterly hostile, almost life-hating environments. They had learnt to co-operate, for they had known there was to be neither help nor encouragement from Earth—only a vast, premeditated lie : their game with Sollis. She Lydia, had beaten them on the return, appropriately for a great-granddaughter of Marjorie Sollis. . . .

How many had died on those first General Transmissions? Marjorie, her great-grandmother, had been amongst them, and again, appropriately, Peters had experienced them at third hand, via the blank, receptive mind of an idiot, and had known them, if only glancingly, for what they were—the ships of the outbases slipping through the wormholes of superspace, searching out fresh worlds orbiting new stars. But they had been such ships as he could scarcely have dreamed of: interlocked man/hypercomputer interfaces, true communities.

She realized now that she need not leave this room of the image of Earth: it was unnecessary: she had been without the community to enlarge it. She need only desire it to reintegrate within it, and that desire she had never lacked. . . .

It was neither a relaxation nor a submission, but a kind of welcoming. The image of Earth did not fade but became less important as her mind warmed itself afresh in the community of Moonbase. She had become a facet of a jewel glittering through a vast spectrum no human eye nor mind could comprehend, a jewel collapsing and rebuilding itself by the instant, the Interface of the City Community of Moonbase, a jewel that could bend space before it and travel to the stars, but also much more: it united in diversity, it created a team, and yet its facets were utterly individual: it was the matrix of the greatest game *Homo Ludens*, Man the Gamester, had yet created, and in this game he need no longer be truly alone.

Cultures before had been determined by their means of transportation, but none more so than that of the outbases: the Interface that had gained the stars had been seductive, so much so that they had transformed entire societies into such Interfaces, telepathic webs in which men and hypercomputers folded themselves into jewel composits of interaction and decision, ruling themselves by the mood of the whole—a concept beyond words but not beyond feeling.

She lingered a moment over the jewel, then let its brightness fade: she did not need to see it for it to be there: it had never abandoned her, even on Earth. By her will, its distant but undiminished power had opened the lock of her prison, lifted her high into the air without need of idle wings, to a rendezvous with a shuttle that moved in the field of its power. Soon it would send her in the General Transmission, and she would be reunited with the even more complex and many-faceted jewel Interface of the New Earth that was Vega III.

POSTLUDE

The games of deceit and deception were over, and the game of the Interface Communities well under way. New games would follow, while things subsisted.

Edward Allen

Crater

"If they are impact craters, we should be able to detect some degree of ellipticity, yet on all the computer results they are circular, or if not, irregularities are due to multiple impact or previous cratering."

Professor Silberg swung his legs idly as he perched on the desk of his computer programmer. They had been working as a team for a couple of years now, and their few grams of lunar sample was a welcome break from the run-of-the-mill problems they usually handled at the tech. industry/liaison group at Portsmouth.

"Well, the programme is spot on, I'm afraid," replied Gammage. "There's hardly any room for error in something as simple as this; either those craters were caused by impact, or by some force that was not moving in relation to the surface of the moon. If they were impact we should find some that occurred at a grazing angle, and even if most of the energy was released by rapid heating, there should still be some directional component. If we assume that it is below the threshold of our analysis, we must assume an impact speed at least two orders higher than the escape velocity for the solar system."

"Then for the time being we must assume that the cause was on the surface of the moon," replied Silberg. "And if that is so, the traces are probably here!" He peered at the moon rock again in its vacuum dome on the side bench of the lab.

"Those small iron globules you gave me are definitely anomalous," mused Gammage. "The density appears to be about twice that of normal iron, yet I can detect no impurity that would give that high a reading. It is almost as though they were compressed greatly at the time of the explosion, and have not expanded again."

"Not possible!" replied Silberg. "Even if they were immediately frozen down to zero after compression, they would still expand.

The electron pressure is far too great to allow them to stay that way."

"Could there be any atomic deformation?" asked Gammage. "I know there shouldn't be, but I'm sure it's iron, and I'm sure it's superdense."

"There was that superdense water reported a couple of years ago," Silberg said thoughtfully. "It might be something of that sort. Can you do a recheck, just to make sure, and I'll have a look at the maths of it. There are configurations that would give us that density, but they're all unstable, so I'll have to see if there's any way of getting stability. If we can, we might as well have a new engineering material!"

Gammage turned back to his samples. Greying, just turned fifty, he had given up hope of making any immortal discovery. He still had a boyish turn of enthusiasm, however, and he peered intently at the globule on the end of the magnet with which he had extracted it from the sample.

Much to his surprise, it was now indented into a perfect hollow on the surface of the magnet. It was also larger, quite definitely. In the space of a few hours it had grown from something the size of a pin-head to something more nearly approaching a matchhead in size. It was not difficult to guess where the extra material had come from either, judging from the end of the magnet.

He reweighed and did another density test, this time finding that the sample weighed half a gram and had a density of twenty-two, slightly better than pure platinum. He put it down on the bench and went off to tell Silberg, who had gone out to lunch somewhere in Commercial Road.

An hour and a half later they were back in the lab, Silberg still half incredulous, but Gammage quite insistent.

"I put it here somewhere," he exclaimed, feeling about the bench. "Nobody could have got in, as I locked the door and only the janitor has a duplicate." The lock was indeed a good one, as the lab had in the past been used for growing synthetic gemstones. "Hello!" he went on, "There's water all over the floor. Maybe the plumbers have been in."

They inspected the trickle of water from under the bench, and Gammage opened the cupboard door to inspect the plumbing.

He straightened up slowly. "I have a feeling . . ." he announced, going over to the fire axe on the wall.

"Hey, what are you up to?" exclaimed Silberg, growing a little alarmed at the expression on Gammage's face.

"Something," said Gammage, in an even tone, "has eaten the water-pipe !"

Silberg bent to look, while Gammage started systematically to destroy the panelling along the side of the lab. Something had certainly had a go at the pipe. It started off like a snail's trail gouged out of the metal, then the metal tapered off in a rough point. The rest of the pipe was missing.

"Got it !" shouted Gammage gleefully, after he had smashed about ten feet of panelling.

He had too. The end of the pipe was sealed by something the size of a large grapefruit. Even as they watched they could see it slowly progressing down the pipe, at about a snail's pace, an occasional drop of water leaking round the edge. Gammage tried to pull it off, then gave it a few tentative taps with the back of the axe head. It was obviously firmly stuck, though, so he resorted to the expedient of turning off the water at the main stopcock and sawing the pipe off a foot from the slowly moving mass.

"Must weigh half a hundredweight !" he gasped as he lifted it onto the bench. They watched it devour the remaining few inches of pipe in silence.

"Do you think it's alive?" asked Silberg doubtfully. He had never met anything like this before.

"Might be a sort of crystal?" suggested Gammage, half-heartedly. "It certainly seems to know what to go for though. I've never heard of a crystal that seeks out a substrate to grow on. They mostly sit in solutions and soak it up."

"Try its density again," suggested Silberg, at a loss for the moment.

This time the density came out at eighteen, although Gammage had a suspicion that it might be altering while he measured it. The surface was certainly changing in colour after its meal.

Also, it was slightly egg-shaped now, although he might have missed that when it was small.

"Shall we feed it some more?" asked Gammage after they had tried all the tests they knew on it.

"If we give it too much it'll get too heavy to move," countered Silberg. "Perhaps we had better contact NASA and see if any more have turned up."

Gammage kept watch while Silberg tried to get some kind of priority on the telephone system. He was back in half an hour.

"Nothing like it," he reported. "They have plenty of glass globules, but no iron ones. They're sending someone over on the first jet."

"I think it has got smaller," said Gammage cautiously. "Shall I run another density and see if it has changed?"

The surface of the object was now raised into fine pimples; somehow it did not seem very friendly sitting there, black, squat and, as they soon discovered, very dense. It was now thirty-four and presumably still shrinking.

The lab steward came in as they were contemplating it sitting like a shorn hedgehog on the bench.

"Results, sir," he said, proffering yards of punch paper.

Silberg rapidly scanned through them. "Just as I thought!" he exclaimed. "There is a stable configuration for iron." He scanned further, then paled. "Get me a line to Trowbridge, the Ministry of Defence," he said quietly. "Tell them it's urgent; we may want something moved in a hurry."

"What's up?" asked Gammage, distinctly uneasy at his partner's change of tone.

"If my calculations are right, this bug will become unstable again if its density goes over fifty-four," Silberg explained. "With all the energy tied up in there keeping that iron compressed to this density, anything could happen. It's about two hundred times as powerful as R.D.X."

"If your calculations are wrong, it might go off before that," added Gammage grimly. "Do you think we should feed it again? That brought the density down last time."

By the time the big magnet, half the tools in the lab and the fire axe had been consumed, the density was down to eighteen again. The weight was now a bit over 120 lb, however, and the colour changes were already running over the surface of the thing. First a dull brownish sheen, shading to shiny dark brown, then black, and ultimately a faint hint of violet on the small protuberances.

"I think it's running a charge," volunteered Gammage. "The bench gets quite hot under it, and I got quite a shock when I cut it off the water pipe."

"Try charging it up again," suggested Silberg. "We can't go on feeding it at this rate; soon it will be too big to move, and sooner or later it's going to detonate. I expect those pimples are blown off and make new ones," he mused. "Some of the fungi are not that dissimilar."

"Can't we get the Navy to drop it somewhere at sea?" asked Gammage. "We can't leave it here. It would take the whole block down if it blew!"

"Have you any idea how much iron there is in terrestrial rocks?" asked Silberg acidly. "If we let this thing go off, it will set a few hundred thousand seeds, which will absorb iron until they can eat no more, and then blow. Given an exponential rate of about a day, as this one seems to be giving us, the whole surface of the world would be churned up inside a couple of months. That isn't counting the really big ones that land on railway lines and ships and the like," he added as an afterthought.

"Well, it seems as though we have a clue to crater formation anyway," consoled Gammage. "I suppose we'll have to get NASA to send it back there."

A few thousand volts seemed to keep the thing quiet for a while. It even began to swell slightly as the current was applied. Quite where it was going they were not sure. It was slightly better than the average conductor, they soon discovered, taking in twenty thousand watts at eighty amps, and putting out about twenty-five and a half thousand at a slightly higher voltage. When they disconnected the return it still absorbed power at the same rate, but did not seem to do anything other than charge the bench to a few hundred volts.

All that night they held it in steady state, slowly increasing the voltage as the thing adapted and tried to shed electrons. It had the disconcerting habit of switching on a magnetic field when anything moved near it. A penknife, some paperclips and half a typewriter were all it caught, however. The other half of the typewriter was blown across the room by the voltage when it hit. The smaller stuff appeared to be vaporized and the vapour sucked back in.

"A few more thousand and the bench will short out," warned Gammage in the small hours before dawn.

"NASA should be sending a special truck," responded Silberg. "M.O.D. are going to get a transporter down from Thorney. I thought I heard a plane a while back, so they may be on their way now."

Within a few minutes they heard sirens echoing in the empty streets, and then there were feet running up the stairs.

The men seemed confident after a brief look at the thing, now giving off malevolent little sparks on the bench top.

"Give it a feed and discharge it," suggested Warth, a respected figure in rocketry. He had apparently flown over at the first intimation that something out of the way was happening. "We had better take the rest of your sample too," he continued. "Luckily the rest of that batch stayed with us and hasn't been opened."

"What are you going to do?" enquired Silberg, feeling some sense of loss now that they were finally getting the thing off their hands.

"Put it straight back on an Apollo and send it back where it came from. We agree with your analysis completely. It's far too dangerous to study down here, although it might be worth sending a team up to study them in their natural habitat. If we can find some method of stopping them seeding, it might be a useful explosive, but that might be a little risky," he added, noticing Gammage's expression.

They fed their monster a few scraps to keep it happy, and finally checked it out at one hundred and thirty-two pounds and a density of twenty-four, which was not too bad. They had about twelve hours before anything would happen, and there were a few hundredweight of bits on the plane in case it needed a feed on the way.

"The critical size ought to be well over a couple of hundred tons," commented Silberg, waving the paperwork he had been engaged on all night. "That is, with lunar gravity. It might respond differently here, however. So far as I can make out the largest lunar craters are still not quite large enough to throw much material free of lunar gravity. Here it would have to be quite a bit bigger before that limit was reached."

"A hole half the size of Europe," agreed Warth. "We had been thinking along those lines ourselves."

Gammage shuddered. The thing they had on their hands was quite a bit better than a self-replicating H-bomb. There was no way of stopping it so far as they knew, and the only way of slowing it down was to make it bigger.

They saw the plane off in the grey light of dawn, and returned to the lab to pack up their notes. They would follow by faster plane to arrive at the Cape about the same time as Warth and his unlikely passenger.

"Pity we couldn't keep it," mused Silberg. "We could have got a very fine electrical supply unit going there. There might even have been a way of taking off power all the time and running it down so that it didn't detonate!"

Gammage was not so sanguine. "Good riddance to bad rubbish," was all he would say, stomping about the lab and getting his print-out together.

They slept most of the way over, arriving not much after midday East Coast time. All was bustle at the site as they drove up with the police escort. Warth greeted them, looking slightly haggard. He had had less sleep than they had. "It ate all the scrap on the way over!" he commented ruefully. "Pulled it all through the bulkhead with a magnetic field. Luckily most of the rest of the plane was aluminium. When we got down it ate most of the first truck we put it on, but it hasn't had anything since."

"What's its weight now?" asked Silberg in alarm.

"About a ton, I should think," replied Warth. "Well within pay-load, so long as it doesn't grab anything else."

They inspected the thing from a safe distance, crackling blue sparks on the concrete pad, well away from anything ferrous. It was now about eighteen inches across and already black.

"We'll give it some more scrap just before we hoist it inboard," commented Warth. "Then we can blast off in a few minutes. The countdown is on now."

"What are you going to hoist it in with?" asked Gammage, visualizing a couple of tons of gantry being gobbled at the last minute.

Warth grinned. "We thought of that one," he said, pointing out a length of steel cable attached to some nylon rope. "We give it the end of that to bite on, then hoist it onto alloy clamps. The nylon will drop off once it reaches the end of the steel hawser. Then we should be able to fire before it starts looking for more."

The day wore on with an uneasy crew watching "Thing", as it was by now universally called, and feeding it on scrap as soon as it started to grow pimples. Finally, at about four and a half tons, mostly eaten in its last feed to keep it quiescent *en voyage*, they blasted off early the next morning.

Lunar landing was only thirty-four hours later, as the rocket had been designed for a substantially greater pay-load, and there was no need for braking provision on lunar approach. The impact was observed just South of Tycho, in a fairly clear area. Eighteen minutes after impact there was another crater on the moon. Not a big one, as lunar craters go, only half a mile or so across.

When the astronomers at Palomar were asked what they would like it called, they did not take long to decide on a name. You can see it on some of the later lunar maps published by a resourceful cornflake manufacturer, on the back of the packets.

"GAMMAGE" it says, in a script that differs slightly from the rest on closer inspection. Actually, they have named the wrong crater, but that can be put right later. Gammage at least is pleased.

Little Big Man

The icewall loomed up fast under James Cassidy as he prepared for his final few minutes of life on Janus Three. Another few hundred miles and he would impact somewhere near the North Pole of this forsaken planet. He cursed himself for not double-checking before takeoff. Now he was caught in a double-bind situation if ever there was one. A little more fuel and he could achieve orbit and connect up with the mother ship, circling some-where on the other side of the planet. Alternatively he could go back down again and wait for another shuttle bringing more fuel. As it was he could neither get up, nor get down at anything less than a few thousand miles per hour.

He slid a cigar out of its fat aluminium casing, a Corona Havana at £10 an inch, and lit up. The recycling system wouldn't cope with the smoke, and half the fire circuits would go on, but that did not matter any more. He blew smoke and watched the jagged terrain getting nearer with a kind of awful fascination.

The thought of sabotage crossed his mind. He was disliked by most of the crew back at Galactic Mining. At six foot five inches, he had on more than one occasion used his weight and reach to settle an argument. He prided himself on getting his own way, not always an advisable attribute when men are living under cramped conditions for a year and a half at a time. He could have sabotage checked out, however. He glanced at his watch and switched on the radio. The ship should be above the horizon any second now.

"Shuttle two, Shuttle two," he intoned, surprised that his voice was so steady.

"Come in, Shuttle two," responded the ship, amongst the crackle and distortion caused by the grazing angle their radios made to the surface of the planet.

"I'm ploughing in, approximate latitude 5°S," he explained. "Not enough fuel to achieve orbit. I can bring her down on retro to about 1,800 knots on snow, so there should be plenty of bits to pick up. I want a full checkout when you bypass on return next year. Cause of failure, etc. Headquarters will want a full report too. They'll probably give you a time allowance for it, so make it good. Over and out." He slipped a syringe of morphia into his leg, more for kicks than anything. He did not anticipate much pain at this impact speed.

"What? What?" came back the radio operator. "Gee, that's terrible! Are you sure? You have over a thousand feet of altitude there, that's about two thousand foot tons you save. Maybe in soft snow you can slide a half-mile or so if you come in low."

Cassidy switched off. He had thought of that as soon as his motor had cut. He was a few hundred miles out for stunts like that. The failure could not have been better calculated, if sabotage it was.

He stubbed the cigar out and concentrated on killing speed as much as possible, so that there would be something to pick up. He set altitude and chose a smooth slope. Firing, he thought he had a chance for a moment. The motor kept going and going as the shuttle slowed over the ground, then, a few hundred feet up, it petered out, and he knew both he and motor were dead. The slope rushed up, blurred, snatched gently as he bounced, then came up in a great wall of blackness and weight.

The taste of sour cigar lingered on, strangely. He relaxed, feeling no pain. There did not seem to be any particular need to think. Utter silence and stillness surrounded him. He wondered vaguely if this was just the last few milliseconds stretched thin against eternity before he expired, or if his brain, somehow more or less intact, was slowly closing down. How long he might have stayed in this condition he did not know; he was brought out of it by cramp in his foot. He ignored it at first. It was just too ridiculous to have cramp in his foot when it was probably twelve miles away, maybe in several directions at once. It persisted, however, and he opened his eyes.

A dim blue light greeted him, and he could just make out the inside of a metal hull. He was imprisoned inside a glass cylinder, which was filled with some liquid. Panic assailed him as it filled his nose and lungs and he struggled to breathe. After a moment he realized that he was not out of breath and relaxed again. He wiggled his toes and gained some relief. By turning his head he could see an instrument panel, distorted through the glass, with a couple of figures bending over it. He wiggled his head violently to attract attention, his arms being pinioned to his sides by the glass walls.

One of them raised a hand to him, and he saw that they had a television screen above the console and were watching him on this as they worked the controls. Suddenly the water receded down the tube, and he was rotated face down. The pressure increased and decreased rhythmically, pumping the liquid out of his lungs. He realized now that it was pale blue and the lighting was normal in the cabin. Sound returned as he cleared his ears.

The glass cylinder withdrew, and he was sprawled face down on a narrow tray. One of the beings came over and pressed a snap buckle, allowing him to swing his legs shakily over the edge.

"James Cassidy?" enquired a strangely flat metallic voice.

He looked at the squat being that confronted him, holding a translator and twiddling the knobs.

"Yes," he agreed. "Who are you?"

"One of the natives," replied the being working overtime with the translator. James wondered why he did not look at him, then realized that the translator was a visual, giving a display that the being read, and presumably translating some minor facial alterations back to the being's language.

"You crashed a year ago," it continued. "We have rebuilt you."

"Rebuilt?" exclaimed James, and then understood that this must indeed have been necessary.

"Rebuilt," confirmed the other. "Made new from parts, reassembled."

"Yes, yes," agreed James, looking round the room.

"If you will talk for ten minutes or so, we will be much better at translation," suggested the other being. "We have only a few thousand words gathered from your ship at the time of the crash, and we do not know much about special sayings and word orders and word pay-loads and different meanings."

James obliged by giving them his life history and that of mining. It also gave him a chance to look around the ward or whatever it was. There was no need to look at his companions whilst talking, as they were engrossed in the display on their translators. They were more or less humanoid, as were most advanced species, a little shorter than himself and hairless. They wore a kind of helmetless spacesuit, which was probably necessary for warmth in these regions. A spare one was handed to him when he mentioned that it was cold. The ward was rough, there was no other word for it. The aluminium was badly finished, most of the bits and pieces were roughly spot-welded together, and the floor covered with some fibrous vegetable material that smelt not unpleasant, but was cracking badly in places. The glass cylinder was unnecessarily thick so far as he could see, unless he had been under pressure to get oxygen into him. Frost was condensing in places on the wall, and he assumed he was still well up north. The instrument console was a masterpiece by comparison. Far too much information displayed for a human, but to beings used to communicating by vision probably just right.

"We used scrap from your ship," explained one of the beings, who had evidently got all he wanted from the translator, and was watching him now. "We only had a few cells to go by, and it was important not to lose time, so we set up here."

"How did you know what I looked like?" asked James, regarding himself in one of the television monitors that served as mirrors.

"Your cells knew that!" exclaimed the first being, surprised. "That is, so long as there were no major modifications made to the apparent pheno-type. If there were we can probably do that too, if you know what needs to be done."

"No," put in James hastily. He checked a scar under his left eyebrow. That had been caused by an argumentative crewman on the Jupiter ferry. The crewman had been put out of the airlock as a hazard to the ship. The scar had disappeared now. He checked the slight swelling caused by a bad break to his shin in a rugger match years ago, a score he had not yet settled. That too had disappeared.

"Wow!" he said, half to himself. "New body!"

"It should age at about the same rate as the old one," explained the being, "so you should be able to discount your present age and start counting again from now."

"What does this cost?" asked James, suddenly realizing that this might be more of a gold-mine than platinum.

"For you, nothing," explained the shorter of the two creatures. "However, we understand that you are a prospector."

James agreed.

"We don't want to be prospected," explained the creature, smiling perhaps. "Our race has followed a different path from yours. We did a little high technology long ago, but realized before it was too late that it would lead to greater and greater demand for fewer and fewer resources, eventually leading to the scouring of nearer planets for scarce materials, and the dumping of wastes back on them again, as the mass of the parent planet increased."

James nodded. Already extraterrestrial mining operations had increased the earth's mass by point nought nought one per cent, and some long-sighted people were predicting that the time might come when we would have gravitational pollution to add to the other problems.

"So we went off in other directions," went on the being. "We can now do most of the things we want with living cells: computers, materials, mining, virtually anything."

"And we might destroy it all if we came barging in?" asked James, wondering how easy it would be to barge in.

"No, we would destroy you," explained the being. "We could easily infect the first mission here with cells that could overcome all your bodily reactions, withstand red heat if need be, and all your disinfectants. We have in fact done this to more than one life form that has tried to invade. Usually we don't destroy, merely alter the genetic program a little to produce the desired change."

"Turn us all into frogs, you mean?" queried James. In his mind he had visions of Zen Four, a world that had obviously had a technology in excess of their own, but now was inhabited by furry little creatures that seemed perfectly happy to play amongst the ruins of their once fine cities. Archaeologists had confirmed that the civilization had perished in a matter of weeks from some form of plague. Palaeontologists had confirmed that there were no precursors to the furry creatures, and the only tenuous explanation of their existence was the much discounted one of a very rapid devolution, the whole species changing back to some ancestral form in a matter of weeks.

"I won't tell anyone," he agreed. There might well be a possibility of some sort of trade later. He knew quite a few people back on Earth who would give half their fortune and more for a brand-new body, ex scars and other damage, that could start ageing from the year dot all over again.

"You haven't had your appendix out, by the way," added the shorter being, matter of factly.

James started to protest that he had, before he realized that he hadn't any more.

"We can do it if it is mandatory," suggested the creature. James declined the offer. If it was brand-new it should do for a while yet.

"There may be some other alterations," warned the being. "Much of the work is computerized, and corrections are written into the programs. Any excess is modified, bad characteristics corrected up to a point and so on, but not to the extent of a change of form or personality."

"Will I still be . . ." James paused for the word. Pugnacious? No, too many overtones. Powerful? Not quite what he wanted.

"Mean?" queried the being, again with that hint of a grin.

"Yeah, that's it!" agreed James. "Mean!"

"Just as mean as ever!" confirmed the being. "I don't think we could have changed that without making you something completely different. You might even be meaner!"

James felt a glow of inner satisfaction. He would soon be back in command, and by God! would he make them jump! They had probably had a party after his presumed demise. The pay-load was probably down, and the ship sloppily run. If there was any hint of sabotage, which he could check for himself now, he'd have the

whole lot out in space and pick up spare pay-load to make up the
weight. He could probably collect a percentage of salary too for
running the ship back by himself. With his new strong body he
could smash a few faces just for kicks.

"When will they be here?" he asked of his new companions.

"Touchdown in less than an hour, not over a mile away," confirmed the taller of the two. "We will take you there, and you
can handle things from then on."

"Too right I will!" agreed James. "When do we start?"

"There is a small flier waiting. We might as well go now," suggested thing number two, as James had mentally dubbed it.

With some difficulty one of them wound open the entire end
of the ward. James noted with contempt the roughly pressed
screw thread that held it. Once outside on the crisp snow under
the stars he felt fitter than he ever had. His new body seemed
to have springs in the legs as though gravity had weakened. Just
as he boarded the flier he turned to take a last look at his erstwhile
home. There was some writing in large letters down the side of
it. He started as he realized that they were English letters. He
peered intently, trying to see what part of the ship had been
cannibalized. Frost obscured them partially, and it was not until
takeoff that he finally made the words out.

"CORONA HAVANA" they said, in faded gold.

The Tree

Alf Rogers had been expecting trouble the past couple of days. Driving his new yellow excavator-cum-digger-cum-packer down the route of the C17, the new South Coast cycleway, he had become increasingly aware that he was one of the front-line shock troops of the squad.

It was all right for the follow-up squad. All they had to do was to tarmac the route he swathed out through the countryside, put up signs and kerbs and do a few simple tests. So long as they confined themselves to the boundaries set by the newly graded and compacted earth, there was not much the environmentalists could touch them on. True, the "Ban on the cycle" brigade had been campaigning more vigorously of late, and it did seem that the cycle might eventually go the same way as the car did in the late 90s, but there were still plenty of people who had an interest in seeing that the cycle stayed, and in any case the situation was somewhat different.

Trouble came at Mile 114 out from Dover. Chugging gently round a contour at five miles an hour, locked onto inertial guidance and not thinking of anything in particular, he came across The Tree.

He fought his first impulse to swerve round the thing, and wheezed to a halt ten feet short, before his supervisor in the back cab had even noticed it was there.

He switched off and pulled out the detailed route map from the shelf under the roller map alongside the steering wheel. His supervisor climbed through and brought out his own schedule.

"Unlisted," he said briefly, then "Keys."

Alf handed over the keys and reached for his sandwiches. There would be no more work today. It did not pay to argue with a supervisor. They had been appointed in the early tens, one supervisor to every piece of plant over five horsepower. Their job was to see that plant was used in such a manner that environmental damage was kept to a minimum. From the outside they were regarded as wise men, preventing companies like Cyclo-trac from tearing up the countryside at five m.p.h. From the inside they were referred to as "that monkey on my back" or worse. Either way their power was absolute, and their appointment had helped to solve the unemployment problem.

The route inspector drew up alongside on his bicycle. Alf climbed down.

"Cor!" said the inspector. "Tree!"

"Unlisted," replied Alf dourly.

Listed trees could be skirted, replanted, or even occasionally knocked down. With an unlisted one, one just stopped until the legal ends had been tied up, an expensive business, as one could lose fifty miles of track before the computers had checked through the body of law relating to trees, land rights, site rights, amenity rights, windbreak rights, and so on. Usually there was hefty compensation to pay to someone at the end of it as well.

"I'll get a local moving order," said the route inspector, reaching for the phone, just inside the cab.

"Can't," rejoined the supervisor. "It's Oak, which is a series three species, and over ten feet tall anyway."

"Then we'll knock it down and pay," countered the inspector, conscious that he represented a multi-million-pound company.

The supervisor flipped through his notes. "Could cost you half a million in computer time and a week's halt for investigation," he cautioned.

The inspector grunted. He knew that one side of the track was National Trust land, with no hope of driving a track for at least a decade; on the other was a greedy landowner who would squeeze the last penny after months of wrangling, before letting them on for a hundred yards or so. Tunnelling was out, as the chalk was an aquifer and rotten to boot. Bridging would bring them into sight of at least three villages, all of whom would gleefully demand line-of-sight compensation. Ahead was the tree.

"I intend to put in for a demolition order," he said, using the standard sentence for such contingencies.

"I witness," chimed in Alf.

"I note your intention," replied the supervisor, and grabbed the phone before either of the other two thought of it.

Alf leapt up into the other cab and drove back to the caravan park at full speed, with the inspector pedalling on ahead and the supervisor shouting over the din in the back. The company wouldn't like the amount of fuel he was using, particularly as allowances were likely to be cut yet again now that the third of the North Sea wells had started delivering salty water. With a total ban on private use, the rest ought to last a good few years yet, however, and it was all good business for the cycle trade.

Back at base there was a flurry of activity. All lines were called into action to feed data to the central computer, and before long people began arriving.

First came the Forestry boys, photographing first, then measuring, soil testing and finally taking one leaf away with them.

The local council rep came next, with the tree doctor. If the tree did get a preservation order served on it, there were very good reasons why the council should do all it could to see that it remained in good health. Trees had been known to die off in mysterious circumstances before now, and it could be a costly business as the investigation could drag on for months and take hours and hours of comptime. The pattern had been set round the turn of the century, when Professor Jenkins, who had proved that the break-up of coral reefs was due to the increased amount of carbon dioxide in the sea, making the species less resistant to attack, had also proved that the spread of Dutch Elm disease to other trees was a result of atmospheric pollution, weakening the species to such an extent that they were likely to go down with anything short of mumps or measles.

Compensation for that had run into many billions, and had removed one or two chemical giants from the face of the earth. The tree population was still declining, and the public were very conscious of the fact that they had scored some major victories over a variety of comers in the last decade or two.

The supervisor handed the inspector a provisional hold order within ten minutes of starting work. Quick, but it only gave a week's protection, and he had anticipated that anyway. He fed it back into his computer outlet and pressed on for a destruct permit. If he could get everything through to the main decision (environmental) control unit in Switzerland before the supervisor blocked him, at least his company would not have to foot the bill if the order were rescinded in the statutory four weeks' revision of decision time that went with a destruct permit.

They were scotched on this in the next quarter of an hour by being served a full evaluation order by the supervisor. This meant that all parties would have to be consulted, and that included the bureau of statistics, whose job it was to keep track of tree population in Europe, and about a score of local hiking, cycling, painting, botanizing, birdwatching and so on clubs, who would not be on computer outlet and would have to have noisy meetings at the town hall before they could come to any decision, rational or otherwise.

Unknowns were beginning to pile up at a worrying rate now. The computer wanted to know whether the tree was planted or self-sown. If planted, when, by whom, were they still living? What subspecies? Did the tree show any unusual resistance to environmental stress? Time of leaf fall, computed against others in the neighbourhood. What was the cost of alternative routing? Did the alternative include any other trees? If so, what species? and so on. All this for a tree that did not officially exist in the records as yet.

The supervisor came over shortly before he had finished his case preparation.

"Ready for Geneva, then?" he enquired, peering over his shoulder.

"Five minutes," he grunted. It was common courtesy to send in their separate computer files at the same time. Not that it made any difference at the other end, but at least it meant that they each knew what the other was sending, and could not pull any fast ones on each other.

Three hours after the discovery of the tree they were ready to send. As the yards of paper wound through the sender the inspector felt suddenly weary. There was no way one could win in this game. If the tree numbers continued to fail there would be no hope of doing anything but avoiding them. If they increased, they would be checked every mile or so, hemmed in on either side and unable to go forward.

Five minutes after the end of sending there was still no reply. Both of them stood awkwardly at the console, unable to think of anything to say. Suddenly the computer chattered briefly. All three craned forward to read the slip of paper.

The message was brief and to the point. "*Noli molestare*," it said. Meaning, simply, don't touch. Not this year, not next year, not ever. Such an order could not be rescinded. There was not even any procedure for questioning it. The tree would have to remain, *in situ*, until it died of old age. So far as it was concerned man did not exist on the earth.

Cliff Lawther

Spider Belt

One

The boy hung by his fingertips to the slimy metal, legs jerking in rhythm with the thin shrieks of terror. Five fathoms below his dangling feet the dark water leapt nearly a fathom higher, to subside in muttered cross-grumblings. And then he had slipped off, to turn over in the air just once before plunging into the surging ocean below the girders. A whitening patch of foam heaved out from the surface, attracting plate-sized flecks of scum towards it as it dispersed outwards.

Jan stopped his downward run through the trellises to grasp the nearby safety rail and numbly stare at the tossing waves as they slapped blindly into pillar and stanchion. Gone! A child scarcely older than the fingers of one hand, sucked under by the churning maelstrom currents deep below the surface.

At the first scream of alarm he had caught a glimpse of the small figure clinging to the narrow steel beam several Levels down, close to one of the colossal concrete legs. One of the little children who had strayed out from Top and lost himself on the catwalks, he had thought in despair, as he ran the gauntlet swiftly downwards. Behind him had clambered the adults, slow and clumsy on the slippery metal rails, shouting hoarse cries of encouragement during their hazardous descent.

A rope snaked downwards. Berenice, well in advance of the fastest moving of the rescuers, had reached the opposite catwalk where the emergency rope was kept ready. To descend further would be near-suicide; the lowest Level was dangerously wet and slippery with the constant washing of tidal and stormy water, softly green with a slimy coating of algae. Since the days of their earliest childhood recollections, they had been warned against venturing near the lethal girders of Level One.

The first two adults arrived, angry at their own negligence in having failed to prevent this tragedy. Old Mackay, blue-stained arms corded with the hauling of nets, brown-stained beard curled and knotted below the heavy glowering wrinkled face, sea-waves of grey hair streaming out behind him in the stiff breeze. And his son, Emlyn, Jan's stepfather, gasping nervously with the effort and the panic, gazing downwards into the green mirror which had always threatened to envelope his soul, as it had Old Mackay's.

"Lost!" the word jerked from Emlyn. "Who, child?"

Jan shook his head, afraid of the senseless passions of his father. He was old enough to sense in his step-parent the frustrated restless yearnings of a bygone youth—yet still too young to understand the consequent moods, changeable as the weather on Top. Jan, ever willing to extend the hand of friendship, and Emlyn, biting at it or casting it thoughtlessly aside.

Together, the three stared at the agitated weed- and scum-strewn surface, a breathing leprous back heaving greenly below their feet; and on the other side stood the girl Berenice, salt tears mingling with salt spray, one small hand twitching the rope as if it would seek out the tossing figure somewhere down there in the floating darkness.

The land of Top was vast, a level table of steel and concrete spanning clear to the horizon and the rusted towers and dilapidated gantries beyond, indented here and there with the great circular wells reaching fifty fathoms clear down to the water-level tidal traps of the energy generators. Nobody lived on Top, where storms lashed rain and snow flurries through summer and winter; though the people from the villages clustering the highest Levels basked in the warm sunlight of a fine day, and children of all ages played timeless games of hide-and-seek amongst the raised windbreaks, or pitted their cunning against the flocks of gulls to steal eggs from the high concrete ledges of the sheersided wells.

Jan had risked his life and his eyes with the other children, their heads turned aside to avoid the beating of wings and indignant squalling of the aroused birds, for the sake of a bag crammed with delicate and delicious robbery and the fame which goes with a hundred unbroken prizes. A reckless fiery flame of a kid, long blond hair encrusted with crystallized salt spray, grey eyes forever fierce in concentration, ears pricked to select the slightest noise above a background of hissing ocean waters.

With him, Berenice always searched in vain for the key to lock up this dancing white flame, and remained constantly pleased that she had so far never managed to find it. She was a year younger in age and older in wisdom than he was, a brave wistful girl with long straight black hair plaited in twists, and hazel brown eyes wide and innocent.

Jan the tornado, transient as the fluttering fire, nerves and muscles entwined to mould any situation at his command; and Berenice the dreamer, a joyful spirit moving cautiously where other children ran hastily.

And Uist, perched upright like a sentry with his tarsus straight and white front facing outwards, neck snaking from side to side in a vain effort to scan through the Levels. The seabird, whose usual vocal contribution was a deep chattering growl, now uttered a plaintive note of warning which lifted Jan from the cold ground to shield his face from the melancholic whistling of the spray-laden wind.

"It's only Estivus. Huh ! *That* creep." Jan turned to look down on the huddled figure of Berenice, who gazed up hopefully from their ragged collection of chalk scribblings.

"Who's Estivus ?" she asked in interest.

"From the next village. Fat Esti. Got a proper mother and father, so he's pampered like a pet. *They're* Level Eighters, don't mix with Threers—too snooty." Jan's lip sneered at the approaching boy, who stopped in sudden uncertainty, then pushed forward against the mental wave of antagonism.

"Little Watty's drowned," Estivus said eagerly, as if it was *good* news.

Jan clenched his fists, unclenched them. He didn't know exactly why he disliked the other boy. Perhaps it was the pink freckled face, chubby and eager to chatter, the red hair like a mass of sea-weed from the lowest girders. Perhaps it was the indisputable fact that he was always top of his teaching station, a clever-clever boy who could sit on his fat backside and waggle sweetsticks and the right answers in everybody's face. Perhaps—or perhaps Jan just didn't like him. As the plump boy approached, Jan circled him.

"We know already." Icy indifference.

"Oh," Estivus said, deflated. "Who told you?"

"Nobody told us. We were there."

"Gosh. Were you? Gosh. Really?" stammered the podgy boy. "No fibs?"

"No fibs. About half the village was there, prob'ly." Which wasn't true, since a dozen doesn't even come up to a tenth part of the *smallest* village.

Estivus lost interest. After all, small ones were getting themselves lost or drowned almost every other day, so it really wasn't all that important. He noticed Uist for the first time.

"What's it?" was his comment, pointing to "it". "Raz'bill?"

"That's a stupid thing to ask," retorted Jan, putting as much scorn in his voice as he could muster. "Everyone knows that razor-bills have been extinct for more'n fifty years. Besides, he's brown, not black. Huh! I thought your dad owned a library."

The last remark stung the most. "He doesn't own it. He runs it for the Ombudsman. Anyway, the place for freak birds is in the museum."

"Uist's *not* a freak!" Jan was startled into shocked denial.

"What is it then?"

"He's a guillemot, p'raps the most rare bird for stretches. He came to us one winter, sick and draggled, like he'd ploughed through a force-twelver. See the white eye-streak. That's 'cause he's a bridled guillemot. My dad told me."

"You haven't got a dad."

Jan clenched hands into fists again. "My stepdad told me. Anyway, what's so special about a *proper* dad." A shrug.

Estivus failed to notice that the older boy hadn't actually asked a question. "'Cause there aren't many, that's why they're special," he said, pugnaciously. "Hardly a boat doesn't return from a fishing trip without—*Oww!!*" The plump boy sat down hard on the concrete sill, eyes streaming with sudden tears, a trickle of blood running out of one nostril. "What did you do *that* for!"

"You *asked* for it, that's why. Don't ever mention my dad again, hear?"

Estivus began to snuffle, his pants getting wet on the damp weather-eroded sill. "You didn't oughta have done that," he whimpered. "Hitting kids younger than you—and smaller," he added, as an afterthought.

Jan looked at him. He hadn't hit him very hard and already the blood was clotting, drying hard. A careless sleeve wiped it away with the tears.

"You're so brave," came the sarcastic comment. "I'll bet you don't know anything except what's within reach of your eyes—and your hands." Estivus took out a handkerchief, blew his nose, and examined the contents with every air of a connoisseur.

Jan felt a bit contrite. After all, the fat kid hadn't actually hurt *him*, just his feelings. "Like what?"

"Yes, like what?" Berenice chipped in from the other side of the sill. Fights didn't concern her, since she was a girl. But mysteries did, since she was a curious child.

Estivus turned, looked, sniffed disdainfully. A girl! Berenice stared innocently back at him, stirring the loose chalk figures with one gloved hand. "Like what?" she repeated.

"Who's she?"

"Like what?" insisted Jan, aggressively.

The plump boy snatched one more glance at Berenice, stuffed his soiled handkerchief back into his pocket and licked his fingers, which had somehow managed to acquire a sticky coating of sweet-stick in the interim.

"Just this," he said, knowingly. "Everyone can see that Top goes on and on f'rever north 'n south and that there's just only sea in the direction of sunrise——"

Jan snorted. "Not a kid hasn't been out along the channels fishing the open sea on a fine day. So what?"

Estivus flung a dramatic hand towards the west. "Nobody's ever been off that way. Bet *you* don't know what's that way."

"Well, I do. More sea, that's all."

"Well you *don't*. My dad told me that it's not all sea in that direction. He's met someone who's been there, so he knows for certain. There's another Top there, just across the water, linked by narrow walks on legs called bridges, and another beyond that, and another—till you get to the shore."

Jan sneered. "That's rubbish. What he prob'ly saw was just the same old Top, only curved round, with a walkway to cut the journey short."

"What's 'the shore'?" said Berenice, inquisitively.

"It's—it's——" The plump boy struggled with words, at a loss to describe the image in his mind. "It's like Top, only it's all earth like the farms and without water underneath."

A gust of laughter forced its passage into the stiff breeze. "That's the *stupidest* thing I ever heard, Esti. If there's no water underneath, what's it got to stick its legs into? Air?"

"No! No, into more earth, and more, and more, and——" Estivus stopped suddenly, appalled at the prospect of so much earth. "And it's not rubbish. Other Tops exist, too. They're prob'ly not all long like ours, perhaps—I mean, my dad read that you can go for days, weeks even, in *that* direction and nothing changes, 'cept it gets colder." He was waving his hand northwards.

"It's just ridiculous," commented Jan, white face scanning the horizon for a break in the level skyline. It was true, he hadn't actually *been* to where the land ended and the rest of the sea began.

Estivus waited to catch his attention. "Not ridiculous," he said, feeling superior now that the nagging seed of doubt had been sown in the other's mind. "You haven't been there, so *you* don't know."

"So what? You haven't been there either. You just rely on some old fairytale your dad's managed to dig up out his musty books."

The plump boy boggled. "I'm going there soon," he said, defensively. "My uncle's taking me in his boat."

"So your uncle has a boat, big fuss. You'll prob'ly never bother, anyway."

"It does sound a nice idea," contributed Berenice, imagining the cosy cabins and whining battery inboard of one of the larger sea-going boats.

"I'm going to see," said Jan, caught in the crossfire of their thoughts.

"When?"

"Sometime." Cautiously.

"Dare you to go!"

"Don't be silly. It wouldn't be a dare 'cause it's too simple. It's—it's like——" Jan stopped, confused. If it wasn't a dare, what was it? Perhaps because it had never been a dare, he hadn't actually ever thought of attempting it. After all, it wasn't as if it was very hard. Just take some food and keep walking until. . . . Until you reached it. Until you reached what?

"*Double-dare* you!"

"*All right!*" Jan pulled himself erect and glowered. "You're so clever. You come too."

"Me? I can't. My mum would miss me if I went."

"Leave her a note."

"I *can't.*" There was a note of wistfulness in his voice.

"Can I come?" asked Berenice, thoughtfully.

Uist gave a chattering growl, threw himself off the lip of the platform and whirred away into the dizzy depths of a nearby well. Journeys to him were trivial matters, not esteemed or revered or decided, simply entered upon without further ado. A pang of envy coursed through both the boys' reflections; a seabird could do anything without thinking that a child or a man would sweat tears over before venturing into.

"All right," said Estivus.

"All right," said Jan.

"All right," whispered Berenice.

The echoing Uist laughed a hollow laugh from somewhere down near the surging ocean.

Two

Berenice clattered down the metal stairway and pushed at the heavy door into their Level Three apartment. It was deserted; her mother was most probably gathering the driftwood that had snagged overnight into the steel nets near the tidal generators.

She went through to the small kitchen. Because she was a re-sourceful girl and expected to follow Jan to the ends of Top today, the bag she packed was heavy; in addition to the usual warm clothing and light waterproof her mother always insisted she take with her and not lose, she had stuffed in enough food to last her until dark.

Taking the food caused her a pang of conscience, for there were few essential items still obtainable through the market; only fresh vegetables were plentiful as this was the end of autumn and the over-producing farms had been designed originally with many more people in mind.

She laced up her boots with fumbling juvenile fingers, pushed her gloves into her coat pockets and went to find Jan and Estivus.

On Top, she met Hab, small elfin face with its bright eyes gleaming as he held out a chunky piece of raw fish to Uist. Hab was a small boy, even for a seven-year-old, an excitable mass of curls through which poked a pair of large ears and not much else. He was intelligent enough to realize that nearly everything on or below Top scared him stiff, and when frightened, as he often was, either burst into tears or swung a fist at anything that moved. Like Estivus, he was fortunate to enjoy the luxury of original parents. He didn't understand what had happened today to one of his school-friends to upset them all down below, so he had come up to Top. Later, he would probably miss Watty and ask ques-tions. Right now, because he was devoted to Uist, he had forgotten everything else around him.

Berenice realized that they would have a hard time getting Uist to go with them without Hab, or of leaving the boy behind for that matter. He was noted for his stubbornness and childish tantrums.

"Where you going?" he asked belligerently as Jan and Estivus drew near, something approaching friendship linking them together now as a result of their recently united cause.

"Nowhere for little boys," replied Berenice.

"Wanna go too," said Hab, spotting her bag.

"Sorry, Hab," said Estivus, in a fatherly tone of voice. "It's too far to walk for a littl'un."

"If you don't take me, I shall scream."

"Scream, then," shrugged Jan, indifferently. Except for the farms, Top was a barren whistling wasteland where a child's cries could go unnoticed for a century.

Hab changed tack. "I'll tell your parents," he offered.

The look of alarm that crossed Estivus' features did not go unnoted. "I'll tell your father. I'll *tell*."

"Oh, bring him along," said Jan in a quiet voice to Estivus and Berenice. "He'll probably get fed up and leave us before we've walked ten minutes, and go home. And he's not got many warm clothes, so he'll get cold in a while."

So, because they couldn't leave him behind, they took him with them, and then found that it was impossible to get rid of him. Hab whined and cried every time they told him to go home, saying that he didn't know the way and he was afraid of the Kraken that lived down at Level One, and . . . and. . . . Finally, they shut him up with a sweetstick and allowed him to trail behind, croaking encouraging noises at Uist, who came and went every few minutes or so.

Apart from the infrequent farms with their glassed-in hydroponics and thin-earth frames, there was little save a flat expanse of weathered concrete, criss-crossed with steel beams and high storm sills, with the inevitable well every quarter-hour or so, and grey-green water grunting fathoms beneath their eager faces. The few people they met looked them over curiously at first, for it wasn't unknown for bands of urchins to emerge periodically on thieving trips. As far as other children were concerned, most of them were probably playing between Levels. Only the gulls shrieked and swooped for titbits over the deserted landscape.

Gradually the character of the surface began to change; vast cracks appeared in the concrete, which had been eroded and washed away by the storm-waters of several years. It looked neglected, as if the material workers never bothered to repair the damage as it was caused. As the second hour wore on, they began to notice an increase in the number of false wells.

"With all that rubbish blocking the trap, how can their 'lectricity be made," commented Estivus, with all the wisdom he could appropriate. "Why they should keep throwing junk into it beats me."

"Perhaps the rubbish was there first and they just built round it," suggested Berenice.

"Wanna go home," murmured Hab, for about the fifteenth time.

"Go home, then," said Jan, in an exasperated voice.

"Don't wanta go on my own."

Jan opened his mouth to say something scary, because he was fed up with dragging the small boy behind him. There was a shout from Estivus up ahead.

"Look ! Look at that !"

They had reached the horizon.

Walking on a gigantic table, they neared the edge, which dropped perpendicularly to an ocean green under the low rolling clouds, reaching clear over in one unbroken stretch to what appeared to be a smaller Top. A crosswind alternately sucked and blew at them, carrying white gulls aloft like so many lumps of chalk thrown up into the sky. The air was filled with their noisy shrieking as they fought for space on the tiny ledges and exposed girders.

Across this vast sea, the lower table of the other Top reared itself out of the water, a turtle-back all lumpy and cracked, with only small areas of concrete visible amongst the jumbled spaghetti of the steel girders.

"Gosh. Look at *that*," breathed Estivus. "I told you. I *told* you so."

They stood on the high edge, savouring the sight and the breeze with awed glances and watering eyes.

"There's a bridge," said Jan.

"Only one?" Estivus turned and looked along the other's out-stretched arm. "P'raps the others have all fallen down."

Chaining the two islands together, the lofty bridge skipped across the water on the inverted apexes of triangular steel spans, some of which were canted at an angle, with visible gaps in the roadway that must have been constructed along the top.

"It's broken," said Jan, with annoyance.

There was something else in addition to the bridge, but closer to them, a black continuous pipe supported inside open steel box-work to run like an umbilical connection between the two land masses.

"There's another bridge in this direction—part of one anyway." Berenice pointed.

They stared hard and were able to distinguish the jutting first few sections a long, long way on the opposite side of them. Of the remainder there was no trace. Presumably, it had been washed into the sea some time in the past.

Jan's heart stirred with the pounding of fresh excitement. The one bridge was useless, but the thick black pipe looked continuous; anyway, given a choice between the two if both had been in good condition, he would have plumped for the lower, thinner one. It looked as if it had never been constructed to allow people across it; it looked, well, more *dangerous*, somehow.

"I'm going across," he said.

Berenice, Estivus and little Hab looked at him in astonishment. Uist sailed down, fighting the crosswind to grip the concrete edge tightly and preen a few ruffled feathers with quick flicks of his serpentine neck.

"You can't," said Estivus, as if it was a fact. "The bridge is broken."

"I'm going across on the little one. *That* looks all right."

Estivus stared at it, blinking as the wind hurt his eyes.

"Have we—have we got time to go across and come back home before it gets dark?" he asked slowly, squinting up into the sky in front of them to where the sun should be, hidden behind the rolling grey cumulus.

Jan shrugged. Berenice looked thoughtful. Hab crooned noises at Uist. Nobody actually ended up making a decision, but the intervening space shortened regardless.

It was a large black pipe, supported on thick concrete legs about ten fathoms above the surface of the whitecaps; thick as a man's height, it emerged from the dark bowels of Level Three and travelled straight across the Sound to disappear a little higher than halfway up the side of the mesh jungle opposite them.

Estivus tapped it with a piece of wormed planking. A hollow boom-
ing seemed to stir and shiver through the pipe as frantic minions
of sound rushed backwards and forwards, bumping into their
echoes on the way.

Estivus slapped his way slowly up the topmost side of the pipe,
eliciting a scream of terror from the frightened Hab by chanting
in a deep voice: "I'm the slimy Kraken from Level One I'm
the——" then interrupting himself to cry: "Hey, look at the
rust on here!" Gripping hard, he heaved and almost fell backwards as a finger's thickness chunk about the size of a stormdrain
cover levered off. Another flake, not quite as large.

Then they were all at it, vying with each other to rip the largest
piece of rotten metal off the ancient pipe. Hands stained with
ochre dust and black paint flecks, they watched the shards twist
and turn in their downward plunge and raise the whitish plumes
of spray as they landed in the water. The pitted surface of the
vandalized pipe looked somehow naked and defenceless after a
time, so they stopped, faintly sad that they couldn't magic all
the bits back up into a heap at their feet and slap them back on
again. All except little Hab, who kept giving little grunts and
heaving witlessly until all his nails had been broken.

" I wonder what used to run through it?" queried Berenice,
thinking aloud.

"Fresh water?" Estivus suggested, still out of breath with the
effort of dismantling the rusty layer.

Jan shook his head, eyes gleaming as they travelled backwards
and forwards along the endless pipe. "No need. Water 'nough on
Top. There's never been a shortage as far back as Old Mackay
can remember." He clambered to the broad top surface as Estivus
had done, wet-shoes gripping firmly the rough layer. "Look at
me!" And off he sprinted.

"Come down, Jan! You'll fall in the water!" shouted Berenice.
"Come back!"

Jan only laughed at her, skip-dancing merrily on the friable
upturned belly of the enormous cylinder. Shards of blackened
rust spun off in his wake as several times he stumbled and fell
to bruise knees and hands, and once his foot plunged through a

completely rotten patch to disappear into the pipe. Yet he ran on, daring the clawing wind to hurl itself at him, daring his sure feet to confuse and mis-step.

After her first attempt to dissuade him, Berenice gave up shouting and began to move slowly along the tiny catwalk, hypnotized into following him with her eyes, frightened that if she looked away for even a moment he would vanish never to be seen again.

The fragile platform swayed alarmingly. Estivus trailed behind, condemned to move at snail's pace by the clinging figure of Hab, who shivered and whimpered, more in fear of being left behind than at the terrifying prospect of dropping vertically into the mottled ocean beneath his feet.

Behind them, unperceived by senses concentrating on other affairs, the first black-streaked fingers of muttering storm-clouds emerged above the protecting wall of Top.

Three

Rain lashed feebly against the door of the abandoned dwelling, sinking down from the highest Level to be caught in helpless swirlings by the storm-winds and to hammer in frustration on the fragile metal roof.

Hab shivered uncontrollably in one corner while the rest of them discussed lighting a fire. "Me c-cold," his small voice chattered. "Me w-wet, m-me cold." Trembling, his automatic pleading had reverted to baby-talk.

"You should have brought a waterproof, silly," fumed Jan, though not unkindly, because he could see that the poor boy was soaking wet, tousled hair running little droplets of water into an already saturated shirt. "You'll dry out when we've built a fire."

Since they neither knew any better nor had much between them in the way of extra covers, all the little one received by way of attention was to have his clothes wrung out and his hair dried with a towel that Berenice had thoughtfully provided amongst her things.

"I'm c-cold," his shivering voice murmured at intervals. "C-cold."

The idea of a fire was eventually abandoned; enough dry, rotten wood had been collected from dusty corners and the shelves of otherwise empty cupboards before they discovered that they had absolutely nothing with which to light it.

As Hab was the wettest, the miserable child was bundled into the protection of two waterproofs, a temporary measure which was better than nothing at all. Berenice huddled damply with a sweater pulled over the knees of her thick trousers, neat plaits now pulled out, hair kinked and bedraggled and the end of her pert nose turning numb. Jan spurned the idea of warming himself with anything except the by-product of his accelerated metabolism and cheerfully handed his waterproof over with the girl's. Estivus whined a bit for his mother and the luxurious comfort of a heated room, sniffing dolefully into the rattling tattoo overhead; after a while, they discovered from his silence that he had fallen asleep, a beatific smile plastered his chubby features. Evening began to grow in darkness from the fading storm.

"Bet it rains all night," commented Jan, morosely.

"We shall be able to get back to Top in the morning, shan't we?" Berenice said, frowning. "My mother will be worried. Ever so."

An encouraging nod. "Course we will. We could go back over tonight, if the storm would let up. It must be blowing a force-niner out there."

Berenice thought of the oily black water lying in wait for them to plunge through holes in a catwalk they couldn't see, winds shrieking malevolently in an effort to dislodge each of them in turn. She shuddered, violently. To fall into the storm-tossed ocean and be swept along the wide Sound, choking on every mouthful of salt spray, icy numbness slowly creeping upwards from the toes and feet. She gathered her legs under her in comfort, frightened of her own thoughts.

Poor exhausted Hab had shivered himself into a fitful sleep, arms and legs twitching slightly. Jan was a battered frigate-bird, fighting gale-force winds down near sea-level a thousand years away. Berenice closed her eyes and eventually she fell asleep.

During the night, the lightning sizzled as it smote its brazen entry into the Levels, illuminating briefly the terrified elfin face of Hab, who had woken from a nightmare and didn't know where he was. His screams and the thunderous cacophony of noise reverberating through the steelwork woke the others and they huddled near each other in shaking anxiety that the next flash would seek out and find them.

But as usual, the threats were empty ones, and the storm subsided to stump away across the steel jungle. Torrential rain slowed to a spasmodic pattering, and then stopped altogether. The gale, however, continued unabated, and had not blown itself out by the time the cold grey sky began to lighten in the direction of the hidden east.

The children were stiff with cold when they awoke. They stared in dismay at the flapping metal struts of the pipe bridge, stretching its flimsy tightrope tantalizingly before them.

"I could crawl over, get some help from the nearest houses," Jan shouted at them, wind whipping the words away.

"No! If you fall, you'll be drowned!"

"It's the only way. The gale could last for days," he mouthed at her.

"It's not safe!"

Jan laughed into the wind, pitting his strength against its freezing breath, defying its awesome power. He stepped from the safety of the massive girder and began inching his way along the catwalk, swaying as the alarmed footpath shuddered under the extra weight. With overworked muscles trying to control limbs numb with cold, he slowly crawled forward on elbows and knees. His head moved from side to side, weighing up handholds, footholds, the feeble distance covered so far, and the terrifying journey still incomplete.

Estivus stared at him, mesmerized in the same way as Berenice had been the day before. Berenice herself was turned away, unable to bear watching, ears pricked to catch the faint wail of terror the wind would carelessly allow her to overhear....

"He's coming back!" shouted Estivus, clinging tensely to little Hab. "It's too far to go! He's trying to come back!"

Berenice swung round in astonishment. Jan had *never* turned back before.

Slowly, far more slowly than he had gone forward, he slid delicately in reverse, huddling flat with every gust of wind, staring behind him with white face and vacant expression. He was shouting at them, trying hard to wave with a hand never free for more than an instant; but the wind swept his words away. Finally he manoeuvred close enough for some scrappy remnants to fight their way clear.

"... up top ... watching. ..."

Clinging, he pointed, upward and above their precarious stance. Following his extended arm, Berenice and Estivus saw the muffled human phantom perched amongst the girders at the highest Level.

Sombrely motionless. Gazing at them.

He hadn't even tried to help them, though a short length of strong rope was coiled over his shoulder and he had obviously been aware of Jan's determined efforts for some time. Nor did he offer the use of his rope to tie them together for the rough crossing, despite eager requests from Jan. It may have simply been the adult in him weighing up the slim chances of them arriving safe at the other side, yet Berenice received the impression that he was somehow *glad* that the children were unable to return. ...

The man was old, a gnarled misshapen levelcomber with an unsmiling gaze icy and fleeting when the bright sunken eyes rested momentarily on the children. His back was bowed, chest and arms massive inside the grease-stained and tattered coat. Small weak-looking legs terminated in the outsize flat feet of someone who had never managed to accustom himself to a lifetime of clambering oddshaped and twisted girders. A thin flouring of grey hair whipped like a torn cobweb in the wind.

With the gale angrily berating every whining cross-brace around them, conversation was limited to essential information. After a while he waved them to follow him and stumbled off, following precisely the black line of the rusty pipe two Levels below. Cautiously, they kept up with him as he plunged deeper into the deformed trellises of the steel jungle, conscious that he was leading them away from home; hoping that he might have a boat, or would direct them to a village which could bear a message to their parents.

For well over an hour they shambled along in the wake of the ancient custodian of this twisted world, fearful that the already weakened, dilapidated struts and catwalks would give way and catapult them downwards, wondering if he was simply trying to lose them—but no, he couldn't, the black pipe was always below them, now straight, now curved, signposted the way ahead.

"What's he *up* to?" Berenice whispered fiercely into Jan's ear.

Jan shook his head. "Look below you," he said. "Down to the water."

She stared, saw nothing at first, then became aware of the eerie, frightening quality of the ocean several Levels below their feet. Never could she recall having observed water which in spite of the shrieking gale was smooth and flat, thick black lethargic stuff scarcely moving.

"Oh Jan, it's scary," she gulped. "What *is* it?"

"Something coming out of the water, a kind of mud, p'raps," he suggested, grimly. "Over by him. Up ahead."

Berenice followed the direction in which his finger was pointing. Below the lowest girders, a mound of thick black treacly substance heaved and groaned, bubbles emerging and collapsing in thin gouts of whitish vapour. A blast of warm air hit them, its embrace transmuted to something repulsive by the faint whiff of rottenness.

Around the anxious children toured a circular catwalk with tall ancient stanchions lancing upwards into the sky, like the tumbled masses of steel in the false wells. Ahead of them was a looming dark building on concrete pillars near which stood the crooked man, urging them with waving arm to come closer, to enter his house.

The black mouth of a doorway gaped idiotically at them; the heavy metal door hung half off its hinges, banging dismally with every gust of wind. Inside, another door of more useful fit silently opened under the old man's touch and closed behind them as they entered the ancient building.

"Gosh. Look at the place," Estivus' voice echoed hollowly as they left the wind behind. "It's *massive*."

Berenice shivered with the sudden change to warmth, merely an illusion since the air had not altered temperature but had simply stopped moving. She stared around her at the colossal musty room, at the empty steel floor with reddish-grey ranks of tall cabinets clustering the walls.

Yellowy dust floated like ghost snow, trapped by the great chamber to float for ever in restless anguish amongst the tall pillars and passage echoes. Three tiers of railed walkways circled the room aimlessly, connected together by only the one remaining ladder, resting places for the dials and plates that had flaked away from the crumbling consoles. A few small glass-and-metal rooms were visible on the topmost level, staring at them with dingy grey eyes.

Towards the centre of the floor, a protruding rusty safety rail prevented them from plunging half a fathom into the untarnished surface of black liquid below a complicated maze of bent piping and bolted gaskets. There was no way of telling how deep the treacly substance was; a finger's depth or fifty fathoms, it was impossible to judge.

Their pipe was there, the large one they had been faithfully following. Held captive by the collars and clasps, it tink-tinked a far-off message of a mindless stanchion tapping in the gale, a tinny recording of the pool a short distance away.

The gnarled man was standing in front of a long-dead console, amused by the expressions creeping across their faces as the information around them failed to register. "Mine," he growled, proudly. "OFFSHORE 93, they called it. Last remaining oil-rig in good condition for several days' walk around——" Then a sudden frown, as he spat the question: "Now, what're *you* doing here?" He stared from one to the other. "A journey of discovery, mebbe? No, that wouldn't be so, not enough kit. . . . It must be stealing, then. From a poor old man like Billow, perhaps? Nobody else here. What's wrong with *him*?"

Jan, who had opened his mouth to say something, now turned to see young Hab behind him, face flushed, fighting for breath enough to say that he wanted to go home, somehow never quite managing to form the words.

"Hab must be ill. He got wet yesterday," said Estivus.

"Wet?" spoke the old man, glowering at the youngest child. "Esposed, probably. Idiot boy !"

"Exposed to what?" Estivus queried, blankly.

"Esposed to esposure. *What else?* Bring him upstairs ! I can light a fire and fry him dry." He turned, grumbling to himself.

They followed, uncertain, though grateful that they had found someone who seemed to know what to do. The room upstairs had been an office of some sort, with the minimum of furniture and a dirty, grease-smelling mass of bedding pulled up near a set of rusted filing cabinets. In one corner, the metal wall had been ripped open and a flap turned up in an inverted scoop to catch and funnel out whatever smoke had emerged from the grey-black sodden ashes on the floor. The wall was smudged with a broad smear of black soot.

The old man ripped up a few rags from a pile inside one of the cupboards, and also withdrew a heavy canister of viscous fluid, to pour some over the cotton waste. Placing the can behind him, he bent over with a small flinty object he had taken from a pocket in his coat, and struck a few sparks. A grumbling roar filled the room; black gouts of smoke rolled upwards from a redly smoulder-ing fire, to lazily sniff their progress out of the crude chimney vent into the heights of the gigantic room beyond. The air swiftly became foggy and close; there was a smell resembling rancid fat amongst the smoky fumes.

"Oil," he stated triumphantly, staring into the shifting glow. "Breath of life."

Estivus stirred uneasily. "Fish-oil?"

"No, silly youngster," corrected the ancient sneering voice. "Sea-oil, millions of tonnes of it, *thousands* of millions, not the feeble bucketfuls squeezed from a day's catch. Prosperity, wealth, the guiding flame of a nation. . . . Oh, but a long, *long* while ago. Over a hundred an' seventy years since the last well played out, 'bout the time of the Great Famine, the time of the estodus, with only a handful of folks remaining, cut off—No, not cut off, cutting *themselves* off. . . . Or so my grandfather used to say——"

Hab gasped softly, hands trembling, eyes glazed. "Wanna go home," he eventually managed to whisper, shivering. "Want m-my mummy."

The old fellow swung round, his reminiscences cut short by the small pleading voice. "So little sonny wants to go home, does he? Well, he can't, can he, and that's a fact. He'll have to stay here for a while, in Billow's home. Just a *little* while. . . ." It was bewildering to sense the abrupt change in his manner of speaking.

Jan stepped back a pace, nearer to the door, some instinctive fear tugging at his nerves. While the old man was clucking at Hab, he caught Estivus' eye and together they slipped out of the smoke-filled office into the mighty silent room below the iron ladder.

"We've got to get outa here, Esti," Jan hissed, fiercely. "There's something strange about everything around us. He's all alone, and I bet there isn't anyone else for stretches around here. An' did you hear him accuse us of stealing? An' how did he know we were crossing at the pipe early this morning? We must have walked for *ages* to get to this heap."

Estivus looked pale under the patina of glistening sweat, his eyes glancing nervously from side to side as if something was liable to leap on him at any moment.

"I don't know how," he said, his voice uncertain. "I don't like this place. It gives me the creeps. That old slimy, Billow, he's jus' like a fat, chuckling spider running up and down his web." His worried expression turned thoughtful. "I wonder if he's got any food. I'm *starving*."

"Esti, you're always starving! If he's got any, it's prob'ly poisoned, anyway. *Listen* to me."

Estivus listened, tensed up.

"I reckon he's a bit barmy," Jan told him, in a confidentially scared voice. "Living here in this spooky place, it's not surprising, is it? Now old spider-man Billow's got young Hab, and us as well, 'cause if we go and look for help, we'll prob'ly never see Hab again. We've got to get all of us outa here, otherwise we'll all go crazy too. And our parents, worrying—we've *got* to get back over to Top——"

"But Hab's too ill, an' there's a hurricane blowing outside!"

"If he's got a boat, we could channel home. We'd just have that break to cross between here and——"

"Yeah, and a force-niner blowing us on to the leg-guards. *Dead* easy."

Jan gave an exasperated snort. "Look, stop interrupting me! There must be a way we could get Hab out while his attention's distracted, take him to the place where we spent the night. We'd be all right there—he'd have no chance of catching any of us once we got off the catwalks. We could sit up there and grin at him for weeks."

"Fall off with starvation, more like," Estivus sneered briefly, before returning his attention to the creaking building. "Besides, Hab'll never make it along an exposed girder without slipping off."

Jan shrugged in disappointment and looked over his shoulder. "Do you think Berenice is all right in there with him?" he said, faintly anxious still. In answer, a gout of black smoke curled up from the makeshift wall-vent as Billow threw a load of oil on the smouldering rags in an attempt to satisfy their hunger.

"He must have temp'rily forgotten about us," said Estivus thoughtfully, following the smoky message. "Let's look around."

"Why?"

"Dunno. Maybe we could find a room to lock him up in, or something."

Jan's eyes sparkled. "Lock him up . . ." he breathed, fascinated by the thought. "Let's make it quick, though—else Berenice will think we've left her behind."

Estivus nodded an eager acquiescence.

The ancient building was a mass of rusted equipment, tangled wires and conduits festooning most of its interior like the strangle-vines that appeared at odd times out of nowhere to infest the farm crops. Decaying passages led to rooms with walls partially fallen in. Floors displayed a tendency to buckle downwards when trodden on, and in particular one floor strip where the weld had sheared displayed the crosshatch of knitted girders with far below a gently swelling oily sea. A fierce draught forced its way up through the gap to whistle eerily around their legs.

"It's not safe," commented Estivus, moving carefully. "The whole darned building is liable to collapse at any moment."

Few rooms remained in either a habitable or lockable state. If the furniture hadn't already fallen apart and blocked up the entrance, the door was either rusted solid to its hinges, or had fallen off them. After a while, they were tempted to give up looking.

"Let's call it a bust and get back before he notices we're gone," suggested Estivus in minor alarm. "This place scares me more 'n more."

"Only one more door." Jan froze as the door swung silently inwards on oiled hinges. He'd been expecting a shriek, a crash, a groan, or just stubborn refusal to budge. "Oh, great wells !" he said. "Do you see what's in there, Esti? *Do you? Do you?*"

Estivus peered round the jamb, let out a gasp of surprise.

"*Food!*"

More replete than a farm storehouse, the room groaned under the weight of hoarded food. Crates leered at them lopsidedly; tins rolled at them across the floor. There were scores of great vats with liquid in them, boxes of dried fruit and vegetables piled up to the ceiling, fish-grease candles, dozens of cartons of things they couldn't even identify. Enough food was assembled in the large store to feed an entire village for several years.

"Food," echoed Jan, walking in through the doorway. "Where did it come from? W*e* don't make things like this——" He picked up a box with a set of airtight tins in it, opened one with his fingernail, sniffed at the contents. "—the label says b-i-s-c-u-i-t-s. What are 'bis-cuts' ?"

"Try one and see."

Jan took one out and nibbled it. "Sweet," he said. "Not so sugary as sweetsticks. Bit pasty tasting, like dried fish."

"Gimme one." Estivus held out his hand. After it was gone he held out his hand for another one, then another, then swiped the tin out of Jan's hands. Munching sounds.

"Nith," his muffled voice concluded. "Very nith."

"Put them down, Esti."

"Why?" There was a world of surprise in that one word.

" 'Cause they're not ours, that's why. And I don't think they're his, either. It's crazy, all this grub for just one person. He must have stole it from somewhere."

"Not from us," asserted Estivus, eyeing up the remaining half of his sixth biscuit thoughtfully.

"Where from, then? Nothing but mysteries around here. Where did all this food come from? And *how* did he know we crossed over yesterday?"

"Listening, inquisitive boy, listening to the singing message of the oil-pipe."

Everything had gone very quiet, the muffled thump-thump-thumping of Jan's heart synchronized perfectly with the pinking of biscuits sliding out of a tin which had suddenly tipped forward of its own volition.

"It tells me lots of things, my friendly pipe does," murmured the voice of Billow from the doorway. "When I'm not happy, it cheers me up; when I'm sad, it cries in sympathy; when I'm lonely, it plays sweet music in my ear, soothing——"

Jan swung round, catching the dilapidated man by surprise.

"No tricks, boy!" came the warning, in a snarling tone of voice. "I may not run as fast as you, but I'm bigger by a long, long way and strong, oh, so much stronger than you. Want to see some *real* muscles?" He stepped full in the doorway so that neither of them could slip past into the corridor, took off his evil-smelling coat in one quick movement and methodically rolled up his sleeve. As he had predicted, his sinewy blue-veined arm bulged with great bulked pads of muscle, massive dollops of them plastered on like white bonemeal cement. Billow grinned at them through stained and blackened teeth.

"See them writhe, boys," he said, mesmerizing them. "All that's left whole. Back and legs hurt in an accident, never worked properly since. But *these*——" He flexed them briefly. "Strong enough to change sail on a railrunner while it's moving at sixty knots. Not many men can say that." A laugh. "Then again, not many left who'll travel the Rail across the rotten bridges. Only me, in fact. Only me."

He stepped a pace forward into the room, an expression of hatred on his face. "Now, kids, coming here to steal food ain't right. Can't possibly let you——"

"Run, Esti!" screamed Jan, springing sideways as the spell broke. "Hide amongst the boxes!" Estivus ran. Jan hid.

Cursing, swearing impotently at them, following them with his eyes, Billow moved aside as a carton tumbled on to his foot, spilling out contents in a mute token of appeasement. Kicking the empty box away from him, he stumbled forward, judging heights and distances to them, lunging in their direction, shambling after their flitting forms. A cry of triumph as he grabbed Estivus' jersey.

"Aargh! Help, Jan! Help me! He's g-got me!" *Then he had wrenched free to cannon into a heap of tins and Jan's foot pushed out to spreadeagle the gnarled Billow face forward on the floor. They ran, sobbing, hearts pounding, gale shrieking up towards them from the rip in the floor, jumping, stumbling, rolling, up again, racing down the passage with Estivus crying his eyes out and Jan white-faced with a terror he'd never felt before, Billow swearing mad limping along after them, keeping close enough for them to hear his voice breathing down their necks prickling with sweat and a fear of the unknown. Cannoning into a doorway, eyes glazed, Estivus sighing stitch, stitch, help me oh please help me, Billow hobbling close, Jan tugging Estivus forward with shaking hands, twisting, dodging those flailing hands ready to grab at them, entering the mighty chamber where the wind stilled, the pipe whispered, Berenice pleaded....*

Locked up, Esti!—Berenice—locked up. *Trying to fight off the hands, shaking, head banged against the swaying console gaping vacuously at them black teeth broken and stained with rust, racing for the door, better the angry gale than the mad Billow, stumbling, fending off the squat form rearing ahead of them, cut off—Rail above the chuckling pipe held in one hand, body bent backwards, Billow lunging forward, slipping, greased muscle*

*sliding into poor Estivus, bones cracking against the safety rail, nose
bleeding just like Jan punched him, sighing, eyes bulging, rusted
stanchion snapping, rails bent suddenly like twisted exercisers,
Estivus' wail of terror as he drops backwards into the smooth
treacle blackness—*

*Black oil pouring out mouth, horrible, doomed creature Estivus
pawing feebly at the slimy pipes, losing a grip he never had, Jan
heaving and sucking breath, reaching down flat to the floor,
hand outstretched to coax poor Esti up again from the pit, Billow
groaning, getting unsteadily to his feet, Jan's hand grabbing
Estivus by the hair as he shoots through the surface, pulling
him limp to the pipework, Billow's strong mad-muscled arm grabbing shirt, jersey, Jan, in one mighty backward heave, jerking
him up, head banged hard, oh, so painfully, against the twisted
clattering rail . . . .*

A shriek of pain. Darkness.

Four

Swim back to consciousness, a fish battered by the concussion of
near propeller blades, sideways, upside-down, twisting in non-
equilibrium while the stimuli approach, recede, approach
again. . . .

Jan thought: *I mustn't let them notice that I can only see them
blurred, why are they wavering in front of me?—Ohh* !" He sat
up unsteadily, head thumping, a sick feeling in his stomach and
smoky fumes in his nostrils. The multiply-dashing figures of
Berenice coalesced into snuffling, gulping girl kneeling close to
him, still tugging at one limp hand as though to drop it would
blot him out of existence.

"Oh, Jan, I thought you had died," she sobbed, haltingly. "You
were so white and still, an' I was scared, ever so——"

In the corner, the fire had been extinguished, evil-smelling
fumes still curling upwards from the filthy charred rags. On the
makeshift bed behind him little Hab laboured for breath, driblets
of sweat rolling down the side of his forehead to soak into the
rough material. He looked desperately ill. It didn't help that the

room was so cold, either. If only a shred of warmth remained in those oily. . . .

"*Estivus!*" shrieked Jan, in realization. "Where is he? I had him, I caught him by the hair——" Snatching his hand from Berenice, he saw the reddened bruised knuckles, the black oil stains, the clinging hairs too few to identify in colour. . . .

Berenice stared at him, uncomprehendingly. "He brought you up—alone. The horrible noise down the ladderway—I heard it—it-it frightened me. I didn't know what was happening—it sounded awful. Then when he carried you up and put you down, I thought, I thought. . . ." Her voice trailed away and her lower lip quivered.

"He murdered Esti," said Jan blankly, shuddering at the vision in the palm of his hand. "He slipped on the floor, skidded into him, pushed him over the rail into—into—If Esti hadn't been there, Billow w-would've. . . . Fat chuckling spider, Esti called him. *We saw the spider's food store, Berenice*—he must have killed more people than—than anything, to get all that—fat chuckling spider. An' he's got us in his web," he finished, in abject despair.

Jan moved carefully over to the door, tried opening it. It was locked, with no sign of a key in the hole. The glass rattled as he shook it; the rusted metal panels beneath remained sturdy in spite of age. If he broke a window he could get himself out quite quickly but not before the noise of crashing glass brought Billow rushing at them. There was no other door leading into the small room, and none of the windows could be opened apart from gaps about a hand in width running around the top.

"I can't see a way out," he said after a long time spent trying to think against the background hammer of his head. "We *can't* get out."

Numb with fear, they sat and shivered in the intensifying cold.

Just before dark, Billow came up the ladder to stare through the dirty window at them and turn away again, satisfied by what he had seen. His mask of kindly stupidity had dropped away com-

pletely, leaving something behind that they were unable to identify, something which appeared horribly evil.

All night they shivered awake, close to each other for comfort,
terrible hunger eating away at their insides. Shadows came and
went with the banging of the gale and the helpless sighing of the
metal walls. Hab was tossing fretfully, running a temperature
which only seemed to climb higher. Exhausted, they started
nervously out of a doze with each creak of the beams and girders,
to examine the charcoal walls anew, and wonder where they
were. . . .

Dawn came, grey fingers of cold light reaching in through the
windowpanes. Hab was moaning faintly, small lungs labouring
harshly with every breath.

With the sleep grateful on his throbbing head, Jan was able
to see more clearly and draw more logical conclusions than the
day before. "The wind's dropping," he remarked, head cocked to
one side. "We've been missing for two days; they'll be able to
get a boat out today and search for us. Those last people we met—
it couldn't have been more than an hour's walk to the pipe from
them. They'll cross and——"

And what? Nobody knew of this old building, tucked away
amongst the intertwining girders and walkways of the endless
jungle. Everyone would think they'd drowned and give up, go
home, leave them at the mercy of mad Billow.

"I'm hungry, Berenice," he said, eventually. "Hungrier than
I've ever been before. I think he means us to starve in here."

Berenice nodded vacantly, and slowly picked up her bag, which
had started out so full and was now so empty. A few clothes,
soiled and damp with the rain. Nothing else.

After the hunger came the thirst, their lips burning as furry
tongues licked to wash off only the dried salty substances. Time
passed, agonizingly slow. Face still glowering, Billow came and
went, satisfied with what he saw.

"We *must* try to get away, Berenice," Jan said weakly, raising
her head where it lolled on his arm. "If we don't try soon, it will
be too late, we'll not have the strength. . . ." The movement inspired him to shrug off the depressed state they had cast them-

selves into. He examined the room again, carefully this time, Berenice's eyes following him hopefully.

"Jan!" she whispered to him, as a thought struck her. "The vent for the fire. Do you think you could squeeze through?"

He glanced up, reached towards it with his hand, touched the angled flap of metal, smears of soot coming off on his fingertips.

"I could get my shoulders through if you helped me up," he said. "With nothing to hold on to at the other side, I'd prob'ly get caught by the legs. If I made any noise——" He looked at her, significantly.

"Try it. I'll help."

Jan hoisted himself into the frame of jagged, ripped metal, squeezing into the space between the flap and the wall. Berenice held his legs while he grunted with the pain of that thin ledge cutting into his stomach. Squirming, he slid gradually through the orifice, gripping flat glass, wafer-thin welded plates, anything to stop the crashing plunge on to the catwalk. . . . As he slipped down, biting his lip, the sharp metal slicing lines into his legs, he jammed his foot against the metal flap, broke fingernails pressing against the squeaking wall.

"I'm through," he sighed, hands touching the cold mesh, one foot swinging free, the other unhooking and walking down the wall as if possessed of a life all its own.

Find help, Jan, Berenice mouthed at him through the grey glass. *Find help, quickly!*

After a few paces, Jan realized the extent of his injuries: the rips in his sturdy trousers where red weals oozed thin trickles of blood, aching, stinging; and a throbbing headache with a gnawing hunger adding its burden to leave him lightheaded and moving in a trance.

Where was Billow?

The empty machine-room floor below waited patiently, silent as a fly-trap ready to spring up from a central hinge. Each mournfully creaking door paused for the moment to shriek open, every rattling window a spying eye ready to shiver asunder. Awaiting the moment, the moment Billow would enter that gigantic room and see him.

Faint and far away, pitting its tiny vocal strength against the mighty combined malevolent stare of floor, doors, windows, came the tinkling hope, a gentle message of succour racing around the metal walls in catch-as-catch-can, easily distinguishable above the squeak-rattling, the mournful creaking, the silent tensed spring vibrations. *Clink, tink.*

Where?

Clink, tink.

At the base of the ladder, shivering in the baleful stare of the room, brave key tinkled in the draught.

Jan slid quietly down the long ladder, weighing up each rusty rung to inhibit the muffled clang of careless tread, slipping on hands covered black with soot. Snatched the key and sped upwards, silent as the night. . . .

"Oh, Jan!" breathed Berenice, bright tears still shining in her eyes.

"I'll carry Hab down the ladder," Jan whispered, quickly. "We must stop spider-Billow from coming after us, or we'll be caught for certain."

She thought for a moment, opened the door to the rusted cabinet, took out the metal can of oil. "A fire," she said, trembling with reaction. "By the door, so he can't come after us."

"Good idea. But—*oh, Berenice!*" he exclaimed. "We haven't got anything to light it with—except sea-stones. The noise will tell him."

"We must. He'll be too busy saving his home. I've seen the insulation between the metal sheets burning. It's slow, smouldering. Once it catches properly, it takes *days* to extinguish. He knows that. We *must* strike the stones."

They lifted Hab, wrapped him in a greasy tattered garment pulled over his face to muffle the laboured breathing and half-cries of alarm. Gently, they lifted him down the ladder, an easy burden, and slunk across the open floor to halt close to the entrance, the empty room ever hanging poised to fall with claws extended. . . .

H

"I'll take Hab up, Jan," said Berenice, weakly confident now that the loathed confinement seemed ended. "Poor child, never should have come with us." Hab heaved breath laboriously, flushed face struggling to form words.

Jan had an inspiration. "Take him as far as the topmost Level, hide him amongst the dwellings there, somewhere distinctive. We can draw Billow away, then circle round and take Hab home."

She nodded, lifted him on her hip as she had seen the other girls do with their younger brothers, and slipped through the door to freedom. Jan waited, nerves on edge at having to remain, began counting under his breath while dribbling black viscous liquid from the can, daubing up the walls, running in tiny rivulets along the crooked floor, dripping silently into the interstices. . . . Fumes drove into his nostrils, making him giddy, hunger free-floating his vision into chunks of shimmering picture, like Top on a day of sunlight scorching.

. . . *five ninety-eight . . . five ninety-nine.* . . .

Taking a rod of steel from the littered floor and the stone from his pocket, he struck it once, twice, three times, just above the liquid. Sparks shot out, glimmered, died feebly, their mission a failure.

Desperately striking the metal, tap-tapping echoing through the building, sound carried by eager messengers to the further-most recesses. Sparks flared, died. . . .

Whoosh! Flame shot up in langorous oily black-red writhings, singeing his hand, jerking his head up one last time to glance into the interior of the preying building, seeing far away through wobbling thermal agitation the stumbling figure, features con-torted into a permanent rictus snarl now vanished behind gouts of lifting, curling smoke.

The echoes had at last summoned Billow into their presence.

Jan turned and ran into the cold wind, the fresh breeze whipping away the sweat from his forehead. Around him, bare girders wrapped his speeding body with their twisted security, a criss-crossed monotonous jungle of peace and serenity. Berenice was well visible near the concrete islands of the topmost Level, moving slowly back to him with exhaustion dogging her footsteps. He climbed eagerly, knew that he had not lost her.

Smoke began pouring from the entrance to the building, whirled away on the wind. Then a mighty puff of air blew out lazily towards them and a dull, trembling boom reached their ears.

"The well of oil in the centre of the floor!" shouted Jan, in realization. "Some of the burning liquid must have reached it. Billow will *never* be able to put that out."

Underneath the great building, flames winked and flared briefly into existence as they dipped downwards from holes in the metal joists. A crackling, grumbling roar as the fires of Hell scrambled outwards in terrible haste from the water below, spreading a great sheet of flame directly under them, black smoke and fumes coiling up towards their tiny figures, reaching blindly, seeking them out. . . .

"*The bubbling on the water!*" screamed Berenice. "*It's alight. Away, Jan! Out of the smoke.*"

They fled, but not before they had seen the squat figure lurching from out of the entrance of the fire-torn building, stumbling across catwalks, climbing to safety, coughing, retching with the ghastly fumes—scorched, but still alive.

"He's coming after us, Berenice. Oh, *run*. He'll murder us for what we've done. *Run, run!*"

Flitting through cross-braces, along narrow, crumbled walks, running on perilous girders across the licking flames far below, they clambered ever sideways, seeking to lose the clinging smoke, the hot buffeting air.

"Hab!" Berenice clapped a hand to her mouth in horror, on realizing they were safe. "He's on the other side of the flames."

Jan started, visibly; he'd forgotten all about the small boy in his haste to escape. "Is he—caught in the smoke?"

She shook her head. "The wind's blowing away from him. I wish I hadn't left him, I really do. But there was no choice, I *had* to—Billow would've caught us otherwise. Oh, *Jan! Jan!*" she screamed.

He was climbing laboriously out of the smoke, creeping relentlessly forward with a single purpose in his insane mind—to seek out and destroy those who had threatened his solitary existence. They jumped up, swung away on clumsy weak legs, relying on handholds to pull them over the difficult stretches, travelling ever away from the fire churning its dark pillar of smoke into the sullen afternoon sky.

And, perhaps an hour's journey behind them, a beacon of hope was lighted within the hearts of others on noticing the magnificent sight. Turning their boat into the tossing waves, they set a perilous course across the Sound with all the haste they could summon. . . .

<h3 style="text-align:center">Five</h3>

They stumbled close to the rail they had seen from far away before realizing the sanctuary it presented them with—a large concrete rail, straddling broad vertical pillars to trace an unbroken curve towards the misty horizon.

Close by them were the broken sheds and buildings of an ancient and dilapidated way station. On the rail was perched a long wooden platform whose top and side wheels hugged grooves with solid rubber tyres. It had a coarse tattered awning of waterproof material stretched across, which flapped dismally with every gust of wind. Further along the rail, shunted off on to thinner skeleton sidelines, more platforms waited; some whole though in dubious running condition, others with axles bent and wheels missing, a few gutted and charred by fire, framework travesties with little recognizable save the outline.

"It's the Rail spider-Billow spoke of!" shouted Jan, recollection arriving quickly. "He told us about it—about being able to ride the railrunner at sixty knots. If that thing goes half as fast"—he raised his arm to point at the wooden platform—"we'll easily outdistance him——"

Berenice had laid a hand on his other arm. "We've no time," she gasped, weak with lack of food and the cold wind sapping her remaining strength. "He's too close behind us."

The youngster shook his head, then reached forward and yanked the rotten sailcloth away, scorning to fumble with salt-faded ties;

he uncovered a mass of ropes, a metal mast, patched sail, a bewildering assortment of impedimenta.

"Help me with the mast," he encouraged her. "If we can run just a portion of the sail aloft, we'll have enough to push us well forward, with this breeze."

Together they struggled with the alloy cylinder, soot covering Jan's jersey and hands; flakes of tarnish settled on their heads and shoulders. Swiftly, he tied the dangling rope to one corner of the cloth, found another corner, tied it to the metal eye on the platform edge away from the wind, hauled up the improvised sail. . . . Their preoccupation with the vehicle caused near-disaster.

Shambling towards them with a look of triumph gleaming in his eyes, he came at them, neither hurrying nor slowing down—relentlessly pursuing them as he had followed them until now, awaiting an opportunity, a time when he knew he *must* catch them.

Unaware of the proximity of mad Billow, the children worked at the wooden handle of a stiff brake, while the sail crack-boomed into the fresh breeze and the heavy craft pitched and swayed under them. Then the shoe had snapped clear of the wheel drum, and their vehicle began to pick up speed. . . .

Behind them, the brief look of disappointment had faded from the gnarled old man's features, to be replaced by something else. Throwing back his head, he laughed a wild cry of triumph which the ceaselessly cleansing wind scooped up and whirled into the air.

"Ride the Rail!" he shouted, in obscure glee. "Ride the Rail, my children. But Billow travels faster and further than anyone yet living. Run until you are weary—then crawl back to me for mercy, begging forgiveness, you miserable misbegotten children!"

Then he turned and regally surveyed the remaining railrunners, of which one in particular appeared to him not quite as unserviceable as it had to the fleeing children.

Six

It had taken the searchers a long time to reach the source of the fire, which was now dying fast as the combustible region shrank into the bubbling oil fountain close by the damaged building. Within the great metal room a funeral pyre to Estivus was still roaring hotly, belching black greasy smoke up through several holes in the roof. The flapping walls of the building smoked from every orifice.

The village Ombudsman drew his heavy cloak together as patiently as he had done a thousand times before and turned to the members of the hastily organized search party. "Cast around," he told them. "Look in every cranny, search each building thoroughly. This fire is recent; whoever caused it must still be nearby. Mackay, wait with me." A far-off figure caught his attention. He frowned. "I worry for your son, Mackay," he told the old man as the small knot of people dispersed. "Emlyn has received the shock badly."

Mackay looked upwards at the circling, whirring creature sometimes skimming the naked girders, sometimes perching momentarily on the concrete sills before flying off. Uist—never still, always searching.

"He follows the bird," the hoarse voice rasped, haltingly. "It is Jan's pet, a seafowl discovered immature and storm-whipped. Emlyn nurses hope . . . that the perceptions of the creature will guide him——"

"I think I understand," the Ombudsman sighed, staring down through the Levels at the bubbling fountain of fire. "Water that burns; an incredible sight for one not used to it——"

"It is called oil, Ombudsman," replied the old man to the unspoken question, dragging memories from the deepest recesses to the light of day. "It has been seen from time to time . . . as thick congealed lumps fouling the girders below Level One.

"Many years ago, eight, nine generations perhaps, when Top was in the process of construction . . . as the last dwelling platform"—he shrugged, thoughts uncertain—"some say an expansion of . . . living space for the other crowded platforms was the reason, or perhaps that food had become scarce . . . or that—well, whatever the reason, Top was built around the then . . . failing gantries that drilled for oil. A *vast* building programme, demanding . . . the resources of an entire nation to make it feasible—and not long after it was finished, the Great Famine struck and . . . supplies of food no longer began to reach the platforms."

Mackay coughed, his voice hoarse with the two days of tiring search. "With the farms, we were . . . self-sufficient to some extent, the power offered from the tidal machines . . . replacing the energy lost to the failing oil generators. Even when Top was being built, they all realized . . . that the oil would not last for ever."

As if living a reincarnated past, the frowning Ombudsman snatched back scraps of long-forgotten questions. "Oil," he said, quickly. "From below the water. Funny how odd phrases stick in one's memory. Yes, but what is it? A sticky substance, like fish glue? It burns well, I can see for myself. Its value could not possibly have been so great as to demand this kind of massive exploitation. The *number* of false wells, Mackay. A thousand? Ten thousand——?"

Mackay nodded. "All of them . . . representing the oil piping and old generators, too dangerous to remove. You ask the question . . . and at the same time supply the answer. It must have been valuable to them—for the very reason of number. It was used to run machines, and in the manufacture of . . . certain substances——"

"*Ten million* machines running day and night could not consume the amounts of this fiery liquid that must have been raised before all the false wells failed," the Ombudsman almost snapped. "How do you explain that?"

Mackay *couldn't* explain it, nor had he ever met someone who could. That same question had been defeating them for decades—*what had the oil been used for?* Nobody knew. Probably nobody ever would.

The Ombudsman gradually became aware of a commotion centred around the windward side of the ragged wedge of smoke. Emlyn raced towards them and halted, breath coming in gasps with the exertion of pushing against the unremitting wind.

"Hab is found alone," he said, his face red. "Alive, but—not well. He is deathly ill, poor child—with pneumonia, it looks like. We—we must get him home without delay——"

"And the others? What of the other boys, and the girl Berenice?"

Emlyn shook his head sadly. "No sign, Ombudsman. There is no trace of the others we can discover. I fear—I fear they may have. . . ." His voice trailed away, unable to sound the thoughts.

May have perished in the water with the burning oil, the other bleakly supplied to his own mind.

"Call the men," he said, surveying the desolate landscape where only the wind moved free. "Those who wish to stay and continue the search may do so. Good fortune to them! The rest can return with me." Wrapping his cloak tighter, the Ombudsman turned his face close to the prevailing wind, so that Mackay and Emlyn would not witness the expression that crossed it.

He may have wished the men good fortune, but in his heart he feared their task would prove hopeless.

Seven

Exhausted, the two children fixed the sail to maintain a forward speed well in excess of a man running, and huddled under the canopy of the remaining sailcloth. Prevailing wind kept them travelling at an even speed across the skeleton landscape. The patchy slabs of concrete which had not crumbled and disappeared into the slushing maw of the turbulent sea flashed past them like tiny islands in a wilderness of twisted girders.

After a while of floating above this metal ocean in a kind of dreamy detachment, they realized that the wooden platform was thundering hollowly across a bridge linking the next great landmass with the one they had just left. Spikes of steel stuck out just below the massive Rail like the short bones of a fish, underlying primitive catwalks through which the whitecapped Sound could be glimpsed a horrifying forty fathoms below them.

There's another Top . . . and another . . . and another.

Where did it all end? With a mythical place called "the shore" which had no legs to prevent it from collapsing and yet no sea into which to fall? Desultorily, Jan searched underneath the tarpaulin of their remaining sail for some tiny thing to ease their predicament. A morsel of food perhaps, lying tucked away in a crevice and forgotten. Berenice snapped momentarily out of her trance of fatigue and bent to help him.

But there was nowhere anything edible inside the low walls of their carriage, just tarred coils of rope lying tumbled in hairy disarray which pulled on their legs and tangled with their groping hands. Jan lifted them out of the shallow recess and placed them well behind the depression, careful not to let them trail out with the wind and snag on passing obstructions.

In the bottom of the platform sloshed a small pool of brackish water. They bent down eagerly to sip their precious hoard, more valuable to them than prime fish-oils. It tasted salty with the accumulated spray and had a smell of wood proofing that made them gag and retch a little, but it was the first drink they had been offered in a long while. They drank with cupped hands, and afterwards they wiped their mouths and smiled at each other.

The broad steel belt of crooked land they had just crossed over to looked little different to the last. Derelict, desolate, without movement or life of any sort save the diving seagulls and the eternally surging subterranean ocean, with no light or smoke to indicate the presence of people. . . .

Jan raised himself wearily, looking back to where the smoky flag still reared up in a stiff sideways wedge. It was tiny now with distance and had faded substantially.

Something caught his attention and held it for several long moments before he realized what it represented.

"Billow!" he shrieked, in terrible dismay. "He's coming up behind us on another moving platform!"

Swooping towards them so fast that their carriage seemed to stand still in comparison, the great unfurled sail belched out forward with the wind howling around it in a mighty devil-sigh of triumph. Already it was approaching the bridge they had so recently crossed, gaining on them by the second.

Jan fell forward on the metal eyes set into the planking, fumbling with shaking fingers at the ropes—ropes that had knotted themselves so tightly with the force of the wind that he could do nothing with them except cry in desperation.

"I can't untie them," he wailed. "I *can't*! We must go faster. He'll catch us!"

Berenice was sunken into the encompassing fold of the flapping tarpaulin, too horrified to do anything except watch the frantic efforts.

Jan worked at the stubborn knots until the rest of his nails split and the blood gathered at his fingertips unnoticed in the cold air; but the rope and stiff sail held out again his puny tugging. Shaking with the cold and his terror he slumped dejectedly on top of the fluttering sailcloth. Berenice said nothing, but her lip trembled and tears started in her brown eyes to roll mournfully in little starts and halts down the marble cheeks.

A bellowing gust of mirth reached their ears, faintly. A massive, rolling merriment. A hunter who sees that his prey cannot escape, toying with it, playing a deadly one-sided game for which the end result remains certain. . . .

Grinning dilapidated face, muddy eyes sunken deep into the wrinkles of an ageless monster, great forearms defying the cold strength-sapping wind to knot their own muscles of steel in anticipation, he reaches forward greedily although ten fathoms separate their approaching carriages. And Jan forces himself to his feet, pulls with all his strength at the planking, trying to rip a club from the old platform.

Muscles, crushing bones, strangling the life from me. . . .

Then a change in the noises around them as the island slips away from under their carriage and vanishes in retrospect. Another bridge, with the tossing waters of the Sound forty fathoms below.

A sliver of timber about the size of his forearm wrenched from the deck, Jan hurls it with all his strength. . . . Billow merely laughs his crazy gurgle, fending off the heavy chunk of wood as if it was a straw, enjoying the game, enjoying it.

"Throw something else, boy!" he snarls, scornfully. "Go on, throw! Knock me over if you can, puny child!"

"LEAVE US ALONE!" Jan shouts in panic as the nightmare

floats in to engulf them. Shaking hands pick up the coiled bundle of rope at his feet to raise the heavy mass aloft and hurl it with all his strength. . . .

Arms reaching forward, the gnarled old man catches the spinning tangle with another gurgle of glee, hoisting it above his head to wave the tumbling coils in derision—

Loops spin out in all directions like an exploding spider's web to dip down with the rushing wind and hook the spikes of the catwalk girders . . . .

"Ohhhhh !" *sighed the old, old man, arching backwards with the irresistible tug from behind, blue veined and knotted arms caught up in meshed handcuffs of rope. Great spider whirled up into the air out of the sling-shot of the carriage, head-over-heels spinning into the great convex sail as a shroud ready to receive him. Sail, mast, Billow, snapping away with a great gasping scream, platform rearing up and sideways, tumbling down, down, down towards the greedy ocean that had waited patiently for so long to begin the work of reclamation. . . .*

And then there was only one platform rolling its gentle progress along the endless Rail, with hardly a rippling disturbance far, far below them as the hungry waters snapped at the morsel that had been so carelessly cast down to it.

Cold, cold sea swallowed the spider and his torn web.

The carriage drifted ever onward while they sat in a trance compounded of hunger and release from fear, their hands too numb to attempt resetting the sail to carry them home.

Vast tables stretched before them, separated by stormy abysses. Clustering steel iced together with concrete, some sprawled long, others mere islands in the turbulent sea, housing several Levels of abandoned dwellings and towering steel derricks, rusted and forgotten like the people of Top. Beautifully desolate in a wild and craggy fashion, they remained permanent homes only for the wheeling raucous seabirds. . . .

And the eroded bridges between the islands, in some places mere fragile concrete ropes stretched across the ocean gulfs, their steel supports precariously balanced or simply non-existent. The fatigued Rail thrummed and shifted under the additional load, but the children were too weary to care about the danger.

Now *they* were the only ones who dared ride the Rail, thought Jan weakly.

Gradually, the character of the scenery around them began to alter, and with the change came a heightening of the lowly sullen storm-clouds into cheerfully raised white cumulus. Surface dwellings appeared in all directions around them, a few bearing smoky messages of occupation. Although the breeze never slackened, the sky began to lighten perceptibly, and below them as they passed between the metal islands they glimpsed a sea they had never seen before, an emerald green gently-lapping water glinting with the reflected light of a blue-torn sky, friendly and inviting.

"Berenice, look," Jan whispered feebly from the bows of their smoothly-rolling craft. "*The shore*. Ahead of us. Great mounds of yellow reaching clear into the sea. Estivus was right. There is a shore. There *is* a place where the water ends, where earth rests on earth and not on legs. . . ."

She stirred, unable to raise herself to look at the wonderful sight they had travelled so far to see. Exposure and hunger had finally caused her numbed body to succumb to a lassitude of spirit.

Beyond the sands, Jan glimpsed the rooftops tumbling back in a tight mass from the gaunt, crumbled-stone castle perched high on a crag of black rock. Houses above the surface, naked and defenceless-looking, yet seeming to offer them security. Some decaying, walls sagging, weeds and grasses sprouting out of cracked tiles. Some fallen in, to lie forgotten until the slowly drifting earth advanced with the flowers to bury and obliterate them.

The breeze which had carried them untiringly from below the horizon gradually lost power as the buildings enfolded them, and their platform began to slow with a diminishing impetus. As they passed near gardens, crossed narrow roads, a few people stopped to stare curiously at them. Some children playing under the Rail rushed out to race after them with gaping faces, but were soon lost in the distance.

Their long ride finished with a dismal crunch as the by now slow-moving carriage ploughed into a mass of rusty plates and wires that had fallen across the great concrete structure to block further progress. Both children pitched headlong with the shock, sprawling across rough timber, sliding into the snagging embrace of rusty fencing.

Jan was revived from his torpid state by a large moustached man in faded blue overalls and a round black cap on his head, who shook him in rough concern.

"Who are you? Where from?" the gruff voice demanded through a mouthful of food, the remnants of a sandwich visible in his other hand. "Stupid children forever riding out to sea. One of these days you be hurt, you be. . . ."

The boy let him ramble on, raising himself with some difficulty to gaze back down the narrowing Rail. Back there was a far-off tangled mess of a place where they had been born and raised without a thought that another world existed within their reach.

Some time yet to come, they'd return, Berenice and himself, to lead the struggling people of Top to a new life of peace and tranquillity, dominated no longer by the cruel and uncaring sea. Not this year, perhaps. Nor the next. But sooner or later they would go home, having repaired the decaying bridges one by one in an effort to re-establish contact with the last sprawling island which for so long had been lost in the infinitely gigantic steel jungle.

For both of them the endless nightmare was over, and the dream had just begun.